SWEET CRAVINGS – BOOK 3

GOING
FOR
Gold

IVY SMOAK

To Matt.
Sorry there wasn't a Jamaican bobsled team.

CHAPTER 1
Saturday
ALINA

My team USA tank top clung to my skin as Kristen and I pushed through the hot, sticky air on our way to the practice arena. We had been blessed with unseasonably cool weather for the first week of the games, but today we were finally getting a taste of the infamous Brazilian humidity.

"So how many do you think we'll see today?" asked Kristen.

"I'm guessing three," I said.

"Less than yesterday? Even though more people are finished with their events?"

"Yeah. It's too hot to be doing that outside. What's your guess?"

"I'll say four."

"You're on."

"Well, I think I already see one." Kristen pointed up to the third floor balcony of one of the skyscrapers that had been built specifically to house all of the athletes for the games. A girl was leaning over the railing. Anywhere else it would have just looked like she was enjoying the view, but in the athletes' village, we had to suspect that something else might be occurring.

We took a few steps away from the building to try to get a better view.

"I dunno, I'm not sure if..." I started. Just then, someone from behind the girl reached around and grabbed her breasts over her shirt. She opened her mouth in a way that could only mean one thing was happening. "Okay, yup. They're having sex."

"That's one," said Kristen.

"How is that girl okay with that? It's so awkward. Anyone walking by can see them."

"Oh come on. Don't pretend like you wouldn't enjoy that."

"Um, no. I'm actually kind of glad that our final game is on the second to last day. Otherwise I'm pretty sure Chris would have tried to make me do something like that."

"Better not let Coach Hammond hear you talking that way."

"I don't think it's any of her business if Chris is into public sex!"

Kristen laughed. "I meant the part about our final game."

"Oh, right. Well what are the odds that we don't make it that far?" Everything was setup perfectly for us to make it to the final. The volleyball portion of the International Tournament of Athletes consisted of two groups of six teams each. For each group, every team would play every other team one time, and at the end of those games, the four teams with the best records in each group would move on to the quarterfinals. We had played four out of our five group games and won all of them, meaning we were guaranteed to finish in the top four and advance to the quarterfinals. Brazil, on the other hand, who had been considered favorites to win gold, had lost three out of four of their games. Their fifth and final group game was against us, and if we beat them, they'd be eliminated. From there it would be a cake-walk to the gold medal podium.

"I actually think Coach is right on this. We shouldn't get too cocky." Kristen stopped and pointed to a girl kneeling in front of a muscular guy in an alleyway between two dorms. "Speaking of getting cocky..."

"Ew, gross pun."

"That's two. And we're not even halfway there. Looks like I'm going to win."

"Good thing we forgot to specify what the loser's punishment would be today." The first few days we had played we had just been counting for fun, but yesterday we kicked it up a notch by saying the loser had to post a picture on their Instagram of the winner's choosing. My Instagram account now featured a selfie of me making a platypus face. Thanks, Kristen.

"Any ideas?" asked Kristen.

I looked around to try to come up with a punishment that wouldn't be too horrible. A group of beautiful, shirtless men were walking towards us with bags of McDonald's. "Maybe the loser should have to buy dinner."

"All the food here is free."

"I know." It was the perfect punishment since I was almost certainly going to lose the bet.

"Nice try. But I think we should have higher stakes. What if the loser has to participate in the very activity we're betting on?"

"Have sex in public?" I asked.

"Yeah."

Of course Kristen would suggest that. "Hmmm..."

"Wait, are you actually considering that?"

"No, of course not," I said, laughing it off. *Shit, am I really considering it?*

"Oh my God, you totally are." Kristen's face lit up in a way I knew all too well. I saw the same face every time I had come back to our dorm room after a long night out with Chris. Even though she hated him and wanted me to date someone else, she still loved making me dish on all the juicy details of our dates. She was not a strong proponent of the old saying that a lady never kisses and tells.

"Well we haven't been allowed to have sex for four freaking weeks! God, I'm so tired of Coach's stupid sex ban. It's like these games are designed to make people crazy horny. They take the most physically fit people in the world, put them all in coed dorms, and then all the coaches tell us we can't have sex until we're done competing. Not to mention there's an unlimited supply of free condoms available."

"You don't have to tell me. I can't wait for our competition to be over so I can have some fun. The guys here are all so hot."

"But it's so awkward to do that in public!"

"Yeah, but it's not really in public. It's more like doing it in the middle of a frat party that only accepts the best looking guys in the world who aren't total douches."

"So not like a frat party at all?" I asked.

"Okay, fine," said Kristen. "That's kind of a bad comparison. But you get the point."

"So if you lost the bet, you really wouldn't mind having sex out in the open?" *Would I? The idea is kind of enticing... God, what is this sex ban doing to my brain? Get a grip, Alina!*

Kristen shook her head. "Nope. So it's settled then? The loser has to have sex in public after our final game."

"Whoa! I never said I agreed to it, I was just saying that I understand why they're doing it."

"It sure sounded a lot like a yes to me."

"It wasn't." *I need to change the topic immediately.* I looked around for something to distract her. The only thing I found was some tan brunette in a thong bikini lying out on a beach towel surrounded by three guys. "If we hang around for a few minutes, that will probably be number three. And maybe number four and five as well. Actually, we probably should discuss the rules on group sex. Does it count as one per group? Or one per pair of guy and girl? Or the total number of people in the orgy divided by two?"

"Wait, isn't that Gabriela Santos?" asked Kristen, ignoring what I thought was a very valid point that needed discussing, especially if the stakes were going to be so high.

Please don't be Gabriela Santos. I had been dreading seeing her ever since I stepped foot in Brazil.

When we got a little closer, I realized Kristen was right. It was indeed Gabriela Santos, the star of the Brazilian volleyball team. She was good, but she wasn't as amazing as the media made her out to be. They just had a hard-on for her because she was gorgeous and had huge breasts. And based on her current outfit, she wasn't afraid to flaunt them.

She also happened to be my arch nemesis. I thought I was finally getting over what she did to me, but I was wrong. The sight of her still made my blood boil.

"Yeah, that's definitely her," I said through a clenched jaw. I took a deep breath to try to get rid of the lump that had formed in my throat and that uncomfortable feeling in the pit of my stomach. "No wonder the Brazilians have sucked so bad this year. They're more concerned with their tans than with practicing."

"Fine with me."

I felt my phone buzzing in my sports bra. I reached in and pulled it out. It had gotten disgustingly sweaty in my cleavage. I made a mental note to find a better way of carrying it. Perhaps I needed to invest in a super stylish fanny pack.

"What's up?" asked Kristen.

I looked at the screen and read the message from my boyfriend, Chris: "Hey babe, you watching?"

"Shit, Chris' race is in five minutes." I typed out a response to let him know I was watching.

"What's the big deal?" asked Kristen. "Just watch it on your phone while we walk."

I shook my head. "This stupid phone won't stream video unless I'm connected to wifi. I'm just gonna run the rest of the way to the arena. See ya there!"

Before Kristen could respond, I stuck my phone back in my sweaty cleavage and took off. I wanted to make sure to catch Chris' race, but I also didn't want to have to see Gabriela for one more second. I hated how just seeing her took me right back. *Screw her.*

On the way, I passed three more couples having sex. *Oh well. I'll tell Kristen that I didn't see any.* I certainly wasn't going to admit that I lost the bet and get forced into having sex in public.

When I finally got to the arena, I sat down on a bench outside the locker rooms, connected to the arena wifi, and pulled up the broadcast on my phone.

The familiar face of Owen Harris popped up on my screen. It was the summer before my freshman year of high school eight years ago when Owen Harris landed the job of being the anchor for the broadcast of the International Tournament of Athletes. My friends and I all had the biggest crush on him with his dimples and deep brown eyes. My parents had no idea why I got so interested in sports that summer, but as a result, I signed up for the volleyball team at my high school. I had been playing since I was a kid, but had never taken it that seriously. It turned out that once I focused hard I was pretty good at it, and now here I was representing the US at the ITAs.

I refocused my attention back on the broadcast. Owen Harris was in the studio relaxing in a comfy looking arm-chair talking about the day's events so far. *Shit, did I miss it already?*

"Before we head out to the aquatic stadium, let's take a look at the updated medal count."

I let out a sigh of relief. Or maybe I was just panting from running in the ridiculous humidity or from seeing Gabriela Santos. Either way, I was glad I made it on time to see Chris' race.

The screen switched to a graphic showing a list of countries and how many medals they had earned. The United States was first with 14 gold, 9 silver, and 13 bronze, followed closely by Brazil who had an identical count, except for 2 fewer gold.

"The US is ahead in the count," said Owen. "But the real story here is Brazil. Bob, what do you make of all this?"

Owen had been joined in the studio by Bob Stimpson, a former four-time gold medalist at the International Tournament of Athletes.

"What Brazil has done here has been extraordinary," said Bob. "Before the tournament started, they were target-ing 30 medals total, and now here they are with that many medals and we're only halfway through the games."

"And it's not like the tournament was front loaded with sports that they're traditionally strong in," added Ow-en.

Bob nodded and shuffled a stack of papers. "That's a great point. In fact, they've been struggling in many of the events that you'd expect them to win. Their men's soccer team has looked okay, but they certainly aren't firing on all cylinders, and their number one ranked women's volleyball team has really failed to impress. They're actually in danger of not even making it out of the group stage if they can't beat the US tomorrow."

No way they'll beat us. Especially if Gabriela has a foursome with those guys.

"Looking at the schedule here," said Owen, "how many more medals do you think Brazil can expect to win?"

"Before the games began, I would have said maybe 10 or 15 more, but we seem to have grossly underestimated their home field advantage. At this point I wouldn't bet against them finishing in the top three."

"Alright, we'll have more on this later, but first let's take it out to the aquatic stadium and see if Brazil can continue to rack up the medals or if Chris Hamilton can bring home a gold for the US after his dominant performance in the heats yesterday. Over to you, Jim."

"Thanks, Owen," said another announcer as the camera switched to a view of my insanely sexy boyfriend stretching next to the pool.

The races were fun to watch, but watching his abs while he stretched was even better. The bulge in his swim suit wasn't bad, either. After dating Chris for two years, I realized that a good standard to measure men by was whether or not they could look hot in a swim cap and shaved legs. Chris certainly passed that test. I still couldn't believe how lucky I was. When I met Chris in college he was the ultimate player. But he gave up that lifestyle for me. Sure, girls still stared at him and tried to make passes at him, but he denied them every time. I was enough for him. My eyes and probably millions of girls back home rooting for him to win were glued to Chris on the screen. And I couldn't help but smile at the fact that I was the one that he wanted. Owen Harris may have been my first major crush, but Chris was my first everything else.

"So here's the lineup for the final of the men's 100 meter butterfly." A list of swimmers and their times in the heats popped up on the screen. Claude Beaumont was his biggest competition for the gold, and he was in the lane right next to him. According to the list, Claude had only been half a second behind Chris in the heats.

Come on, baby, you can do this.

The swimmers were finishing their stretches when Kristen walked into the building.

"Did he win?" she asked.

I glanced up for a second. "Should start any minute."

"Oh. Well, you should probably bring that in the locker room so you're not late."

She was right. Coach Hammond had a rule that we had to be in the locker room five minutes before practice started or we were considered late. And being late meant being benched for the next game.

"Right, okay. Be right in," I said.

With my eyes still glued to the screen, I got up and made my way towards the locker room.

"Alright, it's time to see if Chris Hamilton can do it again. If he can match his time from yesterday, he'll almost certainly come away with the gold," said the announcer as the swimmers all got on the blocks.

A voice on the PA said, "On your marks," and then the buzzer sounded and the swimmers were off. The screen zoomed out to show all the swimmers. Chris had gotten off to a decent start. He was maybe one arm's length behind Claude. *Not a big deal. He always finishes strong.*

I pushed through the locker room door as the swimmers hit their first and only turn. Chris had caught Claude and looked to be a few fingertips in front of him.

"You got this," I whispered.

Chris was two strokes away from the wall when I walked directly into someone. My phone flew out of my hands and crashed to the locker room floor.

"Whoa!" yelled a guy. "What are you doing in here?!"

I looked up for the first time since the race had started. The guy in front of me had his hand on his junk and was scrambling to put his towel back on. My mouth dropped as my eyes landed on his chiseled abs. His chestnut hair was shaggy and stopped right above his baby blue eyes. *His bewildered baby blue eyes. Oh my God.* I had wandered into the men's locker room. *And I'm staring at a naked man that's not Chris!*

All I could think to do was scream and run away.

CHAPTER 2

Saturday

ALINA

"Did he win?" asked Kristen as I sat down next to her at our lockers. "And why is your face so red?"

I shrugged and tried to play it cool. "I dunno."

"What do you mean you don't know?"

"Don't worry about it. Hey, can I borrow your phone for a second?" I had accidently left my phone on the floor of the men's locker room, but I couldn't tell her that. *God, why do I always have to do the most embarrassing stuff?*

"What do you need my phone for? I already put it in my locker."

"Mine uh...stopped working."

"So you didn't see if he won or not?"

"Nope. I was just sitting on the bench when you told me I should hurry. When I looked back down, the screen had gone black. I tried turning it off and on again, but nothing happened. I even tried to take the battery out. I'll tell you, those iPhones just aren't made the way they used to be."

"Okay, you can use my phone. If you tell me what really happened to yours."

"What do you mean? I already told you." *Shit! How does she know I'm lying?*

Kristen raised an eyebrow at me. "Oh come on, you always ramble when you lie. And you can't take the battery out of an iPhone."

"Damn it, fine. I accidentally went into the men's locker room while I was watching the race and I bumped into this guy in a towel. Then I screamed and ran out."

Kristen started laughing hysterically. "Oh my God, are you serious?"

"Yes."

"So you missed your boyfriend's race because you were in the men's locker room?"

"Yes."

"What did the guy do when you bumped into him?"

"He screamed and covered himself. He was as surprised as I was."

"So you knocked his towel off? Did you see his junk?"

Blood rushed to my cheeks as I thought back to the incident. All I remembered was that his abs were amazing. "Not really. I was too busy being shocked that I had wandered into the wrong locker room."

"Did you recognize him? You might have just seen a famous athlete naked! Was it LeBron James? Please tell me it was LeBron."

"Can we please talk about this later? I really need to see if Chris won his race."

Kristen started to open her locker, but just then Coach Hammond poked her head into the locker room and blew her whistle. Practice time.

***

It was impossible to focus during practice. Not only did I not know if Chris had won his race, but I was on edge the whole time hoping that the guy I had bumped into wouldn't show up at the gym. I would have to run away from practice if he did. I couldn't face him after that.

After what seemed like the longest practice of my life, Coach Hammond finally dismissed us. Kristen sprinted with me back to the locker room so that we could get to her phone and see if Chris had won.

There was only one problem. Chris was waiting for me right by the door to the locker room.

Shit. "What do I do?" I whispered to Kristen. I didn't know if I should be comforting him or congratulating him.

"Just play it cool."

"You know I can't do that. Let's pretend like we don't see him."

"Seriously?"

"Yeah."

Kristen and I stared at the ground as we approached the locker room.

"Hey," said Chris. I couldn't tell if he sounded happy or sad, so I continued with the plan to ignore him.

Kristen pushed the door open and walked in first. I followed, but Chris grabbed my arm before the door closed behind me.

Crap. I looked up. "Oh, Chris. You snuck up on me."

He gave me a funny look. "Really? I was standing here the whole time."

I wiped the sweat off my face and let out a long sigh. "Are you sure? I feel like I would have seen you."

"Yes, I'm sure."

"Weird. I guess I'm just super tired from practice. And you must be wiped after your race." I looked at him to try to get a read on how it had gone. It looked like he was smiling slightly.

"I really am. I can't believe Claude broke the world record."

Damn. He lost. "I'm sorry, babe," I said as I gave him a hug.

He pulled back and gave me a funny look. "Why are you sorry?"

"Because you..."

"Beat the world record too!" interrupted Kristen. She had grabbed her phone and apparently checked the results.

"Yeah!" I said. "Gold medal winner! Wahoo!"

Chris laughed. "For a second I thought you had forgotten to watch it. You really had me going."

"Yeah. I thought that would be a fun prank to play on my gold medalist boyfriend. Gotcha." I punched his arm playfully. *Who does that?* "So what do you want to do to celebrate?"

He glanced down at my breasts and smiled.

I laughed. "How about a nice romantic dinner instead?"

"What, are you worried Kristen is going to tattle on you? You wouldn't do that, would you, Kristen?"

"Tattle on her for what? I have no idea what you're talking about." Kristen winked at us and went back into the locker room. She may have hated Chris, but she hated cock-blocking even more.

Chris turned to me and raised one of his eyebrows. "So what do you say?"

I was torn. On one hand, I knew that Coach would bench me if I had sex and she found out about it, which she had an uncanny ability to do. Nina, one of our best servers, would angrily attest to that as she watched our first four games from the bench. But I was also ridiculously horny. I wanted so badly to say yes. I wanted to jump on Chris and kiss him and fuck him right there in the locker room. *Shit! My phone is still in the men's locker room.* "Let's just see what happens. I'll meet you in the village square at six." I gave him a quick kiss on the lips and then disappeared into the locker room.

I immediately ran over to Kristen.

"Sounds like you're in for a fun night," she said. "He's going to be so thrilled when you tell him you want to do it in public."

"What?!"

"You know, because you lost the bet. Don't think I stopped counting after you ran ahead."

"Oh God, I never agreed to that. And anyway, I didn't see any more couples banging on the way here, so really you're the one who has to have sex in public."

"Don't give me that. There were at least three or four more couples banging."

I shook my head. "Not that I saw. So who are you going to bang? Some rando?"

Kristen laughed. "No one, since I didn't lose. Believe me, if I lost, I'd happily admit it. I would love an excuse to bang some hot athlete."

"Do you have video evidence of these people you claim you saw?" I asked. "Pics or it didn't happen."

"No. What kind of pervert do you think I am?" Kristen put her hand over her mouth to pretend to be shocked that I would think such a thing about her.

I shrugged. "Sorry, I win. I'll tell you what though, I'll let you off the hook with the whole public sex thing. Just go into the men's locker room and get my phone and we'll be even."

Kristen scrunched her mouth to the side to make it look like she was actually considering not doing it. "If you insist, I guess I have no choice. How far did you get before you dropped it?"

"I can't remember."

"Oh right, you were too busy ripping some guy's towel off."

"I didn't do it on purpose!"

"Suuure. Alright, let's get your phone back."

I followed Kristen to the entrance to the men's locker room. She opened the door and pushed me in.

"Hey!"

She kept pushing me farther into the locker room. "If I'm going in, you're coming with me."

Oh God. I tried to spin around to get past her and escape, but I didn't stand a chance. She was an outside hitter and I was a libero, which meant she was super tall and I wasn't. She kept pushing me until a group of half naked guys came into view. Some of them were in their underwear. A few of them had towels wrapped around their waists. They all had ridiculously sculpted muscles. It was like I had walked into a museum filled with Greek statues that had all come to life.

"Hey guys," said Kristen, as if it was totally normal for us to be there. *How can she be so confident just walking in here like this?* I wished I had even half her confidence.

Everyone in the locker room turned to look at us. Half of them tried to cover up, while the other half didn't even seem to be phased.

"Alina was in here earlier and dropped her phone. Have any of you seen it?"

One of the guys wearing only a towel looked at me. "So you're the hot girl Bryce was talking about at practice today, huh?"

"Where is he now?" asked Kristen.

The guy stroked his chin dramatically. "I can't remember." He pulled his towel off and put his leg up on a bench to give Kristen and me a perfect view of his penis dangling between his legs. "But maybe you could do something to make me remember."

I put my hand out to block my view of it. "Dude, gross."

"Hey, you're the ones who came into the men's locker room. I'm just trying to get changed."

"Uh, yeah. I'm not going to blow you just to get my friend's phone back. Anyway, your penis is kinda small." Kristen grabbed my arm and pulled me out of the locker room as all the other guys laughed.

When we were safely back in the hall, I turned to Kristen. "So how do we find my phone now?"

"It sounds like some guy named Bryce has it. How many athletes here can be named Bryce? If we search for Bryce in a list of athletes, I'm sure we can narrow it down to two or three guys."

"Good idea. We'll have to do that later though. I've gotta go get ready for dinner with Chris."

CHAPTER 3

Saturday

ALINA

Chris was waiting for me in the village square, an area in the middle of the athletes' village featuring a fountain sculpture of a soccer player. It was surrounded by benches and places for athletes to get free food. He looked amazing, as always, in a slim fit, shiny gray suit. Even though he could pull off a swim cap, I always thought he looked the best when he was dressed up. His brown hair was still wet. It looked like he had just ran his hand through it, because it was sticking up in that sexy way I liked so much.

"You look incredible," he said, staring right at my cleavage. I would have preferred he looked at my face after I spent thirty minutes on my makeup, but I couldn't blame him for focusing on my breasts. After all, I had worn my nicest pushup bra and a low cut dress.

"You too. So where do you want to eat, Mr. Gold Medalist?"

"I don't know. So many options." He looked around. Pizza, fast food, Chinese, Mexican. The junk food options were endless, which seemed crazy in a place full of athletes that should have only been eating healthy food. "Let's grab some pizza so we can eat it while we walk."

"Walk? Where are we going?" I kind of expected he would want to go to a fancy restaurant outside of the village. A nice romantic dinner apparently wasn't what he had in mind though.

"I heard Sword Body Wash is hosting a party at Club Blue over by the water."

"Oh, okay." I wasn't a big fan of parties. I found them sweaty and crowded and gross. But if that was what Chris wanted to do to celebrate winning gold, I wasn't going to argue. This was his big night. "Pizza and a party it is."

We walked over and ordered some pizza. It was cheesy and delicious and everything I had been craving during the past few months of training. Well, not *everything*. I was really craving some sex, but I had decided I couldn't risk Coach finding out that I had done it and benching me. Eating pizza and going to a party would have to be enough for Chris until the volleyball finals were over.

"So why weren't you answering my texts?" asked Chris as we walked and ate. "I was beginning to think you weren't going to show."

"Oh, was I late? Sorry, I lost my phone earlier. And I didn't account for the fact that wearing these damn shoes would slow me down so much." I pointed at my black stilettos.

"Well, I'm never going to complain about you being late because of those." He slowed his pace to let me get a few steps ahead of him. "They make your ass look so good."

"That's exactly why I wore them." I looked back at him with a seductive smile and made sure to shake my ass as much as possible as we approach Club Blue.

The club looked insane. We were still at least 30 yards away from the building, but I could already feel the ground vibrating from the music. There were neon lights everywhere and a line snaked around the side of the building.

"You really want to celebrate by waiting in that line?" I asked.

"No way. A hot girl and a gold medalist? They'll let us right in."

We walked right up to the two gigantic Brazilian men dressed in jeans, black T-shirts, and sunglasses positioned at the entrance to Club Blue. One of them stuck his beefy arm out to block the door as the other one looked me up and down.

"Go ahead," said the bouncer to me in a thick accent. Then he turned to Chris and pointed to the back of the line. "You wait."

Chris opened up his suit jacket to reveal the gold medal around his neck. The bouncers immediately waved us through.

When I saw the inside of the club, I kind of wished they hadn't let us in.

The club consisted of a dance floor in the middle filled with sweaty people and more foam than a professionally drawn bubble bath at a five star hotel. In the front, a DJ with crazy dreadlocks spun records while girls in bikinis and neon colored boots danced in cages on either side of him. The bar to the left was manned by tan men in bike shorts covered in far more oil than could ever be considered appropriate, while the bar on the opposite side of the club was operated by girls dressed just as slutty as their male counterparts.

Chris grabbed my hand and pulled me towards the bar with the female waitresses. *Shocker.* After a few seconds, a brunette in a black bikini approached and smiled at Chris, ignoring me completely.

"What can I get you?" she asked, leaning over the table and pushing her breasts together.

"Let's start with a round of shots. Vodka."

"Sure thing." The girl jotted down his order on a sheet of paper and then put the back of the pen in her mouth. "If there's *anything* else you need, just let me know."

"Do you really think I should be having shots?" I asked. "I don't want to be hung over for my game tomorrow."

"Come on! Don't be such a party pooper."

"But my game..."

"Your game doesn't matter."

"What do you mean it doesn't matter?" *Asshole! Just because you have a gold medal doesn't mean I don't want one too.*

"You've already qualified for the quarterfinals so it doesn't matter if you win or not."

He was right. Kind of. We had won all of our games so far and qualified for the quarterfinals, but Brazil hadn't. The only way for them to avoid being eliminated was to get a victory against us. "Of course it matters. We have a chance to take down Brazil."

"I know. But one shot isn't going to hurt you. You're so good that you could beat Brazil even with a hangover." He flashed me his stupid charming smile that always got him what he wanted.

"Alright, fine. One shot. So how does it feel to have your gold medal?"

"It's pretty awesome. But really I'm just excited to be able to bang you again."

"Uh, about that..."

The slutty waitress interrupted me by putting a tray of vodka shots on our table. I grabbed one and raised it. Chris and the waitress did the same. *Really? She's going to do shots with us?*

"Here's to your first gold medal!" I said and emptied the shot glass down my throat. It burned as it went down. The alcohol hit me almost immediately. I was never much of a drinker, but during training I hadn't been drinking at all. My alcohol tolerance was basically nonexistent.

"Oh my God, you won gold?!" asked the waitress.

"Yup." Chris pulled his medal out and smiled.

"That's so awesome. Come with me." The girl grabbed his arm and started dragging him up towards the DJ booth. He pulled back and downed two more shots before letting her pull him away. I awkwardly followed behind. *What the hell is this girl's problem?*

She whispered something to the DJ. He nodded and then turned down the volume on the record and jumped over the side of his equipment with a microphone.

"Alright, alright people!" screamed the DJ. Everyone stopped dancing and looked up. "Tonight we're joined by another gold medal winner. What's your name, man?" He held the microphone over to Chris.

"Chris Hamilton."

"Let's give it up for Chris!"

The people on the foamy dance floor cheered.

"Any song requests?" The DJ asked.

"Hmm...how about the thong song?"

The thong song was the first song we danced to the night we met in college. At first I thought it was sweet that he would choose that song tonight, but then I realized it meant Chris was going to want to dance with me in that horrible pit of sweat and foam.

"Excellent choice, my man." The DJ jumped back behind his booth and hit a few buttons on his laptop. He turned the volume up and waited for a spot to blend the beats. After a few seconds I heard the familiar sound of Sisqó sounding creepy talking about "the finer things in life." The bumping and grinding immediately resumed on the dance floor.

"Shall we dance?" asked Chris.

I sighed. *Do we really have to?* "Okay, one dance."

The dance floor was even more disgusting and loud than I had imagined. I just kept telling myself that all I had to do was hang in there for one dance.

Chris spun me around and pulled my ass back onto him as I moved to the rhythm. The warm foam on my legs was repulsive, but I tried to ignore it. It didn't take long before I started to feel his erection push against my ass. That combined with the vodka I had drank and his fingers digging into my hips gave me a familiar pull in my stomach. One of his hands wandering up to my breasts just made it even worse. I dipped low and then pushed my ass up against him hard. *God, I'm so horny.*

Chris kept one hand on my back to keep me bent over while his other hand slid down and pushed the hem of my dress up over my ass. I put my hands on his to stop him.

"What's wrong?" he said.

"You can't just pull my dress up in front of all these people!"

"No one will notice. Come on." He grabbed at the bottom of my dress with his other hand.

I pushed him off playfully. "Sorry, babe. You know that I can't until after the tournament." *Shit, he just wants sex tonight.* I had to find a way out, and I couldn't just suggest we leave or he'd try to come back to my dorm room and bang me there. I looked around the club for ideas. After a second I spotted a group of guys from his swim team. I pointed over at them. "Hey, did you see that Bill and Adam are here?"

"Nope. And I'm not interested in them." He grabbed my hips to try to get me to grind on him some more.

"Come on, let's go say hi to them." I pulled him off the dance floor towards their table.

"Yo, Chris!" yelled Adam over the music as we approached. He scooted further into the booth to make room for him.

"Let's see that gold," said Bill. "Maybe that's what we need to get some girls over here."

"First we need to do some shots!" Adam stuck his hand up to try to get the attention of a waitress.

I leaned over and talked into Chris' ear. "Hey, I think I'm going to get going. I'm starting to get a headache and it's kind of late. Congrats again on winning your race." I kissed him on the cheek and walked toward the exit.

CHAPTER 4
Sunday
ALINA

Eight years ago, the genius marketing team for the company that produces Kinesio tape had decided to donate it by the truckload to the International Tournament of Athletes. The results were exactly what they wanted - athletes covered themselves in the colorful tape in all sorts of fun patterns, creating a buzz on social media. The copy cat effect of lesser athletes was nearly instantaneous. Amateur athletes all around the world started plastering the tape all over their muscles in an effort to look like their heroes. Kristen was one of those athletes. For years she thought it was purely a fashion accessory until our trainer in college told her that there were specific methods to apply the tape that would aid blood flow and help muscles heal after workouts. She didn't care. The tape had become part of her pregame ritual, and she wasn't about to change that.

Other girls on the team had different pregame rituals. Some prayed. Others did their hair in a certain way or wore a special headband or blocked the world out with oversized, colorful, noise cancelling headphones, listening to the same playlist of five or six songs that they've listened to before every game since middle school. One girl I used to play with would tape each of her fingers and then rip the tape with her teeth, finger by finger mutating from a sweet teenage girl into a hungry wolf ready to rip the other team to shreds.

Me? I didn't need any of that. I just needed the sound of the crowd cheering.

"Ready?" asked Kristen. Red, white, and blue Kinesio tape ran down her arms and legs.

"Ready," I replied. I took a deep breath and got ready to run through the tunnel onto the court. Butterflies fluttered around in my stomach.

The second we burst onto the court, all my pregame jitters dissipated. The atmosphere was electric. Twelve thousand people were seated around Maracanazinho Stadium, all waiting to watch us play. In any other setting it would have terrified me to be the center of attention of so many people. Public speaking in front of all these people? Forget it. But volleyball was different. I had practiced volleyball for years. I knew I was good at it. Damn good. When I was on that court, it was my time to shine.

Kristen served a practice ball low and hard right over the net. I easily dug it to our setter and got ready for the next serve. We did a few more of those to get comfortable and make sure the other team was watching, and then Kristen started serving high to my left. I lunged for the ball and missed. Not because I was bad, but because we were setting the other team up. High and to the left was actually where I preferred the serves. A little gamesmanship never hurt, right?

After a half hour of warm-ups, we lined up in two parallel lines. The bench players were called first, and then they got to my name. I ran between the two lines of my teammates, them all slapping my ass as I ran. At the end I jumped up to high-five each of our coaches and then took my place on the back line. God, I loved the feeling of the announcer calling my name and everyone cheering. It was such a rush.

While I waited for that to finish, I looked around to find Chris in the audience. Usually it was pretty easy, but normally the crowd was nowhere near this big. Before I could spot him, the introductions ended and it was time to high five the other team under the net.

Including Gabriela Santos.

I went down the line giving high-fives. When I got to Gabriela, she locked eyes with me and smiled, just like she always did when we played each other. And just like always, it crawled under my skin. God, I hated that bitch.

I took a deep breath and tried to channel my hatred into positive energy for the game.

And it must have worked, because we crushed them in the first game of the match. I was getting all my digs, and Kristen was nailing all her spikes. It seemed like it only took a few minutes for us to take them down 25 to 11. The match was best out of 5, so if we could just keep it rolling for two more games, we'd win the match and knock Brazil and Gabriela out of the tournament. After Brazil was gone, there weren't really any other teams that would pose much of a threat to our bid for the gold medal.

Coach Hammond high-fived me as I walked over to the bench to sit down for a second and grab some water. There was an envelope on my spot, so I pushed it onto the floor and...*Wait a second. Did that have my name on it?*

I grabbed the envelope off the floor. Sure enough, ALINA was written on it in bold letters.

"What's that?" asked Kristen.

I shrugged. "No idea."

"It's probably a cute note from Chris. Open it!"

Aw, he's so sweet! I flipped the envelope over and pulled out the contents. At first I couldn't believe what I was seeing. "What the hell?" I mumbled.

Kristen leaned over to get a look. "Oh my God. Is that...?"

"Chris sitting next to a topless girl at Club Blue? Yes, it is." I flipped to the next photo, which was a selfie of Chris and the girl, who I could now see was Gabriela Santos. *That bitch!*

"Alina! Kristen!" barked Coach Hammond. "Get out there!"

I looked up and saw the second game was about to start. I got into my position and prepared for the serve, but my head was still spinning from what I had seen. *How could he hang out with Gabriela after I left? He knows how much I hate her! How far did he go with her?*

"Alina!" Kristen yelling my name brought me back to reality.

"Huh?"

"Why didn't you go for that? That was your ball."

What ball? I looked up and saw we were losing 1 to nothing. *Shit, the game already started?* "Sorry, I thought you had it."

Brazil hit another serve at me, but this time I was ready. I bumped it to our setter, who set Kristen up for a spike. Her spike was saved, and then Brazil set it up to Gabriela for a back-row spike. *No way I'm going to let her win this point. Not after those photos.*

Just as she went to spike it, I caught a glimpse of Chris in the audience cheering for me like everything was totally normal. *Or is he cheering for Gabriela?* The spike should have been easy to deal with, but my brain was distracted by all the anger. I hit the ball slightly off center and it went no-where near where I wanted it to go. Two to nothing, Brazil. *Two to nothing, Gabriela.*

The rest of the game was a similar story. Not all my shots were horrible, but I definitely wasn't as sharp as I needed to be. I tried to avoid looking at Chris, but it was impossible with where he was seated in the audience. Brazil, and Gabriela in particular, seemed to feed off of my poor play. Every time she hit a good shot it just made me more and more angry, which in turn made me play worse.

Brazil won the second and third games. Chris got up to get some nachos or something during the fourth game, so I was able to pull myself together and do enough to get us a victory. *Maybe we can win this match after all.*

Six points into the final game, Chris came back to his seat and our best server, Nina, finally allowed back from her four game spell on the bench for violating the sex ban, jammed her thumb and had to leave the game.

Brazil won.

I couldn't help but feel like it was all my fault. I didn't pay much attention to the post game speech by Coach Hammond. She dropped the f-bomb a few times, probably directed at me for playing horribly. After she was done screaming at us, she calmed down and told us that we'd have double practice tomorrow in preparation for our quarterfinal game against Serbia.

Kristen came over and gave me a big hug as soon as the game was over. "Are you okay?" she asked.

"No. How could I be okay after seeing those photos?" There was a tightness in my chest that I couldn't explain. *Did he cheat on me?*

"Maybe there's an explanation."

"Yeah, there is. He was horny and drunk and likes brunettes with big tits."

"Alina?" said Chris' voice behind me.

"I think it might be better if..." started Kristen, but I cut her off. I wasn't going to hide behind my best friend.

"Hi, Chris," I said. "What are you doing over here?"

"Uh, I came to see you after your game like I always do. You guys almost had them."

"Shouldn't you be over there talking to your new girlfriend?" I angrily pointed at the Brazil bench.

"Huh? What are you talking about?"

"Wow, you're seriously going to just pretend like everything is cool?" *What an asshole!*

"I'm sorry. I really don't know what's happening right now."

"Oh, you don't remember Gabriela's tits in your face last night?" I said way louder than was appropriate in a public place. People in the stands nearby started to stare at us.

"Who?" Chris looked totally lost. It was so scary how he could act like he was innocent. I started to wonder how many other times he had cheated on me and pretended like nothing happened.

"Here, maybe this will help your memory." I grabbed the photos off the bench and shoved one in his face. I could feel the tears starting to well up in my eyes. At first I had just been angry, but now the crushing realization that my boyfriend of two years had cheated on me really started to sink in.

"What the hell?" asked Chris. "Where'd you get this?"

"Fuck you." I threw the rest of the photos at him and ran towards the exit just as the tears started pouring down my cheeks.

CHAPTER 5

Sunday

ALINA

Kristen caught up to me shortly after I collapsed on a bench in the village square. There had been an hour long train ride between me exiting the arena and now, but I didn't remember it. All I could see were those images of Chris and Gabriela burned into my brain. Kristen wrapped her arms around me and cried with me. I didn't care about the people giving us weird looks. I just needed to cry.

Eventually I ran out of tears. I didn't have a tissue, so I just blew my nose in my jersey. It was already covered in sweat and tears. Why not add a little snot?

"I can't believe he did that to me," I said.

"Men are assholes."

"I really thought he was different."

"I did too. He seemed like one of the good ones."

Bullshit. Kristen always hated him. It was sweet of her to not bring that up now, though. I shook my head. "Maybe Gabriela just sat next to him and took that picture to get under my skin." Saying the theory out loud gave me a glimmer of hope that Chris wasn't a total asshole.

"I can definitely see Gabriela doing that. But his reaction made him seem so guilty. If he hadn't done anything wrong, he would have laughed it off rather than asking where you got the picture from."

Damn. Kristen was right. He was so guilty. I buried my face in my hands. Two years of memories, all ruined by

Chris and that bitch Gabriela. I couldn't believe that she had taken everything from me again.

"How about we get some ice cream?" suggested Kristen.

"I don't want to move."

"Okay, I'll get you some. Be right back." Kristen got up and walked over to a nearby ice cream vendor.

I closed my eyes and waited for her to return.

"Rough day?" asked a deep voice next to me.

I opened my eyes and looked over at him. He seemed familiar but I couldn't put my finger on it. I had probably seen him in a commercial or something. He was certainly handsome enough to be in a commercial.

"You have no idea," I said.

"Well, I think I might have something to cheer you up."

Oh God. Is this guy seriously hitting on me right now? "Oh yeah?"

"Yeah. How about a magic trick?"

"You really think magic is going to impress me? I'm not an eight year old boy."

He laughed. "What if I told you I could make your missing phone appear?"

"How'd you know..." Suddenly something clicked and I realized where I recognized him from. He was the guy I had run into in the locker room. I hadn't recognized him because he wasn't naked. "Oh my God." My face started to turn bright red. First I had barged into the men's locker room and ripped his towel off, and now he was sitting next to me right after I had been crying. And I was sweaty and my jersey was covered in snot. I was a hot mess.

He smiled at me. "So you do remember me after all?"

"I'm so sorry I ran into you the other day. I was on my phone and accidently walked in there. I promise I didn't see anything though."

"It's okay," he said, handing me my phone. "Please tell me you'll stop crying now that you have your phone back? It pains me to see a girl as beautiful as you upset."

I forced a small laugh. "Oh yeah, I was totally sobbing inconsolably because I lost my phone."

"Do you want to talk about what's really wrong?"

"Not really."

"Okay. Want to play a game instead? It'll be good to get your mind off of whatever's bothering you."

"What game?"

"Guess the sport. Every time someone walks by, we have to try to guess what event they're competing in. Here, I'll go first." He pointed at an Asian girl walking by who looked like she was twelve years old. "See her? Definitely a gymnast. Your turn."

I looked around at the different options. There were a few people walking by who were in great shape, but they didn't have distinctive characteristics that betrayed their sport. Then I spotted a sloppy guy with a big gut and a baseball cap. I pointed at him. "First baseman on a baseball team?"

Bryce laughed. "Could be. But I'm pretty sure he's just the cashier at the burger stand."

"Oh. Oops. Your turn. What do you think of those two guys over there?"

"Eh, I'm not really into guys," said Bryce.

"That's not what I meant."

"But that seven foot tall guy who just walked by is a basketball player. You're up. You should try to guess the sport of that handsome stud on the bench."

"Ew, don't talk about yourself like that."

"What? Oh, no. I was talking about him." Bryce pointed to some guy on a bench across the path stuffing his face with nachos. "But I'm very flattered that you think I'm a handsome stud."

"The dude eating nachos is definitely a table tennis player. And you...hmmm."

"Come on, it should be easy for you to guess what I am after you saw me naked," said Bryce.

"Why would seeing you naked help me guess what you are? Unless you were a porn star and had a giant penis or something."

"I do have a giant penis, but I'm not a porn star. So I guess seeing me naked would have just been misleading for you."

Did he have a giant penis? My mind raced back to the previous day. All I remembered seeing was his hand in front of his junk and his abs. My God, those abs...

"Are you picturing me naked right now?" he asked.

"What? No." I laughed awkwardly.

"Well you seem to be feeling better," said Kristen. She plopped a bowl of ice cream down in my lap. "Who's your new friend?"

Oh God. Did she hear that whole conversation? "This is uh..."

"Bryce," he said, holding his hand out for her to shake it.

"Oh, the guy who you saw naked who told his pervy friend that you were super hot? Did he give you your phone back?"

Bryce smiled. "Pervy friend? That was just some roided up weirdo. My actual friends are super normal."

I looked away and hoped he wouldn't notice me blushing. *Please don't say anything else embarrassing, Kristen.*

"He's so hot!" mouthed Kristen when Bryce wasn't looking. Or at least, she tried to mouth it. I was pretty sure she said it loud enough for Bryce to clearly hear her.

"Well, I better get going. I promised a few friends I'd meet up with them for dinner." Bryce stood up. "What was your name again?"

"Alina."

"It was great to meet you, Alina." He smiled at me and walked off.

"Damn," said Kristen. "I leave you alone for five minutes and you have the hottest guy at the games flirting with you. Now that's how to rebound."

"I wasn't flirting, I was just getting my phone back."

"That's not what it looked like to me. God, his eyes are incredible."

Yeah they are. "Stop, I wasn't flirting with him. I'm still with Chris." Just saying his name made me feel horrible. The image of him and Gabriela at Club Blue came flooding back into my mind. Any bit of happiness that Bryce had brought me quickly dissipated.

"Well, whatever you were doing, it sure looked like it made you happy."

"Yeah, maybe I'll be happy again some time." I shoved a big spoon full of chocolate ice cream into my mouth to try to keep the tears at bay.

We sat in silence as we both ate an inappropriate amount of ice cream. I didn't know why stuffing my face with delicious ice cream was so comforting, but it was the best. I wished I could date ice cream rather than stupid boys.

"So what do you want to do tonight?" asked Kristen.

I shrugged. I didn't feel like doing anything besides eating more ice cream.

"How about we go get drunk?" she suggested.

Images of Club Blue and Chris getting drunk with Gabriela filled my head and tears welled up in my eyes.

"Uh, okay. No drinking. How about we stay in and watch a movie?"

I nodded.

Kristen gave me a hug and then we got up and headed towards our dorm.

CHAPTER 6

Sunday

ALINA

Our plans for a nice, relaxing movie night were ruined when we got to the dorm and found Chris waiting outside.

"Get out of here," said Kristen, blocking his path to me.

Chris tried to get around her to talk to me. "Can I at least explain what happened?"

"No," snapped Kristen. "She doesn't want to talk to you."

"But I didn't even do anything wrong. Yes, I was hanging out with Gabriela after you left, but nothing happened."

"Yeah, okay," said Kristen. "So she just had her tits out for no reason?"

"Kristen," I said. "Let him explain." Part of me really hoped he was telling the truth. What he had done was bad, but if nothing else happened, it was forgivable. I wasn't going to flush my relationship down the toilet just because Chris got drunk and Gabriela can't keep her top on. It was partially my fault, anyway. If I had just been a good girlfriend and stayed to help him celebrate winning a gold medal, none of it would have ever happened.

"Can we talk in private?" asked Chris.

"Yeah," I said. "I think we should."

"Are you sure?" asked Kristen.

"Yeah. Go ahead and get the movie ready and I'll be right in."

She looked disappointed with me, but she didn't argue.

As soon as she was gone, Chris flashed me his charming smile and tried to hug me. I pushed him off.

"Your smile isn't going to get you out of this," I said. "Start talking."

"What's there to talk about? Nothing happened."

"Well, I wouldn't say that. I mean, those pictures pretty clearly showed you hanging out with Gabriela at Club Blue. You know I hate her."

"Yeah," said Chris, rubbing his forehead. "I was too drunk to realize it was her. I just thought it was some random girl coming to hang out with us. If I had realized it was her, obviously I never would have done it."

"Done it? Done what, Chris?" *What the fuck did he do?*

"Hung out with her."

"That's it?"

"Yeah. Like I said, nothing happened."

"Then why'd she have her top off?"

"I don't know. She just randomly took her shirt off."

"Lucky you. Did she randomly have sex with you too?"

"What? No!" Chris threw his arms up in exasperation.

"You know, I'm pretty sure she fucked three guys yesterday, so she probably gave you AIDS. I hope you enjoyed getting sloppy fourths."

"What are you talking about, Alina? How many times do I have to tell you that nothing happened?"

"If nothing happened, why'd you seem so guilty when I confronted you after my game?"

"How'd I seem guilty? You didn't even give me a chance to talk."

"You got really upset and asked me where I got the photos. If nothing happened, you would have just laughed it off."

Chris shook his head, but he didn't say anything.

"Well?"

"I got upset because I didn't even remember hanging out with her. I thought someone had photoshopped that picture to try to mess with me or something."

"If you can't remember anything, then how do you know that nothing happened?"

"I didn't remember it this morning. But seeing the picture made it all come back. I clearly remember leaving with Bill and Adam and going back to the swim team house. You can even ask them. They'll tell you."

I took a deep breath and tried to process everything he'd said. It seemed like he was telling the truth.

"By the way, where'd those photos come from?" he asked.

"Someone put them on my seat during the first game of the match. That's why I played like shit after that and made us lose."

Chris snapped his fingers. "Oh my God. Gabriela set me up."

"What?"

"She must have seen we were together when we were up on stage. And then when you left, she saw a great opportunity to take some topless selfies with me that she knew would get under your skin. Boom. I'm innocent. I was set up!"

"That conniving little bitch. I can't believe I let her play me like that."

Chris smiled. "So are we good?"

"I do believe you that nothing happened, but I'm still upset that you were hanging out with her topless."

"What should I have done? Just got up and left?"

"Uh, yes. That's exactly what you should have done. How would you feel if I was out with my friends and some guy started swinging his dick around? And then what if I grabbed my camera and started snapping some selfies of me looking super happy next to a big naked penis?"

"That's different..."

"Not really."

"Okay, fine. I should have left. I'm sorry."

It really took him this long to apologize? Wow.

"So are we cool now?" he asked.

"Do you promise that nothing else happened?"

"Yes."

"Okay." I wanted to believe him. I really did. But he just seemed like he was hiding something. There was only one way to find out for sure. "Can I see your phone?"

"Why?"

"So I can see if you took any other pictures."

"Uh, I think I left my phone at home." He had a worried look on his face.

I reached out and felt his pocket where he always kept his phone. It was there.

"Okay, okay. Fine. She might have kissed me once."

"What?!" *You lying asshole!*

"It was just a peck. Nothing, really. I pushed her off right away."

"Are you sure that's all?"

"Yes."

"Next are you going to tell me that she sucked your penis a little bit? Or maybe you guys played just the tip?"

"Alina, stop. I love you. I would never cheat on you." He reached for my hand, but I pulled away.

When I moved my hand, I realized I had been clinching my fists so hard that my nails had dug into my palms. I took a deep breath and tried to regain control. "Maybe so. But I need some time."

"What does that mean? Are you breaking up with me?"

"No. I don't know. I just need some time away from all this."

"Time? How much time?"

"I need to focus on the tournament, Chris. You already have your gold medal, but I don't. I still have three games to play, and I'm not going to let our relationship ruin another game."

"So you just want me to disappear for the next week?"

"Yes. I think that's for the best."

"Come on. This is ridiculous."

"No, it's not. It's ridiculous that you made out with Gabriela and that I had to find out by seeing pictures of it in the middle of my match." Saying it made me want to cry again.

"We didn't make out..."

"I don't know what to believe anymore. Please just stay away from me until the tournament is finished. And if you care at all about me, try not to take anymore selfies with topless whores." I turned around to go into my room.

He grabbed my wrist. "Don't throw all the blame on me, Alina."

"Excuse me?"

"I won gold. I wanted to celebrate and you ran off on me. What was I supposed to do?"

Seriously? I bit the inside of my cheek. "So it's my fault that you cheated on me?"

"You knew what I wanted."

"And I told you that I couldn't." I had lowered my voice slightly. "I'm still competing..."

"And if you were a good girlfriend, you'd put me first."

I pulled my wrist out of his grip. "That's not fair, Chris. You were on a sex ban too. You didn't try to pressure me until you won your event. You're the one that wouldn't put me first. This is such a double standard."

"You don't even care if you win. You're retiring after this."

"I don't care? Of course I care! I want to go out on top. And you know that I need the money to..."

"Right. So money is more important than me?"

"Chris! That's not what I was saying."

"Do you have any idea what I've given up for you? All the girls I turned away in college because we were together?"

It felt like he had slapped me. "It shouldn't have felt like you were giving up anything if you loved me."

"Well it did. Talk to me when you let this go. Oh, wait, you can't. Because you never let anything go. You can't even beat Gabriela in a game because she bullied you..."

"Stop." My voice was barely a whisper.

"That's what I thought. This isn't even about me. You're just jealous that Gabriela..."

"Stop."

"For the record, she had a game the next day too. Yet she stayed to help celebrate my victory. Maybe you could learn a thing or two from your arch nemesis."

"It's not a break, Chris. We're done." I opened the door and escaped into my dorm room, slamming the door behind me.

CHAPTER 7
Sunday
ALINA

"How'd it go?" asked Kristen as she scrolled through a list of movies on the TV. Her hair was wet and she had a towel wrapped around her, which reminded me that I was still sporting my snot covered jersey.

"It went okay," I said in as steady a voice as I could muster. It felt like my whole world had just crashed down around me. The fact that Chris said he felt like he had given up a lot for me was even worse than him giving into temptation with Gabriela. I thought he was happy. I thought I was enough for him.

"Please tell me you didn't let him off the hook."

"I think we're going to take a break." Usually I would have told her all about it and cried on her shoulder, but I decided it was better not to tell her about Chris kissing Gabriela. Kristen would never forgive him for it, and that would cause problems if Chris and I worked it out. I couldn't have my boyfriend and my best friend hating each other even more than they already did. *Do I even want to work it out?*

"A permanent break?"

"Maybe. I'm gonna go take a shower while you pick out a movie." I went into the bathroom and started the water just in time to mask the noise of me crying.

As the hot water poured over me, I tried to picture Chris as the dirt and sweat that was being washed away. It didn't work. The conversation and the pictures kept cycling through my head. *Did he really just kiss her?* It hadn't occurred to me during the conversation because I was so distracted when he admitted they kissed, but there could have been pictures on his phone of them going further than just kissing. And now I would never know. *Will I ever be able to trust him again?*

Stop thinking about him!

I couldn't stop though. He had been my boyfriend for two years. I had seen him nearly every day during that time. I couldn't just pretend like he never existed, because without him there was a big, gaping hole in my life.

Focus on volleyball.

I started running through the game in my head. Yes, most of my mistakes had been caused by Chris, but I had also made some errors in the first game before any of that had happened. I would have to watch the game film tomorrow to see exactly what I was doing wrong.

I took a deep breath. Volleyball was only a temporary patch for the hole in my life, but it was already making me feel a little better. And I was sure Kristen would pick a wonderful movie that would make all my problems disappear for the next two hours.

But she didn't.

She had put on black leggings, a black tank top, black sneakers, and pulled her hair back into a tight pony tail with a black headband. She had gone through my drawers and laid out a similar outfit on my bed.

I looked at her and raised an eyebrow. "Are we going to rob a bank instead of watching a movie?"

"You tell me. What's Operation Red Rip?"

"Uh, what? Did you do a line of coke while I was in the shower?"

She tossed me my iPhone. "Your alarm went off while you were in the shower. It said to get ready for Operation Red Rip and to wear all black."

Did Bryce give me the wrong phone? I swiped my finger across the screen and looked at the homepage. All the apps were the same. I checked the texts next. Lots of missed texts from Chris. *Definitely my phone.*

Then another alarm started playing. It was titled, "Operation Red Rip - Meet at the village square."

"Did Bryce add weird alarms to my phone?" I asked.

"It would appear so."

"You don't really expect me to go, do you?"

"No. I expect *us* to go," said Kristen. "Now hurry up and get ready! We're going to be late."

"But what about our movie?"

"We can watch our movie any time. But we can't go on a secret mission with your sexy new friend any time." Kristen got up and started stretching her quads.

"He's not my friend. He's just a guy who was nice enough to return my phone."

"Well, whatever he is, he sure seems to make you happy."

I thought back to my conversation with him on the bench. For those few minutes, I had forgotten about everything else. And right now I just wanted to forget. *Damn it.* I hated how Kristen always made so much sense. "Fine, I'll go."

I threw on the all black outfit she had picked out for me and added a little eye makeup and I was ready to go. I usually would have been concerned about going out with wet hair, but it was so hot out that having wet hair would probably just help cool me down.

A few minutes later we arrived at the village square. But Bryce wasn't anywhere to be seen. There was just a trio of guys in Canadian track suits sitting on the side of the fountain. *Wait a second! That's Bryce. Is he really Canadian?* I thought back to my brief conversation with him. He hadn't said "eh" a lot or been overly polite. And he hadn't mentioned maple syrup or hockey at all.

He and his two friends ran over to us. One had brown hair that was buzzed close to his scalp and the other had perfectly coiffed dark hair. They were both about the same height as Bryce, which was probably a foot taller than me.

"Hey, Alina!" said Bryce. "I'm glad you guys came. I was starting to think we'd have to start without you."

"What the heck is Operation Red Rip?" I asked.

"You'll see. Follow us." He pushed a Razor scooter toward Kristen.

"Where's mine?"

"Oh, we didn't realize your friend was going to come so we only brought one extra. You'll have to ride with me." He got on his scooter. "Hop on."

I raised an eyebrow.

"Come on. I won't bite."

Kristen gave me a shove to force me onto his scooter. He immediately kicked it into motion, giving me no choice but to wrap my arms around his waist to keep from falling off. My hands ended up on his abs, which felt as incredible as they looked when I had seen them in the locker room. I quickly moved my hands over to his hips. It seemed wrong to be feeling up Bryce an hour after breaking up with my asshole boyfriend. And it made me wonder what he was doing right now. The thought made my stomach churn.

The wind whipped my hair around as we zoomed past the dorm buildings. We had gone into an area of the village that I didn't recognize.

"Where are we going?" I asked.

"Dorm 16."

"Why?"

"Sorry. Classified."

"Oh yeah? How about now?" I reached up with one hand and tickled his armpit. It seemed like a good idea. It wasn't.

He laughed and pulled his arm down to block me from tickling him, which in turn pulled the handlebars sharply to the right. As the front wheel turned at a 90 degree angle from where it should have been, the scooter stopped dead and Bryce and I flew over the handlebars.

I went airborne for a few seconds and then came to rest in a bush directly on top of Bryce. My face was an inch away from his.

"Ow," he muttered.

His minty breath wafted up to my nose. I locked eyes with him for a second. The twinkle in his baby blue eyes was enchanting. Even though I had just caused him to crash his scooter and flip into a bush, there wasn't a hint of anger in his eyes. Only amusement and a bit of desire. *Shit, what am I doing?*

I quickly crawled off of him and wiped the leaves off myself.

"Oh my God, Alina!" screamed Kristen as she pulled her scooter up next to me. "Are you okay?"

"Codenames only!" yelled one of Bryce's friends.

"Really, dude? They just flew into a bush and you're worried about code names?" Kristen scanned me for any major injuries. "It looks like you're okay."

"Yeah, I think I'm fine," I said. Nothing was in excruciating pain, so that meant no sprains or breaks. A quick glance confirmed that I had a few scratches on my arm, but that was about it. "No thanks to Bryce's driving..."

"My driving?" said Bryce. "Sorry, I must have missed the part in the scooter manual about how to deal with a spontaneous tickle attack."

I smiled and tried to look innocent. "I don't know what you're talking about."

"Green Tiger, " said one of Bryce's friends, looking at his phone. "The eagle is in the bird bath."

"Huh?" asked Kristen.

I looked over the guy's shoulder at his phone screen. He was looking at a video feed of an empty dorm room similar to the one Kristen and I shared.

"What in the world are we doing?" I asked.

"No time to explain," said Bryce. "We've gotta move."

The handlebars had broken off our scooter during the crash, so Bryce just took off running. I chased behind him, but he was sprinting way too fast. Luckily we only had to run one more block before we arrived at Dorm 16.

Bryce's friends grabbed the scooters and hid them in the bushes out front and then we all huddled up.

"Alright," said Bryce. "Red Wolf, you'll stand guard out here. Pink Ocelot, you're my eyes in the sky..."

"Pink Ocelot?" I asked, looking at the guy who had just been addressed by that name. He was the one with the perfectly coiffed dark hair. "Is that seriously your code-name?"

He shrugged. "I thought it sounded cool..."

It doesn't. "Interesting. So what are Kristen and..."

Pink Ocelot cleared his throat. "Codenames only, please."

"Geez, okay. Sorry. We'll get codenames. Kristen, what do you..."

"God damn it!" yelled Pink Ocelot.

I jumped when he yelled at me. Bryce glanced at me and laughed.

"Guys, we're wasting time." He pointed at me. "Your name will be Sex Panther."

"Sex Panther?" I asked. "Isn't that the cologne in Anchor Man that's illegal because it contains bits of real panther meat?"

"Shit, you're right. I knew it sounded good. How about Blonde Tigress?"

"I like it." I pointed to Kristen. "What about her name? How about something super girly? Maybe Pink Ocelot?"

"Hey!" yelled Pink Ocelot. "That's my codename."

Bryce laughed. "Okay. Blonde Tigress, you're coming with me. Brunette Giraffe, you go with Ocelot."

"Really?" asked Kristen. "She gets a super sexy name and I get stuck being a giraffe?"

"No time to argue," said Bryce. "Red Wolf, do you have the final pieces of our disguises?"

"Yes sir." Red Wolf reached into the pockets of his track suit and pulled out three fake mustaches. All three of the guys grabbed one, peeled off the back, and put them on. Bryce's was a perfectly twirled handlebar mustache. Ocelot had a Hitler stache.

"Alright, let's roll," said Bryce. Red Wolf stayed in place while Bryce and Ocelot sprinted up the stairs to the lobby of Dorm 16.

Kristen looked at me with a confused look on her face. "Want to run away?"

"No way. I'm too curious now. And plus, I couldn't possibly deprive you of spending some more time with Pink Ocelot. You guys seem perfect for each other."

Kristen rolled her eyes. "Oh God."

"Pssst," whispered Bryce from the door to the building, waving his arm for us to follow.

"Here goes nothing," I said to Kristen and we both ran up the stairs.

CHAPTER 8

Sunday

ALINA

Kristen followed Ocelot over to a couch in the lounge to the right of the lobby while Bryce pulled me into the staircase.

"Why not take the elevator?" I asked.

"The elevators all have cameras. The stairs don't."

"Why can't we be caught on camera?" *What kind of crazy shit are we going to do?*

"What kind of secret agent are you? That's like spy training 101. Never be caught on camera, even in disguise."

"Okay, you're right. Being caught on camera would be bad. Because we're going to...steal something?" I asked, hoping I'd be able to get some information out of him.

"Nope. Try again."

"Kill someone?"

"What? Wow, that got dark in a hurry. Come on, isn't it obvious? We're going to pull a classic ITA prank!"

"Is that a thing? I don't think it is."

"Of course it is!" said Bryce. "Don't you remember all the pictures of toilets without dividers at the games two years ago?"

"Yeah. I thought that was just a weird cultural thing."

"No way. That was an epic prank orchestrated by Lars Berg."

"The Swedish skier? I remember him from when I was a kid."

"Yup, that's him. Apparently he only came back to the sport to pull that prank. He did horrible in his event that year, but he won an unofficial gold for the best prank of the year. Or maybe you remember in the 90s when Sally Jones threw a banana peel onto the track and caused Uma Longhorn to slip. After that the CPG declared..."

"CPG?" I asked.

"Committee for Pranks at the Games. They host a private party at the end of the games where they award a prize for the best prank. Anyway, after the banana incident, the CPG made a new rule that pranks are only permissible that don't interfere with an actual sporting event."

"How have I not heard about this before? Is it mainly a Canadian thing?"

"Canadian?" Bryce looked confused. "What makes you think I'm Canadian? It's not like I say 'eh' a lot and love hockey and maple syrup."

"Oh my God! That's what I first thought when I saw you in that track suit. I was so surprised that you were Canadian."

Bryce burst out laughing. "Wow, I guess this disguise is even better than I thought."

I tried to fake a laugh to hide my embarrassment. *How did I not realize that was a disguise?* "Just kidding. I knew you were American this whole time."

"Really?" asked Bryce. He didn't sound convinced. "Because I'm pretty sure you actually thought I was Canadian."

"Okay, fine. I admit it..."

"Shit, someone's coming," said Bryce. He put one hand on my hips and the other on my face and pushed me against the wall.

I gulped. I looked into his eyes for a second before he pressed his lips against mine.

Holy shit! Stop!

But I couldn't stop or the person would see us. I decided the best course of action was to just stand there with my lips closed while Bryce pretended to kiss me. Actually, he wasn't really pretending. He was passionately kissing me, occasionally flicking his tongue against my lips in hopes that I would let him in. It was so hard to resist kissing him back. I never realized how hard it would be to not kiss someone back, especially someone who looks like Bryce. It was like trying to not hit someone back after they just punched you in the face, only instead of getting a busted jaw, I was getting incredible horny. *Stupid sex ban.*

"Get a room," muttered the guy as he passed us. If a little kissing in a stairwell bothered him, I wondered what he thought about all the public sex that was happening in the athletes' village every day.

When we couldn't hear his footsteps any longer, Bryce gave me one more kiss and then pulled back.

"Sorry about that," he said with a huge smile that made it seem like he wasn't actually sorry at all. "Standard spy procedure. Although I feel like you could have sold the kiss a little better."

I laughed awkwardly. "Sorry. I kind of have a boyfriend."

"Kind of?" he asked.

"Uh, yeah. I mean no." I sighed. "It's complicated."

"Well it's not a big deal. It was an undercover spy kiss, so it doesn't count for anything. It's like an actor making out with a co-star on film. Just part of the job." He feigned a very serious face.

"Right," I said, trying to convince myself that I wasn't a horrible person for not pushing him off me. *God, I'm just as bad as Chris!* I looked away from Bryce.

After a few awkward seconds, Bryce cleared his throat. "Let's keep moving. We have some boxers to freeze!" He turned and started sprinting up the stairs two at a time.

He didn't stop until we got to the fifth floor. God was he fast. I was in great shape, but I couldn't even come close to keeping up with him. I was glad that it wasn't any higher. I ran enough stairs at practice every day. I didn't need to be doing more in my free time.

Bryce pushed through the door and stopped in front of room 524. "Game time." He pulled a walkie talkie out of his track suit and pressed the button. "Pink Ocelot, what's our status? Green Tiger, over."

"Green Tiger, the nest is empty. Mission is a go. Pink Ocelot, over."

"Copy that, Ocelot. Over." Bryce put his radio back in his pocket and jiggled the door handle. It was locked.

"How are we gonna get in?" I asked.

"You really think I wouldn't come prepared?" Bryce asked as he pulled an access card out of his wallet. "Ready?"

"Are you sure we should do this?" I asked. It had all seemed fun at first, but now we were breaking into someone's room. I never did stuff like this. The closest I had come was when I snuck under the fence to get into the neighborhood pool when I was a kid, and I had worried about the cops showing up at my door for months afterwards. "Aren't we going to get kicked out of the games if they catch us?"

"Relax, Blonde Tigress. No one's going to catch us. And anyway, we're just playing a little harmless prank." Bryce gave me a reassuring smile.

I took a deep breath. I had always been so uptight. Maybe it was time to live a little. "Okay, let's do this. What's the plan?"

"Okay, your job is to find his underwear drawer, soak all of it in the tub, and then put it in his freezer. Got it?"

"Yeah. What are you doing?"

"You'll see." He winked at me and slid the access card into the lock. The light turned green and I heard the click of the door unlocking. We looked both ways down the hall to make sure no one had seen us before creeping into the room.

I immediately started rummaging through his drawers. My heart was pounding out of my chest. I wanted to get in and out as quickly as possible. *Come on! Where is your underwear?* I tried a few more drawers before I came to one filled with tighty whities. I grabbed them all and transported them to the bath tub. It only took a few seconds for them to get soaked, and then I stuffed them into his freezer next to some hot pockets.

"Done," I said.

Bryce poked his head out of the closet. "Me too. Let's get out of..."

Click.

Shit! Someone's here! I looked around frantically for a hiding spot. The closet was really the only option. I jumped in and Bryce shut the closet door. For the third time tonight, I found myself with my face a few inches away from Bryce's.

Oh my God. I'm going to get caught and end up in a Brazilian prison as someone's lady-bitch.

"Stop breathing so heavily," whispered Bryce.

Stop talking! He'll hear us! I peered through the slits in the closet to see whose underwear I had just frozen. He was a ridiculously muscular Asian man, and he had just stripped off all his clothes. *Fantastic. Now I'm a peeping Tom too.*

The guy approached the closet. I pressed myself more firmly against Bryce's chest. *God, he smells amazing.* I thought I was going to shit my pants when he reached towards the door, but it was just to grab the towel that was hanging next to the closet. Then he disappeared into the bathroom and the shower started.

Thank God.

We waited a few seconds before emerging from our hiding spot. On the way out, Bryce grabbed the guy's dirty underwear and threw it in the freezer.

I let out a sigh of relief when we were safely out in the hallway. "That was insane," I said. I couldn't believe I had just broken into someone's room and frozen their underwear. My heart was still pounding.

"We're not off the hook yet." Bryce pointed to the maid who had just rounded the corner. "Act natural."

She was blocking the only path to the stairs, so we had no choice but to walk right by her.

"Lovely evening, eh?" said Bryce as we passed her.

I held in my laughter until we were safely in the stairwell. "Nice accent," I said.

"Thanks," replied Bryce. "We better split up though. We can't risk anyone else seeing us together since you're not in disguise. Wait here for five minutes before you come down. Kristen will be waiting for you outside. Thanks for a great night, Blonde Tigress." He smiled at me and then took off down the stairs.

CHAPTER 9

Monday

ALINA

I went back to my locker after our second practice of the day. I was exhausted. Coach had nearly killed us as punishment for our loss the previous day against Brazil. And to make matters worse, I had barely gotten any sleep last night. My mind kept going back and forth between Bryce and Chris. I felt guilty for what had happened with Bryce. But I hadn't kissed him back. That's exactly what Chris had claimed Gabriela had done to him. It had seemed like he was lying though. Maybe Chris had kissed Gabriela back. Or maybe he had initiated it to begin with. It may have even gone further than that. Now I just felt angry and guilty and confused.

Plus I was on edge the whole day thinking that the police would show up any minute and haul me away to prison. I yawned. I really needed to take a nap.

I grabbed my stuff out of my locker and noticed that my phone was blinking to signal I had a new message. I turned it on and a message popped up from "My Favorite Athlete."

Who the hell is that? I didn't remember ever putting anyone in my phone with that name.

I clicked on the message to bring it up. "Make sure you don't miss the highlights tonight. Operation Red Rip - Success."

Bryce! That sneaky little bastard had put his number in my phone, and I guess also stolen my number.

"Why do you look so happy?" asked Kristen.

I turned my phone so she could read the text.

"Ah, I should have known it was your new boyfriend."

"He's not my boyfriend!"

"Suuure. You even have him in your phone as your favorite athlete. And here I was thinking that *I* was your favorite athlete." Kristen made a dramatic sad face. "By the way, did you ever figure out why it was called Operation Red Rip? I mean, I know you froze some guy's underwear, but what does that have to do with the color red or the word rip?"

"Right, since all of their codenames make so much sense," I said. "Pink Ocelot probably named the mission."

"Pink Ocelot," said Kristen with a laugh. "What a weirdo." She looked strangely happy about him.

"Oh my God, do you like Ocelot?"

"What? Psssh. No." Kristen turned away from me so I couldn't see her expression. "What time do the highlights usually come on?"

I checked the time on my phone. "I think around now. Let's see..." I clicked on the ITA broadcast app on my phone and Owen Harris popped up.

"We have some new developments in the Yao Kai incident, but first let's take a look at the updated medal count."

Yao Kai incident? Is that the guy whose underwear I froze?

A chart popped up on the screen. The US had 19 gold, 13 silver, and 19 bronze, for a total of 51. Brazil had 20 gold, 16 silver, and 16 bronze, for a total of 52. It didn't matter if they ranked it by gold medals or total medal counts. Either way, Brazil was ahead.

"The US had a strong showing today in wrestling to pick up a pair of golds and a bronze, but Brazil had an even better day, racking up a total of 10 medals and bringing their total ahead of the US for the first time in these games. To analyze the significance of this, let's bring in our medal analyst, Chip Nickels."

The shot panned out to show Chip sitting next to Owen at his desk.

"Well Owen," said Chip, "I don't think anyone saw this coming. I know I didn't. And the sports books in Vegas certainly didn't either. A few weeks ago you could have bet on Brazil winning the medal count with 30 to 1 odds. If Brazil can keep up this performance, Vegas is going to be paying out a lot of money to a few very lucky people."

"Do you think Brazil will be able to sustain this success for the next few days?" asked Owen.

"You know, I actually think they can. I just looked at a list of events that they could still medal in, and they could potentially get 50 or 60 more medals."

"Right, but most of those athletes are only in because Brazil is the host nation and got automatic qualification for all the events."

"Well, regardless of how they got in, the Brazilian athletes are really performing at these games. As a sports geek, I'm kind of hoping that they continue to do well and end up tying the US in overall medal count so that we can see our very first tiebreaker."

"Can you walk us through the rules for the tiebreaker?" asked Owen.

A new graphic popped up on the screen and slowly started scrolling up.

Article IV, Section 8 - Medal Count Tiebreaker

1. At noon GMT of the final Tuesday of the games, the committee will calculate if it is mathematically possible for two or more nations to end up with the exact same number of gold, silver, and bronze medals based on the current count and the number of athlete's still yet to compete.

2. If a tie is possible, the host nation will have 24 hours to choose a tiebreaking event. The event can be any event that is not currently featured in the 2017 games. The host nation must specify if it is a men's, women's, or coed competition.

3. The top five nations in overall medal count at noon GMT on Wednesday may select one (or a team, if required) of their current athletes to compete. Only athletes that have competed in the games are eligible.

4. If the medal count ends in a tie, the tiebreaker event will take place before the closing ceremony.

5. If there is no tie at the end of the games, the tiebreaker event will not be held.

"It's pretty simple, really," said Chip. "It will happen in three phases. First, tomorrow the ITA committee will calculate if it's mathematically possible for Brazil and the US to tie based on how many athletes they have left to compete. I'll tell you right now, it's going to be possible since they both have so many athletes."

"Okay. Step two?"

"Once they determine it's possible, the host nation, in this case, Brazil, has 24 hours to announce what the tiebreaker will be."

"And they can choose anything?" asked Owen.

"Yes," said Chip. "The only restriction is that it can't be a sport that's already a part of the games."

"Has there been any indication of what they might choose?"

"Not really. Although one interesting point is that the athletes who compete in it must be chosen from the athletes already at the games, so I suspect they would ask all of their current athletes if they are talented at any obscure sports. Anyway, the final phase is to look at the medal count at the end of the games. If the US and Brazil have the exact same number of each medal, they'll go ahead with the tiebreaker. If not, the event will be cancelled."

"What are the odds that a tiebreaker will actually be needed?" asked Owen.

"Probably less than one percent. But I can hope, can't I? Looking at the schedule, it looks like the last opportunity for either country to win a medal will be the women's volleyball final. Can you imagine if the US and Brazil both make it there and are playing to see which nation wins the medal count?"

Great. The fate of the US might rest on my ability to not lose my shit when I have to play against that slut Gabriela.

"That really would be something. Well, thanks for joining us, Chip. It's always a pleasure to have you on here. Now let's turn our attention to the developing story about Chinese gymnast Yao Kai."

Finally! "Kristen, they're showing it!" I said.

She leaned in closer to get a better look at the screen.

The graphic next to Owen Harris changed to a picture of the man whose underwear I had frozen. Owen stifled a laugh. "First, let me apologize for the obscene footage we aired earlier. We're sincerely sorry to those of you who were watching live. For those of you who didn't see it, here's a censored version."

Oh God. What happened?

Footage started rolling of Yao Kai powdering his hands and then hopping up onto the rings. He did a few moves before turning upside down and spreading his legs as far as possible. As he did, his pants tore clean in half.

Kristen and I started laughing hysterically. While I had frozen Yao Kai's underwear, Bryce must have cut a slit in his pants that would rip as soon as he did anything acrobatic. Turning upside down and doing the splits on the rings was more than sufficient to get his pants to rip, and due to the frozen underwear, Yao Kai had been going commando.

"After changing into a new pair of pants, Yao Kai performed well and led his team to a silver medal. When interviewed afterwards, he took a surprisingly lighthearted view of the incident."

The screen switched again to show Yao Kai talking to a reporter. They started talking in Chinese and then a voiceover cut in.

"Can you tell us what happened during the warm-up?" asked the reporter.

Yao Kai smiled. "I ripped my pants. It happens sometimes in gymnastics."

"Is there a reason why you weren't wearing any underwear? Do you usually perform like that?"

"I performed well today, so maybe this will be the start of a new tradition. But seriously, the real person you should be interviewing is the person that snuck into my room and froze my underwear last night."

At least he took it well.

The broadcast switched back to Owen Harris at his desk. He looked extremely serious, but I could tell that laughter was bubbling just below the surface. How could it not be? "Yao Kai's claim that his underwear was frozen prompted an investigation by the ITA committee, which has revealed that his pants were likely tampered with before the incident. Security footage from his dorm didn't reveal any suspicious activity, but one maid reported seeing a mustachioed Canadian man near Yao Kai's room at around 9 p.m. last night. They've released the following sketch."

A picture popped up next to Owen that looked nothing like Bryce, besides for a Canadian track suit and his ridiculous fake handlebar mustache.

I should have been concerned that the ITA committee was looking into it, but the sketch was so far off that there was no way they would ever link it back to us. And anyway, last night had been the most fun I had since arriving here. Actually, it had been a long time since I had that much fun.

"We'll continue to monitor this story," said Owen Harris, "but as of now, we have no idea why a Canadian would want to sabotage the Chinese gymnastics team. The Canadians didn't even send a men's gymnastics team to these games, so it doesn't appear that the sabotage was intended to gain a competitive advantage. Moving on, let's take a look at how the US won two golds in wrestling..."

Yuck. Who wants to watch big sweaty dudes wearing onesies and molesting each other? Not me.

I closed out the broadcast and typed out a text to Bryce: "I wonder if they'll ever find the mustachioed Canadian responsible for that heinous crime."

My phone buzzed with a text a second later: "I don't know, but he sure seems like a real bad ass. Where do you want to go for dinner?"

Did he just ask me out? Or demand that we go out? I smiled to myself.

"What's he saying?" asked Kristen.

"I think he just asked me out on a date."

"Oh my God, really?"

"Yeah. But I don't think I should go. This week is supposed to be about volleyball, not boys. That's why I'm taking a break with Chris." Saying his name made me feel nauseous. I still hadn't told Kristen the whole story about my conversation with him. I kept saying taking a break, but that wasn't really what it was. I had told him we were done. And he hadn't contacted me since.

"No, it isn't. You're taking a break with Chris because he's an asshole and cheated on you. As much as I want us to win gold, I also don't want you to miss out on getting to know Bryce. Here, let me see what he said. He probably didn't even mean it as a date. It was probably just as friends."

I handed her my phone. She immediately started typing a response to him.

"Hey!" I yelled. I grabbed for my phone, but Kristen turned away from me so that I'd have to reach around her to get it. Her arms were so much longer than mine that I didn't stand a chance. I gave up and sat down to try to lull Kristen into a false sense of security before my next attempt to get my phone back, but it didn't work. Instead, it just gave her time to finish the message and hit send.

"What'd you say to him?" I asked.

"Told him he could choose the place and asked where we should meet him."

"*We?*"

"Yes, we. That way you can hang out with him without feeling like it's a date. No harm in that, right?"

"Are you sure you're not just hoping Ocelot will be there too?" I asked. I was totally on to her.

"Ew, no. Why do you think I like him? I'm doing this for you."

"Sure..."

CHAPTER 10

Monday

BRYCE

"Alright, I have a challenge for you," I said.

"Please tell me you finally want to see who can fuck more girls by the end of the week," said Alex, aka Red Wolf.

"No. I was going to challenge you to find me a girl here at the games who's hotter than Alina. I think it's impossible."

"Oh God damn it," said Alex. "Will you please just fuck her and quit talking about it?"

"I think it's romantic how he's so smitten," said Tim, aka Pink Ocelot.

"It's not getting on your nerves at all?"

"Well, maybe a little," admitted Tim.

"Alright. How about you go for a run, and when you come back, we'll pretend like Alina doesn't exist?"

I was going to think of something clever to say, but then I had an idea. I snapped my fingers. "You're a genius, Alex! If I go right now, maybe I'll conveniently bump into Alina as she's leaving volleyball practice." I was only half joking.

Alex shook his head. "I think you totally missed the point of what I just said. Maybe instead you need to go find a nice Brazilian prostitute."

I glanced at my phone to try to ignore Alex. Somehow he always managed to steer the conversation back to his favorite topic: Brazilian prostitutes. I'm pretty sure the only reason he trained hard enough to be a part of the ITAs was so he could come to Brazil to find himself a nice prostitute. He didn't even like running that much. I was hoping to see a text from Alina, but instead I saw I had a missed call from my sister, Emily.

"Be right back," I said, ducking into the hallway to call her back. I leaned against the wall and dialed her number.

"Hey, Bryce!" she said. Despite all we had been through as kids, she always managed to be so positive. It was infectious. But today there was something else in her voice.

"Hey, Em. What's up?"

"Nothing, it's okay now I think." The bubbliness from her voice was suddenly missing entirely.

"What is it?" I asked.

"Well when I got back to my dorm today after class I got a weird feeling, like someone had been in here."

"Was the door open or something?"

"No, no. Nothing like that. It just felt off. A few things looked like they weren't how I left them. It was like when we used to know Max had been in our room." For a year and a half, Max had been our foster brother. He loved stealing stuff from our room whenever he had the chance.

"Weird. Maybe it was a maintenance guy or something?"

"Yeah, maybe. Anyway, don't worry about it. You need to focus on your race."

"I'm actually having a little trouble with that."

"Is Alex keeping you and Tim up all night by banging poor, sweet Brazilian girls?"

"Surprisingly, no. It's this girl Alina. I can't stop thinking about her."

"Is she some sexy foreign girl?"

"No, she's American," I said.

"Is she cool, or do you just like her boobs?"

"Don't worry, it's not another Michelle situation."

Em made a gagging sound. "Thank God. She was the worst. Just keep in mind that I have to be sisters with whatever girl you end up with. Don't screw me on this."

"I'll try not to. Anyway, I dunno if anything is going to come of it. She's in a relationship or something right now. It's complicated."

"But you like her?"

"Yes."

"Then it's not complicated. Go get her."

I smiled. Em always had a way of making everything seem so simple. "Alright. Thanks for the advice. I wish Tim and Alex could be as sensible as you."

"Let me guess: Alex told you to fuck her and forget about her, and Tim told you to send her a dozen roses and a singing telegram?"

"Something like that, yeah."

Em laughed. "Those two..."

"I wish you'd been able to come," I said. I had tried to think of a way to get her here to watch my race, but it was just too expensive. All the money we had went towards her schooling.

"Me too, but you know I'll be watching from here and cheering you on. Hey, I gotta run to class, but call me soon to tell me how it's going with Alina. I want to hear all about her."

"Will do. Oh yeah, if you have a chance, watch the highlights tonight of the men's gymnastics."

"Why? Oh my God, did you..."

"You'll see."

"I can't wait. Bye, Bryce!"

"Bye, Em. Stay safe."

Click.

I stayed leaning against the wall for a few seconds thinking about what Em had said. I knew she was tough and could take care of herself, but I still worried about how she thought someone was creeping around in her room. I tried to think of someone on campus that I could have check in on her, but no one came to mind. All the people I knew there had already graduated.

Tim poked his head out of our dorm. "Dude, come check this out."

I went back in and walked over to Tim's computer. He had found a BuzzFeed article featuring gifs of Yao Kai splitting his pants. Tim seemed to think the one where someone had photoshopped an image of a kitten in place of Yao Kai's penis was particularly hilarious.

"Who were you talking to?" asked Alex. "Please tell me it wasn't Alina."

"No, it was Em," I said.

"Did you tell her to get a flight here? She can share my bed; I don't mind."

I punched him in the arm. "How many times do I have to tell you that I'll kill you if you ever touch Emily?"

"What if she's the one who comes onto me? I can't help it. Girls just love me."

"Yeah, not gonna happen. How's your search for a Brazilian prostitute coming?"

"Not bad. I picked up some literature the other day..." Alex held up a stack of fliers with half naked women on them.

"You better not bring them back to this room," said Tim. "I don't want to end up in Brazilian prison."

"Yeah, that would be awful," said Alex. "Especially for you, Tim. You'd definitely be the first one to be someone's bitch."

Tim smiled, as if Alex had just given him a compliment. "You know, I've always thought I'd be popular in prison. It's the one place where my baby-smooth skin would come in handy. It's a blessing and a curse..."

Alex and I glanced at each other and tried not to laugh. We still weren't entirely sure if Tim was gay or not. He had a lot of girlfriends, but the things he said were just so freaking gay.

I was about to add a comment about Tim's inability to grow facial hair, but my phone buzzing in my pocket distracted me.

I pulled out my phone and read a text from Alina: "I wonder if they'll ever find the mustachioed Canadian responsible for that heinous crime."

Hmm...how to respond. I started typing out a response: "I don't know, but he sure seems like a real bad ass."

"Was that Alina?" asked Tim.

"Yeah," I said.

"Did you ask her out to dinner?"

"No."

"And you think *I'd* be the bitch in prison? You can't even ask a girl out."

"Oh snap," said Alex. "Tim's right, you are being kind of a bitch about this girl. You've been talking about her all day and then you don't even ask her out?"

"I was just waiting for her to respond." I added, "Where do you want to go for dinner?" and hit send. "There, I asked where she wanted to go for dinner."

Tim put his hand on his head. "You didn't ask her if she wanted to go first? Chivalry is dead."

"I like it," said Alex. "Way to man up."

"Do you even have proper Brazilian evening dress?" asked Tim. "This is a disaster."

"What is this, Downton Abbey?" asked Alex.

Alina's response popped up on my phone: "Wherever you want. Where should Kristen and I meet you guys?"

Damn. Her inviting Kristen was a pretty clear sign that she didn't want it to be a date. Em's advice ran through my head. *It's not complicated. Go get her.* "Well, she thinks you guys are coming. And her friend Kristen is coming. Who wants wingman duty?"

"Is Kristen her friend from last night?" asked Tim.

"Hmm...I don't know who you're talking about," I said. I wanted to see if I could trick Tim into saying her codename outside of a mission, a clear breach of spy protocol.

"You know. The tall one with the dark hair."

"Oh, you mean Brunette Gir..."

Tim slapped me. "No! No codenames."

I should have been shocked, but slapping was Tim's go-to move when he got upset. Whenever anyone questioned him about it, he insisted that punching was "too brutish."

"Alright, fine. Yes, Kristen is her friend from last night. Now help me figure out where we should take them. We need somewhere real nice."

"I read about a steakhouse in the city that's simply to die for," said Tim. "I think it's called Carne Duro."

"My Portuguese is a little rusty, but doesn't that translate to Hard Meat?" asked Alex. "As long as we aren't going to a gay strip club, I'm in."

Tim grabbed his phone and brought up his trip advisor app. "Oh, my mistake. It's actually Carne Deliciosa. Carne Duro must have been...never mind. Here, I'll make a reservation." He clicked a few buttons and then said, "Done. Tell the girls we'll meet them at the north village exit at 6:30."

CHAPTER 11
Monday
ALINA

I finished blow-drying my hair and glanced down at my phone. I had been silently willing Chris to text me all day. He was doing a great job staying away from me, which is what I had requested. But that was before I had told him we were done. And this silence didn't feel like he was respecting my boundaries. It felt like we really were over. I knew we needed to have another conversation. I refused for it to end by me slamming the door in his face. I didn't think he really meant the things he said, but he still said them.

If he called me right now, I'd answer in a heartbeat. I'd hear him out. But he wasn't calling. And I couldn't help but think that he was hanging out with a bunch of sleazy women, catching up on all he had missed out on in the last two years. I put my elbows down on the sink and my face in my hands. It really was over. Gabriela had won. Again. I just felt so defeated.

A knock on the bathroom door made me jump.

"Hey, are you almost ready?" Kristen asked.

"Yeah, just a sec." I glanced down once more at my phone. Chris had cheated on me. I had found out. And now we were done. He hadn't reached out to try to fix things, because there wasn't anything else to talk about. Even if I could forgive him, I couldn't trust him. Maybe if this had been the first time that he hadn't been faithful.

But this wasn't the first time we had a conversation like this. I just never had photographic evidence before. I was like putty in his handsome hands and he knew it. *Screw you, Chris.*

I took a deep breath and looked in the mirror. All the under-eye concealer in the world couldn't hide the fact that I had been crying, but I applied a little extra hoping it would help before unlocking the door.

"Wear this one," Kristen said and tossed me a sparkly, low-cut dress when I walked out of the bathroom.

"I want something a little more conservative." I tucked a loose strand of hair behind my ear and opened up the closet.

"It's a date, not an office meeting."

"It's not a date either. What if Gabriela set Chris up? Maybe I should call him..."

"No. Chris is an asshole. Chris has always been an asshole. And Chris will always be an asshole."

"Just because you don't like him..."

"Alina, you're my best friend and I'm trying really hard to be supportive. I know I've told you this a hundred times, but apparently you need to hear it one more time. People don't change."

She was referring to Chris being a player. We had had this conversation a bunch of times. And I always chose not to believe her. Because there hadn't been proof. Now that there was, could I really look the other way? I pulled a dress out of the closet. It was short but didn't have such a plunging neckline. "How about this one?"

She smiled and nodded. "Keeping a little to the imagination. Good choice."

"Are you sure you don't want to just grab takeout and watch that movie we skipped out on yesterday?"

"Bryce seems like a nice, normal, drop dead gorgeous guy. You need this."

"I need time." I felt empty and lost. I thought Chris was my future. I bit my lip. There was no way I was going to start crying again. *Fuck*.

Kirsten gave me a sympathetic smile. "Trust me, tonight is going to make you feel better."

I thought about my reaction to Bryce kissing me during Operation Red Rip. I had wanted to kiss him back. I pulled on the dress I had picked out. Bryce had cheered me up after that horrible game. He didn't care that I had snot all over my jersey. He sat with me and made me laugh. And during Operation Red Rip he had made me forget all about my breakup with Chris. He made it feel like I could breathe again. I didn't know anything about him, but I liked the way he made me feel. When I was with him everything seemed like it was going to be okay.

"What do you think?" I asked and turned toward Kristen. She was wearing a dress much more similar to the one she had wanted me to wear. Apparently she didn't want Ocelot to imagine very much.

"Perfect. Come on, or we're going to be late." She linked her arm in mine and pulled me toward the door.

CHAPTER 12

Monday

BRYCE

I couldn't believe it, but I actually had butterflies in my stomach as we waited for the girls to arrive. It was like I was back in fifth grade again.

"Dude, what's that guy's deal?" asked Tim, signaling with his eyes for us to look behind him.

Alex and I turned to see what he was looking at, but nothing stood out. All I saw was a big fence separating the athlete's village from the rest of the city, a few guards at the gate, and a guy leaning against the fence smoking a cigarette.

"Who?" I asked.

"The smoker. He keeps staring at us. Now why don't you idiots quit making it so obvious that we're talking about him."

"He's probably just mesmerized by the hair gel dripping down your forehead," said Alex. "I think you might have used a little too much. I'm concerned you might get a stain on your dinner jacket."

Tim got a worried look on his face and whipped out his compact mirror to check on his perfectly quaffed hair. He checked a few angles and then snapped it shut. "I don't know what you're talking about. My hair looks fantastic, although I'm not sure how much longer it will last. Not even Paul Mitchell's finest gel can last long in this heat. The other day in Cosmo I read..."

"Hey!" said two girls.

I spun around. Alina and Kristen were standing behind us. I probably should have been more subtle, but I couldn't prevent myself from giving Alina the up-down. Her dress was fairly conservative on top, but it hugged her tiny waist perfectly and showed off her great legs. I snapped my focus back to her face. "Hey, Alina," I said, going in for the hug.

I got a nice whiff of Alina's perfume. Cherries? Maybe. I could never tell the difference between all those scents. It all either smelled like cherries or cookies. Whatever it was, it smelled good.

"So now that we're not on our secret..." Alina started, but Tim put his finger across her lips to shush her. She swatted his hand away. "Sorry, I just wanted to find out your real names."

Tim stepped back and smoothed his ridiculous maroon dinner jacket. "This is Alex, and I'm Tim." He locked eyes with Kristen and gave a flourished bow. "It's a pleasure to see you again, m'lady."

"I figured bringing him would give us good entertainment for the evening," I whispered to Alina as Kristen introduced herself to Tim.

He, of course, kissed the back of her hand.

Alina stifled a laugh and whispered, "Is he always like this? I think Kristen has a crush on him."

"Unfortunately, yes. He is."

"Is he gay?" she asked.

I laughed. "Officially? No. Unofficially..."

Alex cleared his throat. Alina and I quit whispering and looked up. He was standing awkwardly by himself while Tim taught Kristen how to do a proper curtsey and Alina and I whispered to each other. It was obvious that he held the unenviable position of being the fifth wheel. I would have tried to get Kristen and Alina to bring a third volleyball girl, but I wouldn't wish Alex on anyone.

"Sorry," I said.

"So where are we going?" asked Alina.

"Some steak place. Hopefully it'll be good. Tim said it had pretty good reviews on trip advisor."

"Perfect," said Alina. "I've been craving some meat."

"Yeah, Alina loves meat in her mouth," said Kristen.

Alina started to turn red. "Oh my God. I didn't mean it like that. I meant steak meat, not penis meat. Not that I don't like penises, it's just I'm really hungry for steak. And I should stop talking now."

Kristen cut in. "Sorry, Alina's having a little trouble thinking straight. Our coach has banned us from sex for the past four weeks. Did your coach give you guys a sex ban too?"

I tried not to show my excitement. I knew Alina had a boyfriend, but with things being "complicated" between them and Alina being horny as hell, things could get interesting later in the week.

Tim laughed. "Yeah. We aren't even allowed to masturbate. It's been kind of funny, actually. It's like boner-city in the showers after practice. A little hot water and boom, boner time." He turned to Alina. "You probably know all about that though after you wandered into the men's locker room the other day."

Alina caught my gaze and raised an eyebrow slightly. She didn't need to speak to communicate a very clear, "What the fuck is wrong with Tim?"

I shrugged. I had no explanation for the odd shit Tim said. *Does he really check everyone out in the shower?* I made a mental note to stay away from Tim in the locker room.

"Shouldn't we get going so we aren't late to dinner?" asked Alex.

"Good idea," I said.

As we walked through the gate, I glanced over at the guy that Tim had accused of being creepy. The dude stared at me for a second and then flicked his cigarette and ground it into the sidewalk with the heal of his scuffed Timberland boots. There was a pile of about three dozen other cigarette butts in the same spot. *Does this guy do anything other than stand here and smoke?* He pulled out his phone, typed out a text, and walked away.

"Alright, our Uber should be here any minute," said Tim.

Just as he finished his sentence, a black car with an Uber sticker in the window pulled up.

CHAPTER 13

Monday

ALINA

"Wow, that was quick," I said.

"It really was," agreed Bryce. "He must have known you couldn't wait much longer to get some meat in your mouth."

Oh my God. Why did I ever say that? I couldn't think straight with him standing so close in that damn fitted suit. *The way it hugged his arms...* I hit his arm playfully. "Just get in the car."

Bryce opened up the door.

"Is there enough room?" I asked. There were five of us and only three seats in the back of the car, so the answer was no.

"Sure there is," said Kristen. "We can just sit on their laps."

"Works for me," said Bryce.

Tim got in first, followed by Kristen. She sat on his lap way more seductively than was appropriate.

"What about seatbelts?" I asked.

Kristen gave me a death stare. "I'm sure Bryce will be happy to put his arms around you."

I glanced sideways at Bryce to try to catch his reaction, but he was already climbing in after Alex. There really wasn't any room to sit besides on Bryce lap. I slowly got in, trying not to expose myself in my tiny dress, and sat on Bryce's lap. He put his hands on my hips and the smell of his cologne filled my nose. God, he smelled so good. His right hand left for a second to close the door, but then immediately gravitated back to my hip.

I swallowed hard. I was sure I wouldn't have felt what I was feeling if there hadn't been a sex ban. There's no way his touch would send shivers down my spine. There was no way I'd be noticing how big and strong his hands were. I tried to shake the thoughts out of my head and stared out the side window.

"Where to?" asked the driver in a thick accent.

"Carne Deliciosa," said Tim.

The driver nodded and pulled into the street. I lurched forward slightly, which caused Bryce's fingers to dig into my hips. It didn't matter what I tried to tell myself. I liked the feeling of his hands on me and I liked the feeling of his fingertips digging into my hips even better.

His grip eased up on me, but every time we hit a bump or came to a stop, his fingers would dig into my hips again. My body stiffened when he started to trace small circles with his thumb along my lower back. I wasn't sure if he was doing it absentmindedly or on purpose, but it was making my heart race. I put my hand on the armrest on the door to steady myself. If I wasn't careful, I'd melt into that touch.

"Alina?" Kristen said.

"What?" I turned away from the window.

She was staring at me like she had been trying to get my attention for awhile. "Do you have any guesses?"

I cleared my throat. "Um...what are we guessing?"

Alex laughed. "She's been trying to guess what sport the three of us are here for. Basketball, cycling, fencing...nope, nope, and nope."

"Oh." I turned around to see Bryce's reaction to those guesses.

He was staring at me so intently with his blue eyes that it made me gulp.

I immediately turned back around and stared at the headrest in front of my face. It seemed like he was doing that with his hands on purpose. Maybe he was trying to see how I reacted to his touch, and I was certainly reacting to it. "Do you guys play tennis?"

"I already told Kristen that we don't play with balls," Tim said.

"Right." I coughed awkwardly. "Soccer? I mean, not soccer. There's balls in that. I mean one ball."

Bryce laughed behind me. His laugh was electric. It was like I could feel it radiating through me. His right hand had slipped down when he laughed and now his thumb was dangerously close to my ass.

"You two have one more guess," Alex said. "Make it a good one."

"What happens if we get it wrong?" Kristen asked.

Alex shrugged. "What do you guys think we should make them do?"

"So many options," Tim said.

Bryce's hands were making it hard to concentrate, but I didn't want to lose any more bets. I was still worried Kristen was going to force me to have sex in public. There was no way I'd have another punishment hanging over my head. As if the last couple days weren't punishment enough for awhile. I thought about how fast Bryce had run during Operation Red Rip. All the athletes in the ITA were in incredibly good shape. But they weren't all that fast. "Track," I said, before they could even come up with a punishment.

"Bingo," Tim said.

Kristen almost looked disappointed that she wouldn't owe Tim anything. She was totally crushing on him.

The car came to a stop outside of the restaurant and Bryce's fingertips dug into my hips one last time. "Thanks for being my seatbelt," I said and lightly touched his hand. I immediately removed my hand from his, opened up the car door, and stepped down onto the curb.

Bryce smiled as he climbed out of the car. "No problem."

"He liked you being on top of him," Alex said and slapped Bryce on the back.

Oh my God.

"So, Alina, you and Kristen both play volleyball, right?"

I turned my attention to Alex as we walked toward the restaurant. "Yes."

"So why are you so much shorter than Kristen?"

I laughed. "I play in the back row so I don't need to be tall."

"Interesting."

A hand on my lower back almost made me jump. I looked up at Bryce smiling at me. He removed his hand as he opened the door for everyone. I had my doubts about what Bryce wanted before tonight. But it was becoming pretty clear and I wasn't sure if I was ready. I knew that I was a mess right now. When I looked into his eyes, though, I wasn't thinking about what I had just lost. I wanted to hold onto that feeling.

Even if this wasn't a date, I was going to enjoy myself tonight. I wasn't going to think about Chris. At all. Because he damn sure wasn't thinking about me.

Tim said something to the hostess and we followed her.

I felt Bryce's hand fall to my lower back again, guiding me toward our table. I was almost disappointed when we reached our table, a crescent shaped booth in the corner of the restaurant, because Bryce's hand dropped from my back.

Alex scooted into the booth first. "Girls," he said and tapped the booth on both sides of him.

Kristen laughed and scooted in on one side of him. As long as Bryce was planning on sitting next to me, I didn't care who was on the other side of me. I slid in beside Alex.

Bryce sat down beside me and put his arm behind me on the booth, without touching me. "Alright, let's play a game while we wait for the waiter," he suggested.

"What game?" I asked.

"It's called ask a friend. We go around the table and take turns asking anyone at the table any question we want, but instead of them answering, someone else at the table has to answer for them. Alina, do you want to start?"

"Sure. What's Bryce's favorite food?"

"Really? That's a super lame question," said Alex. "But if you must know, his favorite food is a nice juicy rib-eye."

"Oh. Well what kind of question should I have asked?"

"Let me give you an example. What's Alina's number?"

"Why is that question any better?" I asked. "Half the people here already have my number."

"No. I meant how many people have you had sex with?"

"Oh..." My face started to blush.

"One," said Kristen. "Her boyfriend. Er...her ex boyfriend. Or whatever they are."

"Okay, next question," I said quickly. "Kristen, I think it's your turn." I could feel Bryce staring at me.

Kristen tapped her finger against her mouth while she thought of a question. "What's Tim's biggest fantasy?"

"Based on our conversation earlier, I think he wants to be someone's prison bitch," said Bryce.

Alex laughed and Tim looked slightly annoyed. From the brief time I had known Tim, I thought that Bryce's guess might not be far off.

"Nope, try again," said Tim.

"Well if he was normal he would just want to have a threesome," suggested Alex.

"With two guys or two girls?" asked Tim.

"Two girls I hope," said Alex.

Tim shrugged. "Oh, I've done that before."

"What?!" yelled Alex. "How did you not tell me about that?"

"I dunno. What's the big deal about having a threesome with two girls?"

"Wait, are you being serious?" I asked. "I thought it was like every guy's fantasy to have a threesome."

"It was okay I guess. It was just kind of tiring and I felt like I didn't really get to fully satisfy either girl. I'd much rather just focus on pleasing one woman at a time. If anything, a threesome makes more sense if it's two guys and a girl."

"A devil's threesome?" asked Bryce. "Is that your fantasy?"

Tim thought about it for a second. "It's not my fantasy, but it makes way more sense than two girls and one guy."

Bryce laughed. "How does it make more sense?"

"Simple anatomy, really. Do I need to draw you a picture?"

"No you don't..." started Bryce, but it was too late. Tim had already flipped over the menu and started drawing naked figures.

"Look," said Tim, holding up a drawing of two stick figures having sex while a third watched. "Guys only have one penis, so they can please one girl at a time. That leads to one girl feeling left out." He drew a frowny face on the third wheel to make his point. Then he drew a picture with a girl sandwiched between two smiling men. "Girls, on the other hand, have three holes, so they could easily please two men at once. Not to mention that girls take a lot longer to please than men do, so it makes sense for multiple men to work together to give a beautiful woman the attention she deserves."

"I think his logic is sound," said Kristen.

Tim smiled at her.

I shifted uncomfortably in my seat, realizing that I was starting to get damp between my legs. *God, what is wrong with me? This sex ban is turning me into a freak.*

Our waitress appeared and pulled out a notebook. "Are you all ready to order?"

"Yes, I think so," said Tim. "Ladies?"

Kristen ordered a stupid salad, but I had to go for Bryce's favorite. A big juicy rib-eye. I couldn't resist. We were at a steakhouse after all.

"Nice choice," Bryce said. "I'll have the same." He put his menu down and then leaned in a little closer to me. "Couldn't pass up the opportunity for meat in your mouth?"

I laughed awkwardly. The restaurant suddenly seemed stifling.

Before I knew it, our wine glasses were being filled. Kristen took a sip of hers. She always could hold her alcohol better than I could. There was no way I was drinking before tomorrow's game, though. And the longer I sat here with Bryce so close in proximity, the more parched I got.

"Okay, my turn," Tim said when the waitress walked away with our order. He rubbed his hands together. "On a scale of one to ten, how attracted is Alina to Bryce?"

Bryce seemed to stiffen. "Dude. Ask a different..."

"An eleven," Kristen said and winked at me.

Holy shit. I could feel my cheeks turning red.

"Bryce thinks Alina is an eleven too," Tim said. "Stop looking at me like that. It's true."

Bryce cleared his throat. "I'm sorry. I forgot to tell you that my friends are the worst."

I was embarrassed that Kristen told the whole table I was attracted to Bryce. But I wasn't upset with his friends for getting him to confess that he was attracted to me. This was definitely a date. I avoided Bryce's gaze and fidgeted with my hands under the table.

"The worst?" Tim asked. "You know that you're in love with me."

"I don't know how many times we have to tell you this," Alex said. "There's a difference between loving someone and being in love with someone. Bryce and I love you like a brother. But we aren't in love with you, man."

Tim shrugged. "I really don't understand the difference."

"Do we need to draw you a picture?" Bryce asked and started laughing.

His laughter was infectious. Soon I was laughing and couldn't stop. I thought that our friends announcing that we were attracted to each other would take the night on an awkward turn. But who was I kidding? I thought Bryce was hot. And sweet. And funny. It was nice to know that he was attracted to me too. I was still laughing when I looked up at him.

There was that twinkle in his blue eyes again. It took my breath away. And I knew I was in trouble, because I didn't ever want to look away from those eyes.

"Can I steal you for a second?" Bryce asked.

Kristen gave me two thumbs up, not subtly at all.

"Um, yeah, sure." I slid out of the booth after him. "I was hoping to get some water from the bar."

"I noticed that you weren't drinking any wine." His hand fell onto my lower back again. Those really big, manly hands. *Stop it.*

"We have a game tomorrow. I really shouldn't be drinking."

He nodded. "My race is on Wednesday. I'm going to skip the wine too." His hand left my back and he waved down the bartender. He ordered two waters and leaned against the bar. "Where are you from?"

That wasn't what I was expecting him to ask me. "Wilmington, Delaware. You?"

"Pasadena most recently. I've moved a lot. Did you go to school in Delaware?"

"I went to the University of New Castle for the last three years. I just graduated."

"What about for freshman year?"

I felt that familiar lump forming in my throat. I tried to swallow it down. "NYCU."

"Why'd you transfer?"

Our waters had arrived, but Bryce made no movement to head back to our table. He was staring at me intently, waiting for me to respond.

"You don't have to..."

"No. It's fine. It was so long ago." I smiled, pretending it was nothing. "It was silly, really. There was this girl who played the same position as me. She wasn't happy that a freshman was competing for the same spot as her on the team. And she didn't take it well. She hazed me. At least, that's how she put it."

Bryce lowered his eyebrows slightly. "How would you put it?"

"She bullied me until I broke and ran home. I don't know. Like I said, it was silly." I laughed awkwardly.

"It's not silly."

Something in my chest tightened. Chris had always told me it was stupid and that I should get over it. That it shouldn't bother me anymore. But he didn't understand. He didn't know what it felt like to be humiliated every day for months. To dread leaving your dorm room each morning. To always be on edge. Bryce wasn't looking at me like he thought I was ridiculous. He was looking at me like he understood. "And how would you know what it's like to be bullied? Bullies don't pick on guys that look like you."

"I didn't always look like this. I was a scrawny little kid."

"I can't picture you as scrawny or little."

He shrugged. "Let's just say that I run because I had something to run from."

He wasn't just handsome, sweet, and funny. He was real. And honest. I barely knew him, but I trusted him more than I had ever trusted Chris. I wanted to know what he was running from. Actually, I wanted to know everything about him. But before I could ask, he had another question.

"How complicated is it?"

I sat down on the stool beside him. "Complicated."

"Enlighten me."

I bit my lip. I wanted to know more about him. I didn't want to talk about Chris. Maybe it wasn't complicated at all. "He cheated on me."

"Then he must be an idiot."

I laughed. "Thanks for saying that."

"I don't really see the complication, though."

"We've been dating for two years. He made one mistake." *That I know of.* "I don't know if that means I should throw it all away. And you've seen what people do in the middle of the athlete's village..."

"Wait, he's here?"

"Yeah, he's on the swim team."

"What's his name?"

I didn't see why telling him that mattered. "Chris Hamilton."

His jaw seemed to tense.

"What, do you know him?"

"No, I've seen him around." He shrugged his shoulders like it didn't matter. But I had seen him clench his jaw. He had reacted to hearing Chris' name.

"I told him it was over right before Operation Red Rip. And I haven't heard from him since. I guess it really isn't that complicated. He seems perfectly happy with my decision."

"Are you happy with it?"

"I'm trying to focus on winning the rest of my games."

"Well, I personally think you made a great decision."

"You do?" My heart seemed to flutter.

"You deserve better than him."

"What, like you?"

He raised his eyebrow. "I never said that. Are you hitting on me?"

I laughed. "Like you aren't hitting on me."

"Let's just say that I wouldn't mind making things a little more complicated for you."

It took me a second to realize I had stopped breathing. I wasn't sure if him liking me complicated things, or made them way less complicated. Because from everything I knew about Bryce, he was worth taking a chance on. He seemed to understand me. And I couldn't stop thinking about his hands on me and his perfectly sculpted torso.

Especially when his gaze was fixed on me like that. My whole body felt overheated.

He picked up both glasses of water. "I think our food is ready." He nodded toward our table.

Our dinner had just been served. Alex and Tim looked like they had both moved a little closer to Kristen. It seemed like she might be getting close to achieving that devil's threesome Tim wanted so badly.

"I know how much you're craving meat in your mouth," Bryce said. "I'm surprised you're not running over there."

I laughed and grabbed one of the glasses out of his hand so that one of his would be free. "I'm never going to live that down, am I?"

Bryce smiled. He placed his free hand on the small of my back, just like I hoped he would. This time I didn't try to justify the shivers that went down my spine. It wasn't just the sex ban. I liked Bryce. I really liked him.

"What's actually going on between Alina and her kind of boyfriend?" Alex asked as we sat down.

Apparently they had continued playing the game while we were away. Which didn't really make any sense, since I wasn't there to answer the questions for Kristen.

Kristen shrugged. "He cheated on her with her arch nemesis. And they're taking a break. Hopefully a permanent one."

I could feel Bryce's eyes on me. When I told him about Chris, I had left off the part about who he had cheated on me with. I didn't want him to pity me. But he wasn't looking at me like that. I couldn't really place the expression on his face. It almost looked protective.

I cut into my steak and took a big bite. Despite the teasing, I really did like meat in my mouth.

"On a scale of one to ten, how interested is Kristen in that devil's threesome?" Tim asked.

"At least an eight," I said when I finished chewing.

Kristen laughed.

"Whoa. No. I'm not your third," Alex said.

"Why not?"

"Because I'm not gay."

Bryce and I both laughed.

"I'm not gay either," Tim said. "I fully appreciate the female body in all its grace and beauty." He was staring intently at Kristen.

She blushed.

How was Kristen attracted to this guy? Despite what he had just said, he was clearly gay. I took another bite of my steak. For the first time since seeing those photos of Chris and Gabriela, I felt completely relaxed. I hadn't laughed like this in such a long time. Maybe things had been going south between me and Chris for longer than I had realized. Or maybe I had been too focused on volleyball. But how could I not be? This was the biggest competition of my life. Chris wasn't allowed to make me feel guilty for caring so much. He had put me second while he trained too. *Stop thinking about him.*

When I was upset, I tended to eat way more than usual. I was the first one done with my steak.

"You weren't kidding about liking meat in your mouth," Alex said.

I shrugged and looked at Bryce out of the corner of my eye. "I never joke about meat in my mouth."

He choked on the sip of water he had just taken and everyone at the table laughed.

"Do you think they have anything good for dessert?" Kristen asked.

"I'm completely stuffed," Tim said as he pulled his napkin off his lap with a flourish and placed it on the table.

"Me too. But Alina never goes anywhere without getting dessert and she always lets me steal one bite."

"How do you keep such a slim figure?" Tim asked me.

"I'm an athlete? Maybe they have some Brazilian delicacy I haven't tried."

"Have you tried a brigadeiro yet?" Bryce asked.

I turned toward him. "No. What is that?"

"They're these little chocolate balls that Bryce can't stop eating," Alex said with a laugh.

Bryce ignored him. "They're these sweet, gooey, absolutely delicious chocolate things with chocolate sprinkles. Or you can get coconut instead of sprinkles. You have to try them."

Chris had this way of making me feel guilty about ordering dessert. "You don't need that," was something he said to me all the time. I never knew if it was because he was being cheap, was in a rush, or if he was just calling me fat. Either way, it always made me feel horrible. I loved dessert. Was that really so bad? And how was I supposed to own a bakery if I didn't taste other people's creations and scope out the competition?

And after one bite of a coconut covered brigadeiro, I realized that Bryce wasn't just a great guy. He also shared my taste in desserts. There wasn't a single thing about him that I didn't like. And the more time I spent with him, the more I realized how lacking my relationship was with Chris.

CHAPTER 14
Monday
ALINA

I wanted Bryce to press me against a wall and kiss me again like he had during Operation Red Rip. This time I'd kiss him back. I thought about his tongue tracing my lips. I had wanted it then, before I even knew anything about him. And everything I had learned since then, I liked. Not to mention that I had never been this instantly attracted to anyone in my life. Except maybe Owen Harris.

But Bryce was being respectful. His hand wasn't even hovering on my lower back as we waited for our Uber outside of the restaurant.

"What time is your game tomorrow?" he asked.

"2 o'clock."

"Do you mind if I come cheer you on?" His shaggy hair blew in the warm Brazilian wind. He ran his hand through his hair to get it out of his face.

I smiled. Everything he did seemed to exude sex. "No, I don't mind."

"You can count me in too," Tim said. "Those spandex shorts really do something to a man."

Kristen blushed under his gaze.

"But we might be a little sweaty, because that's the same time that our practice ends."

Kristen whispered something in his ear and Tim smiled.

Alex cleared his throat. "Ubers in Brazil really are fast."

An SUV had just pulled to a stop in front of us. I couldn't deny the fact that I was eager to sit on Bryce's lap again. To feel his fingers on me. Bryce seemed equally excited, because he was the first one that approached the car.

He opened the door and hopped in. I was about to join him, but before I could, the tires squealed and the car sped off, nearly running over my foot in the process. I screamed and jumped back. The hasty getaway left the smell of burnt rubber lingering in the air.

"What the hell was that?" asked Kristen.

"I dunno. That jackass almost ran over my foot."

"I guess that explains how he got here so quickly. He's a crazy driver," said Alex.

Tim glanced down at his phone. "I think that was actually someone else's Uber. The map shows that ours is still two minutes away."

"Is Uber Psycho a new service option that they offer?" asked Kristen. "Or is that a Brazilian exclusive?"

I laughed for a second and then started to get worried. "Wait. What if he just got kidnapped?"

"Relax, Alina," said Kristen. "The car had an Uber sticker on it, so it must have been legit. He probably just took someone else's Uber."

I looked around, but there was no one else waiting to be picked up. And her logic about why it had to be legit wasn't terribly convincing.

"Why don't you text him?" suggested Alex.

"Good idea." I pulled out my phone and typed out a text: "Are you okay?"

But there was no response.

CHAPTER 15
Monday
BRYCE

"Dude, what was that?" I asked as the driver floored the acceleration.

He eased off the gas and turned back to look at me. "Where to?" he asked in a thick Brazilian accent.

"The athletes' village. But first can we go back and get my friends?"

"Não entendo. You have map?"

"What?"

"Map." The driver picked up his cell phone and pointed to it.

"Uh, yeah. Hold on." I pulled up google maps and put in the village square. It calculated for a second and then told me to take a right in 800 feet. "Right up ahead."

"Give map," said the driver, reaching back with an open palm.

I handed him my phone. He looked at it for a second and then closed the app and put it in his cup holder. I guess he knew how to get there.

"Can I have my phone back?" I asked. I wanted to text my friends to make sure none of them had been run over by my crazy Uber driver. They must have been thinking the same thing, because I heard my phone buzz to signal I had a new text.

"Ten minutes."

What? "Okay, great. Can I have my phone back?"

The driver responded with something in Portuguese that I didn't understand.

Oh well. I guess he'll give it back when we get there.

His driving had improved considerably once I told him where we were going, so I decided to just lean back and take in the sights. I hadn't really explored the city that much yet, so it was nice to get to see it. At first we were just driving through the new part of town. Most of it had been built within the past few years with the hopes of capitalizing on all the tourists coming to town for the games, but there were also some shops that looked like they had been there for decades. We passed a ton of restaurants with patios packed well beyond what could be safe or comfortable.

And then the scenery started to change.

Glamorous restaurants and high-rise hotels gave way to shoddy looking apartment buildings and warehouses connected to a grid of makeshift wires and satellite dishes that looked more like something you'd see at an elementary school science fair than in a city connected to actual electricity. The ride grew bumpy as the quality of the roads quickly deteriorated.

Why did the Uber driver have to pick the route through the sketchiest part of town possible?

I turned away from the scenery and let my mind wander to Alina. She ordered steak instead of a stupid salad. She liked dessert just as much as me. She was funny and sweet. And she deserved way better than Chris Hamilton. I had seen him around the athletes' village. Maybe he had only cheated on Alina once, but if I had to take a guess, I'd say it was way more. I never would have thought that Alina was his girlfriend after seeing him with a different girl every time we had crossed paths. The fact that one of the many times he cheated on her he chose the girl that had picked on Alina in school made it a million times worse. The guy was a total dick. But it wasn't my place to tell Alina that. I couldn't butt in on her decision. She needed to realize that she deserved more on her own. And I'd be waiting when she made the right call.

I leaned back and put my head on the headrest. Alina was gorgeous. It was going to be hard to control myself around her. But I needed to give her time to get over Chris. I wasn't interested in being her rebound. I wanted more than that. She knew I liked her. Now I just needed to wait. But after dinner, all I had wanted to do was kiss her. Each time I touched her I felt this spark. I couldn't exactly explain it, but I knew it wasn't a feeling I wanted to let go.

The SUV came to a stop outside of an unmarked, run down building.

"We're here," said the driver.

"Um, sorry, this isn't right. I said the athletes' village. For the International Tournament of Athletes." I looked out the window. We were in the middle of the slums, far away from the cushy hotels they had built specifically for the games. If I hadn't grown up in places similar to this, I probably would have been terrified. But I wasn't in America. I was in Brazil, which automatically made this situation more alarming. "Let me bring up the map again," I said.

A giant Brazilian man with a shaved head opened the car door before the driver could respond. He was wearing a black suit over a black button down. Even Lil Wayne would have thought that the amount of gold chains around his neck looked tacky. Despite his laughable fashion decisions, the man had an aura of danger about him. I was quickly realizing that this situation was more sinister than a simple misunderstanding with an erratic Uber driver.

"Follow me," said the man. His English seemed to be much better than my driver's. And his tone didn't leave much room to disagree.

When I hesitated, he pulled back his suit coat to reveal a Glock tucked into his waist band.

Shit. I put my hands out to show I wasn't going to make any sudden movements. "Alright, I'm coming." I slowly slid out of the back seat and followed the enormous Brazilian. I looked around to size up my options. Follow the guy with the gun, or make a run for it. I could probably sprint to a nearby corner and get around the side of the building within a few seconds. If he was anything like the thugs I grew up with, the ones who held pistols sideways when they shot to try to look cool, he had no chance of hitting me. But there was a chance he was ex military or something, in which case I'd be toast.

I decided to cooperate and see where this was going. There was no reason to provoke him if it wasn't absolutely necessary.

The big Brazilian knocked twice on a door that was really just a random collection of plywood and sheet metal. The door swung open and he stepped to the side to let me pass. As I tried to slide past him, the smell of Brazilian barbeque mixed with musky sweat stung my nostrils.

The inside of the building was much nicer than the outside, besides for the fact that the enclosed space intensified the smell of my kidnapper. We were in a dimly lit hallway with wainscoting and gaudy chandeliers hanging from the ceiling. We passed a few open doors. I couldn't be sure, but I thought I caught a glimpse of three men counting piles of cash in one of the rooms. As we progressed down the hallway, the sound of rap music grew louder.

The hallway ended in a staircase that led down to the back of a gentlemen's club. Tan girls in very skimpy lingerie and heels danced on poles while men covered in tattoos reached for them. I quickly realized that classifying this as a gentlemen's club was far too kind. At best, this was a strip club. Possibly a brothel. *Maybe they were supposed to bring Alex here instead? He would love it.*

Directly in front of me, a man with a short mohawk wearing a crisp white suit sat on a leather couch. Two strippers in white lingerie sat on either side of him. Three men just as large as the guy who had escorted me down the hall stood in front of the couch to prevent anyone from approaching from the VIP section of the club.

As soon as he saw me, the man in white stood up and smiled. "Boa noite," he said, holding his hand out for me.

"Boa noite," I said and shook his hand. Before coming to Brazil I had learned a few phrases, and that happened to be one of them.

"I'm Rodrigo, and this is Isadora and Giovanna. Thank you for coming to see me. How was the drive?" His English was surprisingly good, despite his thick accent.

"It was okay. Although I would have preferred if your driver had taken me to where I wanted to go rather than kidnapping me."

"Kidnapping is such a strong word. I just wanted to talk to you discretely, so I figured that was the best way to arrange such a meeting." Rodrigo gestured to the chair next to his couch. "Please, take a seat."

I couldn't run away now. There were too many people in my path that could stop me. I hesitantly sat down and Rodrigo did the same.

"Before we begin, would you like anything to drink?"

"No, thank you." I didn't want to give him a chance to roofie me. He was giving me kind of a rapey vibe.

"Alright then, we'll get right down to business." Rodrigo took a sip of his drink and leaned back on the couch with one arm around each of the strippers. "Are you much of a gambler, Bryce?"

I shrugged. "I've never really gambled much unless you count my yearly fantasy football league."

"What does the winner of your league get?"

"I think most years it's like $500."

Rodrigo shook his head. "Doesn't it just drive you crazy watching the games and not knowing if your players are going to perform or not?"

"Yeah, but isn't that kind of the whole point of gambling?"

"No. No, no, no. The point of gambling is to make money. At least, that's why I gamble."

"Okay."

"Do you know what a parlay is?"

The term sounded vaguely familiar. It took me a second to remember, but then the voice of my college stat professor filled my head, describing a parlay in his accent from God-knows-where. A parlay is when you only get a payout if a series of events all occur. So, for example, you could have a five part parlay that depends on the results of five different games. If you get any of them wrong, you get nothing, but if you guess them all right, the payout can be quite large. The more scenarios and the less likely they are to occur, the more money you can make for getting them all correct. The small investment combined with the extremely low probability of winning a large sum of money made parlays a lot like playing the lottery.

"Yeah, I know what they are," I said.

"Good. I recently made a parlay that included a number of events from the International Tournament of

Athletes. My odds of winning are less than a percent of a percent. I don't like those odds much, do you?"

"No."

"Then maybe you can help me make them better."

"Sure. Just cut your losses and invest in something with better odds. I know a guy who does financial planning if you're interested."

Rodrigo laughed. "Ah, so you're a funnyman, are you? I should have known you'd be funny after that prank you pulled on Yao Kai."

I tried to maintain my poker face. "I don't know who's giving you your intel, but that wasn't me." *How the hell did he know that was me?*

"Good, deny it to the end. See, I knew you were the right man for the job."

"I'm sorry, but I'm really not. If you're trying to rig the games, you'll need to get a ton of the top athletes on your payroll. I couldn't possibly rig however many events you have in your parlay. It'll never work."

Rodrigo shook his head and turned to one of the strippers next to him. "I don't get it, Isadora. Why doesn't he want to work with us?"

"It is possible he wants a payment," said Isadora with a sexy accent.

"What kind of payment do you think he wants?"

"I could suck his cock." Isadora stood up and un-hooked her bra. It fell to the ground to reveal her oversized, tan tits. On paper, she was attractive. Big tits, tiny waist, flat stomach, toned legs - every physical trait a man might describe he wants in a woman. But none of it was real, especially her smile. Sure, her lips formed a smile, but her eyes just weren't in it. Seeing her just made me kind of sad, not horny. I'd take a real woman over Isadora any day of the week. Especially a real woman with a volleyball ass like Alina's.

"Not a bad idea. What do you say, Bryce? Is this what you were holding out for?"

"No, I just really don't think I can help." All I wanted to do tonight was get to know Alina better, not contract HIV from some Brazilian stripper.

Isadora made a pouty face. "You like Giovanna more, yes?"

The other stripper stood up and dropped her bra. Her tits looked exactly the same as Isadora's. They must have had the same surgeon.

"You're both very beautiful, but..."

"Maybe you want us together?" The girls started kissing and rubbing each other's tits.

"Come on, Bryce," said Rodrigo. "You can have both of them at the same time. You'd really pass that up?"

"I'm sorry, I just don't think I'm the right man for the job."

"What if they fuck you?"

"Right here?" asked Isadora. "In middle of club?" She glanced at Rodrigo. She must have gauged his reaction, because she quickly added, "Yes, this will be such fun."

I sighed. I clearly wasn't going to get out of here without agreeing to give Rodrigo what he wanted. It didn't mean I had to follow through. "As lovely as you ladies are, I think I'm going to have to pass."

Anger flashed across Rodrigo's face.

"But," I continued, "I will help you. I'll need a nice budget to work on, though. Rigging events isn't easy."

Rodrigo clapped his hands together as the girls sat back down next to him. "Now we're talking! I knew you'd come around."

"So how are we gonna do this?" I asked. "Do you have a list of events and your desired results?"

"Not exactly." Rodrigo pulled a smartphone out of his pocket and tossed it to me. "Check the drafts folder every morning. If I have any jobs for you, I'll put them in there. Delete the drafts immediately after you read them so that there's no trace of what we planned."

"Okay. Done."

"If you need money for supplies, I have ways of getting it to you."

"Good. And payment for my services?" I asked. If I was going to pretend to help him, I had to act legit. He'd know something was up if I didn't want money.

"Ten grand, once everything is finished."

"Twenty."

"Fifteen."

"Deal." I stood up and we shook hands. I was just glad this shit was over. I'd dump the cell phone as soon as I could and hopefully never hear from him again.

Just when I reached the door, Rodrigo said, "Hold on."

I spun around and looked at him.

"There's one more thing I wanted to show you. Isadora, can you grab my computer?"

Isadora walked past me into the hallway and returned a second later carrying a laptop. She opened it and put it on Rodrigo's lap. He typed a few things and then turned the laptop around so I could see it. It looked like some sort of crappy quality YouTube video.

"Does this look familiar?" asked Rodrigo.

"Not really."

"Let me switch to a better view." He hit a button and the screen changed to a video feed of Emily sitting at her desk in her dorm room typing on her computer.

I balled my fists. *That mother fucker.* While Emily was out, Rodrigo must have had someone sneak into her room and plant cameras. I suddenly realized that I had slightly underestimated Rodrigo. I originally thought he was some two-bit thug trying to intimidate me into helping him. But that wasn't the case. He had probably been planning this for months, setting up an international network and thoroughly researching his marks. There was no doubt in my mind that he knew my entire history and that I'd do anything to keep Em safe. He was three steps ahead of me.

"I hate to be unpleasant," said Rodrigo, "but it would be bad business to not have an insurance policy to keep my assets from skipping town in the middle of a job."

"I assume you've done your research about me," I said.

"I have."

"Did you happen to come across any information about my last foster parents? The one's who weren't very kind to my sister?"

"Yes. Horrible tragedy."

"Was it?" I said, raising an eyebrow. Maybe Rodrigo's research hadn't been that thorough after all.

"Now you're a tough guy, huh? Nice try, but I'm not buying it. Call the police, mess up a mission, or try to fuck me over in any way, and my friend Vitor is going to blow your sister's brains out." He pretended to put a gun to his head and pull the trigger. "Are we clear?"

Every word out of his disgusting mouth made my blood boil. I was going to kill him. "Are you sure that's how you want to play this?" I asked.

"Yes."

"Alright then." *Big mistake, asshole.* "I hope you're making the right choice."

"Enough with the tough guy shit. Just check your emails every morning and don't do anything stupid that's going to get your sister killed. Isadora can vouch for me; I'm not fucking around."

For the first time, I could see emotion in Isadora's eyes. She nodded her head slowly. I wondered what horrible thing Rodrigo had done to one of her family members, but whatever it was, it had been enough to scare her into being his sex slave.

"Don't worry, you'll win your bet," I said.

"Good. Then your sister will live and you'll be fifteen thousand dollars richer. Everyone walks away happy."

"We'll see."

He ignored my comment. "It's a pleasure doing business with you, Bryce. I hope you aren't as disappointing as my last operative. I'd hate for this to end the same way that it ended for him. Cristiano will drive you to wherever you need to go."

CHAPTER 16
Monday
ALINA

"Guys, this isn't funny. He left before us. He should have been back by now."

"Alina, I'm sure he'll be here any second," Kristen said. "His crazy driver probably got lost or something."

My phone buzzed and I quickly swiped my finger across the screen.

"Holy shit," Alex said.

I looked up and saw that they had all received the same text message alert. It was about a missing ITA athlete, last seen in a town on the outskirts of the athletes' village earlier tonight. There was a picture of him in the alert. I had seen him before. His name was Liam. He was on the Canadian swim team. He had competed in a few races against Chris.

"What if whoever picked up Bryce was somehow involved with this guy disappearing?" I asked. "Maybe they saw the three of you dressed up as mustachioed Canadians the other night and..."

"Shhh!" Tim hissed. "Keep your voice down. Don't bring up the operation in public."

"No one is targeting Canadian athletes," Alex said. "Everyone loves Canadians."

"Yao Kai isn't thrilled with Canadians right now. Since we ripped his pants and he thinks we're all Canadian."

"So you think the Chinese government is going around kidnapping Canadian athletes because of a prank? It's China, not North Korea."

"I don't know." My phone buzzed again. But it still wasn't Bryce. It was another alert. The director of the ITA was suggesting that all athletes stay inside the athletes' village until Liam was located. For our own safety.

"Okay, I'm going to call him," Alex said. Before he made the call, his phone buzzed again. Alex laughed. "He's fine. Apparently his Uber driver got him back super fast and took the bumpiest route possible. He felt car sick so he went back to our room. I told him to lay off eating so many brigadeiros."

I took a deep breath. *Thank God.* "What a relief."

Alex smiled at me. "I'll let him know how worried you were."

I laughed. "I mean, we were all worried." I wasn't sure why I was denying it. They had all been joking around and I had been worried he was kidnapped with Liam.

"Mhm," Alex said. "Come on, Tim, let's go see if he's okay." He slapped Tim on the back.

Tim bowed slightly. "Ladies."

Kristen giggled.

Tim immediately grabbed her hand. "Until tomorrow." He kissed the back of her hand.

"See you later, guys," Alex said and started to walk away.

"Guys?" Tim dropped Kristen's hand and ran after Alex. "They're women. You're always so disrespectful."

I tuned out the rest of their conversation and turned toward Kristen. "You like him?"

"What? Psh." Kristen walked past me in the direction of our dorm.

"Are you denying it?"

"I'm not the one denying anything." She raised her eyebrow at me.

"What is that supposed to mean?"

"Clearly you like Bryce."

Kristen knew me better than anyone. And she always knew when I was lying. I was starting to feel butterflies in my stomach just thinking about seeing Bryce at the game tomorrow. Bryce. Even his name was sexy. "Yeah, I do."

Kristen squealed. "I knew it!"

I couldn't hide the smile that had spread across my face. There were a million reasons why I shouldn't be feeling the way I was feeling right now. But I didn't care. "I really like him, Kristen."

She threw her arms around me. "I told you everything would be okay."

"But..."

"No buts!" She pulled away from me. "You can get over Chris, win Gold, and get Bryce. For once in your life you're allowed to have it all. If you don't stop worrying, you're going to miss out on living, Alina."

Yesterday I felt like I had lost everything. I needed time.

"We're in Brazil. Did you ever think we'd end up here?" She looked up at the stars above us. "We worked so hard. We deserve to enjoy this moment."

I looked up too. She was right. I took a deep breath. It was time to start living. I'd never forgive myself if I let Chris ruin the most amazing week of my life.

CHAPTER 17

Monday

BRYCE

My hands were shaking as I clicked on Em's name in my phone.

"Hi!" Em said after just a few rings. "Are you calling me to tell me you won over that girl you're crushing on already?"

I put my face in my hand and exhaled. I just needed to hear her voice. I needed to know that she was okay.

"Bryce?" This time her voice sounded concerned.

I cleared my throat. "Yeah. It's me. Sorry, the reception here is pretty shoddy."

"Is everything okay?"

It will be. "Yeah. You were right. I was calling to brag about my date."

Em laughed. "It went that well for you? What happened to the complication?"

"She was dating the biggest scum bag on Team USA. He cheated on her with this girl that used to bully her in school. He's a complete asshole."

"Wow. What a dick. So they're definitely done?"

"I think so."

"Well, it sounds like things just got a little less complicated. When's your next date?"

Less complicated? Yeah, right. Hearing Em's voice had calmed me down, but things were definitely still complicated. What the hell was I supposed to do when I got

Rodrigo's first demand? What was he going to want me to do?

"Bryce?"

I ran my hand through my hair. "Sorry, I'm still here. I'm going to her game tomorrow."

"That's so cute."

I laughed. "So cute!" I said in a high pitched, valley girl voice.

"So cute!' she said in an even higher pitched, squeakier voice.

We both laughed.

"I have to get back to studying, Bryce. Good luck on your second date. Love you!"

"I love you too, Em." I looked down at my phone as soon as the line went dead. I had three text messages from Alina asking if I was okay. I smiled to myself. She was worried about me. Granted, she should have been. I was fucking kidnapped. But my friends hadn't texted me at all. Alina cared, and that was a really good start. I was about to text her back when I saw I had a few more unread messages. The first was an alert about a missing ITA athlete. A Canadian swimmer named Liam Clark. He had last been seen in a town near the athletes' village earlier tonight. The other message was another alert. The director of the ITA was suggesting that all athletes stay inside the athletes' village until Liam was found. For our own safety.

I didn't think it was a coincidence that news about the disappearance of an athlete came through right after I had talked to Rodrigo. He was most likely Rodrigo's last operative. And I had a sinking feeling that Liam wasn't just missing. Rodrigo had said he'd hate to see it end the same way for me as it ended for him. Liam was most likely dead.

Instead of texting Alina back, I sent a message to Alex, saying I got sick on the way home. I couldn't talk to Alina right now. The butterflies in my stomach had disappeared and now my insides felt like they were twisting. Maybe I was going to be sick.

I pulled the phone out that Rodrigo had given me. There weren't any new messages in the drafts folder. Maybe he'd never send anything. Was it possible he had more operatives? I couldn't be the only one. How was I supposed to get any results by myself? And if I got caught sabotaging the games, I'd end up in some Brazilian prison. I wasn't Tim. I wouldn't do well in prison.

What the fuck was I going to do?

CHAPTER 18
Tuesday
BRYCE

My morning walk over to the practice arena had quickly become one of my favorite parts of my daily routine at the ITAs. I would always leave a few minutes before Tim and Alex and grab a breakfast bar at my favorite food stand and then take the long way to the practice arena. They were both awesome, but living with them was a little much. These few minutes every morning were exactly what I needed to stay sane.

But today, my walk served another purpose. It was the first time I could look at Rodrigo's phone since last night without Tim and Alex looking over my shoulder.

I took a deep breath and pulled the phone out of my backpack. *Maybe there won't be any messages. Maybe Rodrigo will have forgotten about me.* I clicked on the email folder and smiled when it came up empty. Then I remembered that he said we'd be communicating through drafts to leave less of a trail. *Damn.*

I opened up the drafts folder and clicked on the message:

Your expertise is required for two events taking place tomorrow. Win your race, and make sure that Marco Kramer loses in the Table Tennis finals. I don't think I need to remind you what's at stake here.

I already intended to win my race, but knowing that Em's life depended on it did make me slightly more nervous. Sabotaging the competition crossed my mind for a split second, but I quickly buried the thought. I had worked my whole life for this race. I could do this.

Marco Kramer was a whole different matter though. A quick Google search told me that he was heavily favored to win gold. How was I going to sabotage him with only one day of planning? For Yao Kai, we had done a week of surveillance and learned his every move before breaking into his room. Not to mention that I had the help of my friends. I was going to have to go solo on this one since it was going to effect an actual event.

Shit, shit, shit. How am I supposed to do this alone? And how will I live with myself knowing that I robbed a man of his dream just so fucking Rodrigo can make a few bucks?

The morning air suddenly felt stifling. I sat down on a bench and tried to regain my composure. There had to be a solution to this. I just had to think.

I sat there for a good five minutes thinking through every possibility, but nothing was coming to me. It was all too risky or too awful or both. Sometimes I found that I thought best when I wasn't actively trying to think about something, so I pulled out my other phone and started scanning the news. The top story was about Liam being missing, and the second story was something about the ITA Committee announcing that Germany, China, Russia, Brazil, and the USA will take part in a tiebreaker event if necessary at the end of the games. I clicked on the article and read it on my way to the practice arena. There was a list of events that experts were hypothesizing Brazil might choose to be the tiebreaker. Since they were the host nation, they got to choose. The most popular theory was that they would choose footvolley, which as the name would imply is volleyball played only with feet.

The end of the article mentioned that the odds of the tiebreaker actually happening were extremely small, which made me think that maybe the tiebreaker was Rodrigo's ultimate goal. After all, if he wanted to make money fixing the ITAs, the best way to maximize his investment would be to bet on the outcome least likely to happen.

I got up and started walking toward the practice arena. Luckily there was something else that helped distract me from Rodrigo. Or someone else, rather. Alina. I knew that she needed time to get over her ex. It was good that I hadn't gotten to say goodbye to her last night, because I would have ended up kissing her goodnight. And if I gave into kissing her, I knew it would lead to more. I wouldn't be able to stop myself. It wasn't the sex ban that was getting to me, though. It was more so the fact that I hadn't had sex since I broke up with my last girlfriend six months ago. I guess it was a self-inflicted sex ban.

It wasn't just a lack of sex that had me wanting Alina, though. I had never been so attracted so instantaneously to anyone. And it wasn't just physical. She was easy to talk to and funny. I'm sure we didn't have similar childhoods. I wouldn't have wished my childhood on anyone. But she seemed to understand me. Maybe it was because of what happened between her and that bully at NYCU. Or maybe it was something else. But I wanted to know more about her. I wanted to take the time to get to know those things.

Certain parts of my anatomy disagreed with me. And I could tell that the same thing was on Alina's mind. The way she pressed her thighs together when Tim was talking about devil's threesomes. The way she reacted to my hands on her hips. The way she looked at me when she bumped into me in the locker room. The way she looked at me even when I was fully clothed. I knew because I was looking at her the same way. Like I wanted to rip all her clothes off and fuck her in the first place we could find to be alone. And now I was starting to get hard. *Shit.* I shifted my athletic shorts. They were horrible at hiding boners.

I opened my locker and saw a flyer for a prostitute laying on top of my stuff. There was a message written on top of it: "Dude, I think I found the one!"

It took me a second to realize that Alex had put this here. *Why didn't Rodrigo kidnap him instead?* I was sure he would have loved to help Rodrigo in exchange for some quality time with Rodrigo's girls. It was a match made in heaven.

Wait a second! That's it! All of a sudden, a plot started for form in my head. I knew what I had to do. And it was absolutely perfect.

I pulled out my burner phone and created a new draft:

Consider it done. I need your help though. Send Isadora to the north village exit tonight at 8. Have her bring her favorite sex toys.

The sound of wet feet slapping against the tile floor made me hit save and throw the phone in my locker. I looked up just in time to see Tim skid to a stop at the end of the hallway. He put one hand on the wall to stop his slide and grabbed the top of his towel with his other hand, just barely saving me from getting an eyeful of his junk.

"Dude, you've got to come see this!" he yelled.

"What is it? A naked girl?" I hoped the answer was yes, because that was the only acceptable reason for a man to be so worked up after coming from the showers in the men's locker room.

"No time to explain. Just come look."

"Oh God, did you find Liam? Please tell me he's alive."

"What? No. Come on, hurry!"

"I'm coming." I slammed my locker shut and reluctantly followed Tim into the foggy showers.

After passing a few shower stalls, Tim turned to me and whispered. "Okay, don't be obvious about it, but walk past and look in that shower." He pointed at one of the shower stalls on our right.

"Why shouldn't I be obvious about it? Unless there's a naked girl in that shower, I'm leaving."

"Just look. I promise it's worth it."

A guy with a towel around his waist exited a shower stall at the end of the hall and came towards us. As he passed, he gave us a weird look.

We stood there awkwardly until he was out of the hall. "This is getting weird," I said. "I'm leaving." I turned to walk away.

"If you don't look, I'm going to yell pervert."

"You wouldn't..."

"Three, two..."

"Okay, okay. Fine. I'll look."

Tim smiled triumphantly as I walked toward the shower stall that he so badly wanted me to see. The curtain was mostly pulled, but it was cracked enough for me to be able to look in. I faced straight ahead as I passed, just looking out the corner of my eye into the stall.

There was no body, and there was no naked girl. In fact, there didn't seem to be anything at all. I stopped and pulled the curtain back more.

"Dude! What are you doing?" whisper-yelled Tim. "You're going to freak him out!"

Him!? Was Tim seriously trying to get me to check out some dude in the shower? I was about to tell Tim that there was no one in there, but I decided to mess with him instead. I leaned back out of the stall and turned to Tim. "It's okay. He said he wants to meet you."

Tim's eyes got wide. "Seriously?"

"Yeah, come on." I beckoned him over.

He hesitated for a second and then approached. The eager look on his face dissipated when he saw the stall was empty. "What the hell? Where'd he go?"

"Where did who go?" I asked. "Did you really want me to look at some guy showering?"

"Well it sounds weird when you say it like that."

"Is there another way to say it?"

"Uh, yes. You could say I wanted you to see an interesting physical specimen."

"That might be worse. Actually, it's definitely worse."

"Seriously, where could he have gone? He was there one second, and now he's gone."

"The other set of lockers?" I said. "Or maybe this interesting physical specimen of yours has magic powers and turned invisible."

"I hadn't considered that, but I guess it's possible. That's the only explanation of how his penis could be that big."

"Are you fucking kidding me?" I said, no longer whispering.

"No. Dude, you'd understand if you saw it. This thing was insane. It was bigger than most fully erect penises, and I don't think he was even hard."

I couldn't help but laugh. Tim was already the weirdest person I knew by a long shot, but this just confirmed it. "Tim, can you do me a favor?"

"Track down the penis magician so that we can learn his ways? Yes. Challenge accepted."

"What? No. Not even close. In fact, that's the exact opposite of what I was going to ask."

"Oh my God." Tim's eyes widened and he took a step back from me. "You want me to kill him because his monstrous penis is too powerful for mankind to handle? I think that's a little extreme."

"Never mind. I was going to tell you to not mention this to anyone to save you from endless teasing at the hands of Alex, but I can see that you're too far gone to help. Just don't mention my name when you tell people about this. And anyway, what are you doing showering *before* practice?"

"I always shower before practice. A gentlemen always presents himself..."

"Okay, whatever. Just hurry up and get ready so we can finish practice early and catch some of the girls' volleyball match. Or should I just tell Kristen you were too busy checking out dudes in the shower so we had to start practice late?"

CHAPTER 19

Tuesday

ALINA

We crushed Serbia in the first game. I was sitting on the bench gulping down water when Kristen nudged me in the ribs.

"They're here."

I turned around to see where she was looking. Bryce, Tim, and Alex were squeezing their way past some other spectators. Bryce smiled and winked at me as soon as he caught me staring. Tim blew Kristen a kiss and Alex slapped his hand, clearly embarrassed by what Tim was doing.

But I didn't dwell on what Tim and Alex were doing, because my gaze was stuck on Bryce. He was still sporting his workout clothes. He had this sweaty V down the middle of his T-shirt that made me gulp. Some of his hair was sticking to his forehead. It was somehow sexy and adorable at the same time.

I had dreamed about him all night. I wasn't sure if Kristen had gotten in my head or if I was a lot kinkier than I had originally thought, because I had dreamed about being with Bryce in the village square. Or at least, near it. He had pulled me down an alley in the village square, pressed my back up against the wall, and kissed me like he had during Operation Red Rip. Only this time, I was encouraging him to go farther. His hand slowly traced up my thigh while his other hand unzipped my dress.

The ref blowing the whistle drew me out of my daydream.

I squeezed my thighs together.

"You okay?" Kristen asked.

"Mhm." *I'm just ridiculously horny.* I took one last long sip of my water and got in the circle that my team had formed.

"Two more games like that first one, and we're going to the semi-finals," Coach Hammond said. "Stay focused and let's get this done."

The ref blew the whistle again and I ran onto the court. I looked back over at Bryce. He was waiving a poster in the air. It read, "I Dig Alina - Go Team USA." Tim was holding one that said, "Kristen Loves Juggling Balls - Go Team USA."

Bryce digs me.

Kristen laughed in front of me. She turned around. "Tim is really trying to get that devil's threesome going."

"Pay attention," I said and gestured to the other side of the net. I smiled to myself and looked at the girl that was about to serve for Serbia. I thought I might be nervous with Bryce watching me. Instead, it made me play even better. I wanted to impress him. I wanted to forget about Chris, win gold, and win over Bryce. It was just like Kristen had said. I could have it all.

The hitter on the other side spiked it hard. I dove to the left and bumped it perfectly to our setter. I was on fire.

***

The crowd went wild as Kristen landed the final spike on Serbia's side. I joined the hug in the middle of the volleyball court. We were soon surrounded by all the members on our bench too, laughing, crying, and scream-ing. *We're heading to the semi-finals!*

After shaking hands with the other team, Kristen and I rushed toward the exit. I wanted to see Bryce. All I could think about was kissing him. I wanted to jump into his arms. Him bringing that sign and cheering me on was such a sweet thing to do. I just hoped he was going to kiss me back. Kristen seemed just as eager to see Tim, even though she would never admit it.

"Is that Chris?" Kristen asked, stopping in front of a row of bleachers. I almost ran into her as she abruptly stopped in the middle of the crowd exiting the stadium.

I turned toward where she was looking. Chris was standing on the stairs talking to some tan brunette girl with big breasts. She was a Gabriela Santos wannabe. He was holding a bouquet of flowers and smiling at her.

If I hadn't been about to go meet up with Bryce, I probably would have burst into tears. Chris had seriously come to my game to give some random girl flowers? What an asshole. He never brought me flowers. He said they were a waste of money because they died so fast. Appar-ently this girl was worth the wasted money. Chris leaned in and whispered something in her ear. The girl laughed and touched his bicep.

I rolled my eyes. "Who cares if it is?" I said. I brushed past Kristen.

"Alina!" Chris' voice made me cringe. I looked over my shoulder to see him running down the steps. Before I could say anything, Kristen was walking toward him.

For some reason, I felt frozen in place. The stadium was too loud for me to hear what they were saying. So I just watched the scene unfold in silence.

Kristen poked him in the middle of the chest and said something. Chris laughed and lifted up the flowers. Kristen pointed over his shoulder at the girl he had clearly been flirting with. Chris shrugged and looked over at me. He gave me one of those looks that used to get him anything he wanted. But today I wasn't fazed.

He put his hand on Kristen's shoulder and lightly shoved her to the side so he could get past her.

My feet unfroze and I walked over to him. "What do you want, Chris?" All the joy I had felt from my team's victory seemed to evaporate.

"To give you these." He held up the flowers. "Congratulations, babe." He leaned forward to kiss me.

I put my hand on his chest to stop him. "Chris, stop."

He pulled back and gave me a funny look. "I stayed away for a few days to give you time to cool off. Let's move forward, okay?"

"Is that an apology?"

"Yes. We've already talked about this. Gabriela tricked me. We shared a kiss. End of story."

"Shared a kiss? You said she kissed you and you shoved her off."

"Yeah, that's what I meant."

"Those two things are different, Chris. How do you expect me to trust you?"

He smiled again. "Babe, come on. It's me. Don't do that thing you always do."

"What thing?"

He sighed. "Where you don't let things go. You need to learn how to forgive people. If you had forgiven Gabriela years ago, this whole thing wouldn't have been that big of a deal. And she couldn't have used your own anger against you. You're not even mad at me. You're just upset with her. So how about you come back to my room and we can celebrate your victory how we should have celebrated mine."

Each word out of his mouth made me even more angry. "You're such an asshole, Chris."

"Because I'm right?" There was that damn cocky smile again.

"Why do you always have to be right about everything? I told you that stuff about Gabriela so you'd support me, not hang it over my head. How could you do this to me? With her?"

"I said I was sorry."

"Actually, you didn't say you were sorry. You just shoved flowers in my face."

"Well, I'm saying it now."

I stared into his eyes. He didn't look sorry. Last night I had promised myself that I wouldn't let Chris ruin this week for me. Yet, here he was ruining this victory. I should be celebrating right now, not fuming. This wasn't what love was. Love was putting the other person first. It was supporting them. It wasn't hooking up with their arch nemesis during the most important week of their life. This relationship was so one sided, and I had been too blind to see it before. "I don't forgive you, Chris. And I don't believe it was only one kiss." I turned around to walk away from him.

"Alina." He grabbed my wrist. "I'm choosing you."

"Over Gabriela? I didn't realize that was a choice you were debating."

"You know what I mean."

"Well, I'm not choosing you."

"What the hell does that mean?"

"It means that what we have isn't healthy. All you care about is physical needs, not emotional. You don't love me because you're too in love with yourself."

"God you're pathetic." He said it under his breath, but I still heard him.

"You know what? How about you just be you. And I'll be me. And one thing's for damn sure. We're not together anymore, Chris."

"Fine. If that's what you want. Good luck in the rest of your games. If you end up facing Brazil in the finals, you're going to need it. Gabriela's so much better than you." He tossed the flowers at me and walked away.

My whole body felt cold. It wasn't just what he said, but the way he said it. He wasn't talking about Gabriela being better at volleyball. He was talking about their kiss. Or whatever else they did. And it didn't matter how horrible Chris had been the past few days. His words cut through me just like they would have when we were happy. His opinion had always mattered so much to me. I wasn't good enough for him. I wasn't as good as Gabriela. It felt like I was a freshman at NYCU again. Gabriela had spread rumors about me to the rest of my team to the point where none of them would even look at me. Then she found a way to barricade my dorm room from the outside so that I'd miss important practices and games. And finally, the night before our term papers were due, she snuck into my room and smashed my laptop and shredded all my papers. After that, I went home and never went back. But this time I couldn't run home.

"Why didn't you tell me the whole story?" Kristen asked.

I took a deep breath. How much had she heard of that? The expression on her face made it seem like she had heard all of it. "I don't know. I didn't want you to hate him anymore if we got back together. You don't have to worry about that now."

"Alina." She put her arm around my shoulders. "I'm so, so sorry."

And even though she hated Chris, I knew she meant it. "I can't believe he kissed her back," I said.

"I know."

"You were right about him. Why didn't I listen to you?"

"Because he's pretty. And you never had a boyfriend before."

I laughed.

"Can I tell you something, though?" She let go of my shoulders and stood right in front of me. "I'm actually glad that you two dated."

"Seriously?"

"Because now you'll recognize a good thing. In comparison."

"You mean Bryce?"

Kristen smiled.

"I'm already sold on Bryce. Do I look okay?"

"You look like you just played three games of volleyball."

"So...bad?"

Kristen laughed. "But he's already seen you after ugly crying with snot all over your jersey. And he still likes you."

"Still." I wiped some of the sweat off my face with the back of my hand.

"Come on." She grabbed my arm and pulled me toward the exit.

Bryce was standing by the door with his friends. I chucked the flowers in the trash right before we reached them, but not before Bryce had seen them. He glanced at the trashcan and then back at my face.

"Congrats on the win," Alex said. "Who knew our volleyball team was so good?"

Kristen laughed. "Everyone except you, apparently. We're favored to win gold. And we're going to win."

"I like my women confident," Tim said.

I tuned them out and looked up at Bryce. He was smiling at me. I suddenly felt extremely self conscious.

"You dig me, huh?" I asked. "I like the volleyball pun."

"I'd never lie on a poster." He had rolled the poster up and was holding it in his hand. I thought he might give it to me, but the fact that he didn't was even better. It meant he wanted to use it again.

"Congratulations, Alina," he said and leaned in for a hug. I didn't hesitate to hug him back. He smelled like his cologne and sweat. I'm pretty sure the combination was my new favorite smell in the world. I could easily feel the muscles in his back through his shirt. I had the urge to trace every muscle with my fingertips, but kept my hands rooted in place. I reluctantly pulled back when I felt like I had probably been hugging him for too long. But he hadn't stopped hugging me either. Maybe he liked having me in his arms just as much as I liked being in his.

I nervously tugged the bottom of my jersey. "Are you feeling better?"

"What?"

"Last night, Alex said you weren't feeling well..."

"Oh, right." Bryce laughed. I loved the sound of him laughing. "I'm good. My Uber driver just took the bumpiest route possible. That combined with eating way too much Brazilian steak was not a pretty sight."

"I'm sorry about all the texts. I thought you'd been kidnapped." I smiled up at him. He was going to think I was so ridiculous.

"It's okay. It was nice that someone was looking out for me."

The way he said it reminded me of when he was talking about the reason why he was such a good runner. Because he had something to run from. I wanted to ask him about it, but not in front of Kristen and his friends.

He leaned in close to me. "As much as I love my friends, maybe you and I could hang out tonight just us?"

"I'd love that." I coughed awkwardly. "I'd like that I mean." *Love? I can't say love this soon. I'm going to freak him out.*

Bryce smiled at me. "We'll catch you guys later," he said as he grabbed my hand.

I immediately interlaced my fingers with his. Again, I couldn't help but notice his large, manly hands. My hand felt so small in his.

Kristen looked down at our intertwined hands. "Have fun," she said with a wink.

CHAPTER 20
Tuesday
ALINA

Bryce kept his hand in mine as we sat down side by side on the train. He scooted in close to the armrest, the only thing that was separating us. The train's air conditioning was on full blast, but I could feel Bryce's body heat radiating off of him. His hand was so warm. I felt safe and happy when I was with him. This was how I should be feeling after my game. I wanted to rest my head on his shoulder and close my eyes. But falling asleep wasn't exactly the best use of the only alone time we'd gotten since he'd given me my phone back on that bench.

"You were amazing today." Bryce traced the lines on my palm with his thumb as he spoke.

I wasn't sure if my cheeks blushed because of his compliment or because of the way he was touching me. My whole body felt warm. "Thanks."

"Really. I don't think you lost a single point. I've never seen volleyball like that."

I laughed. "We have a really good team."

"And they're certainly lucky to have you."

Kiss me. But Bryce didn't move any closer to me. Maybe because I was a sweaty mess. He had just come from his practice too. A long shower and some nicer clothes might make our first real kiss better anyway. But I wanted to run my hands through his hair and feel the muscles in his back again. I shifted a little closer to the armrest. Maybe he'd get the hint.

"Speaking of people being lucky to have you, I'm guessing Chris came to the game?"

I knew a few ground rules about dating, even though Chris had been my only boyfriend. And one of those rules was that you don't talk about an ex on a date. "Yeah. But it's definitely over. We don't have to talk about that."

Bryce continued to trace my palm with his thumb. It was so soothing. It felt like I could tell him anything. And his silence made it seem like he wanted me to.

"At dinner when Kristen said he hooked up with my arch nemesis, she was talking about the girl that bullied me in school. Gabriela Santos. She plays for Brazil. During our match against Brazil I got this envelope on my seat. I opened it up and it was pictures of Chris with Gabriela. And she was topless. I was so upset, we lost the match. It was all my fault. I just...she just...I couldn't play against her. She did it on purpose to mess with me, I know she did. She has this way of crawling under my skin. And she used my relationship with Chris against me. Chris said he didn't know it was her. And that nothing happened. But then he kept changing his story. Eventually he said she kissed him. But then it was him kissing her back too. And I don't know what else happened, and I don't want to know. I don't want to think about it at all."

I realized I was rambling. But for some reason I couldn't stop. "He said it was my fault. That if I didn't still resent Gabriela I wouldn't be upset about the whole thing. But that's not true. I'd still be upset with him for cheating on me, no matter who it was with. And he said it was my fault for not celebrating the way he wanted to celebrate after he got his gold medal. But I couldn't. My coach has a sex ban, and I couldn't risk being benched. We have to win gold. I need the money." I swallowed hard. I don't know why I didn't stop talking. Now Bryce was going to think all I cared about was money. Which wasn't true.

I looked down at our hands. "I mean, it's not just about the money for me. I know that there's more important things than money. I want to win. I want to beat Gabriela." I put my face in my free hand. "And there's more important things than revenge. This is all coming out wrong."

Bryce laughed. "Hey." He put his fingertips under my chin and tilted my face back to his. "I get it. Beating your arch nemesis, especially after what she just did, will be the most satisfying feeling in the world. That's not revenge. That's overcoming something. And everyone here wants the money that comes with gold. There's nothing wrong with that being an incentive for victory."

"All I meant to say was that Chris and I are done."

Bryce laughed again and his fingers dropped from my chin. "I'm glad to hear that." He squeezed my hand. "Tell me about why you need the money."

"I..." I let my voice trail off. Chris had told me my plan was dumb. That I should be using my education after I retire from volleyball. Or that I should go pro. I didn't want to do those things, though. They didn't make me as happy. And Bryce wasn't Chris. He loved dessert. Maybe he'd understand. I looked up into his blue eyes. "My grandma owns a bakery. But she has beginning stages of Alzheimer's and has to retire. The bakery is kind of in disarray. It needs new ovens and basically a remodeling in general. My parents don't want to front the cost of all that. They're planning to sell it. But it was my dream to take over for my grandma. I love baking. All my best memories from my childhood were in that bakery. I need the money so I can take over the lease and buy the necessary equipment to keep it going. This is my only shot. They're selling the bakery at the end of the month if I can't take over."

"See, that's a good reason." Bryce smiled. "Is your grandmother's bakery in Wilmington?"

"Yeah. It's the cutest little shop. And it's actually in a really good location. If I could fix it up, I know it could do really well again."

"I envy you."

I laughed. "Why on earth would you envy me?"

"Because you know what you want to do after all this. I just graduated too, and I have no idea what I want to do."

"Are you going to keep running after the ITAs?"

"I don't know. It depends on a lot of things." He looked out the window. We were passing some of the beautiful mountains in Rio. But it didn't seem like he was actually seeing them. He seemed lost in thought.

"You said you run because you had something to run from. What was it?"

Bryce shrugged. "Everything. I felt like all I did was run. We grew up in foster care. Bad foster parents, even worse foster siblings. It wasn't...easy."

My heart seemed to constrict. That was why he knew what it was like to be bullied. "You said we?"

Bryce smiled. "Yeah, me and my little sister, Em."

"Is that why you're so good at comforting girls when they cry?"

He laughed. "I guess I've had quite a bit of practice." He looked down at our hands, rubbing his thumb against my palm again.

I loved that feeling. I never wanted him to stop touching me. "Why do you run now?"

He looked back up at me. "I need the money too. To pay for Em's college. I don't want her to have to start her career with a bunch of debt."

"That's really sweet."

"Or horrible, since I'm motivated by money?" He raised his eyebrow at me.

I laughed. "Well, sweet and horrible. Maybe I could come to your race tomorrow and cheer you on?"

"I'd love that."

I bit my lip. It was almost like he said it because he knew I said love earlier by accident. "Where does Em go to school?"

"Penn U."

"Oh, in Philly? That's actually really close to where I live. Do you visit her a lot?"

"Not as much as I'd like to. But if I win gold tomorrow, I'll be able to more often. Me and my greedy ways."

I gently nudged his arm with my free hand. "You knew what I meant." My hand hesitated on his arm a moment too long. God his bicep felt amazing. "Sorry, I..." I let my voice trail off and laughed awkwardly as I removed my hand.

His eyes lingered on my lips. I watched his Adam's apple rise and then fall. *He's going to kiss me!*

"You're making it really hard to be respectful." He leaned forward slightly. I could smell his cologne. I wanted to lick his skin and taste it.

I took a deep breath. All I wanted was his clothes on the floor of the train. "What if I don't want you to be respectful?"

Phones buzzing and ringing all around us both made us jump. Bryce dropped my hand and pulled his phone out of his pocket. "Shit." His eyebrows lowered.

"What's wrong?"

"They found Liam."

"Is he okay?"

"No." He leaned forward, putting his elbows on his knees. "They found his body."

"Oh my God." I put my hand over my mouth.

The train squealed as it started to come to a stop.

"I'm sorry, I have to go." He slid his phone into his pocket and stood up.

"Bryce, I'm so sorry. Did you know him?"

"What? Yeah. Kind of." He ran his hand through his hair. His face looked pale.

"Do you want to go get dinner and we can talk about it?"

"No. I'm sorry, I have to go," he repeated when the train stopped moving. He lifted out a single rose from his backpack and handed it to me. "Congratulations on your win, Alina." He leaned forward and kissed my cheek. And the next thing I knew he was pushing his way past the other athletes getting off the train. I looked out the window to see him run off the train. He stopped in the middle of the street and bent over with his hands on his knees. It looked like he was going to throw up. Maybe he still wasn't feeling well.

I tried to shove my way through the other athletes too, but I wasn't as big as Bryce. It took me a few minutes to get off the train. And Bryce was already gone.

CHAPTER 21

Tuesday

BRYCE

I pulled my phone out as I walked toward the village square. There was a text message from Alina, asking if I had gotten sick again and if I was feeling okay. She asked if she could bring me soup. No one ever worried about me. For some reason her concern made me feel warm and fuzzy. I meant what I had said to her earlier. It was nice that someone was looking out for me, that someone actually cared. Em worried about me to a certain degree, but I was the one that took care of her, not the other way around.

I typed out a text. "Sorry about running out on you. You're right, I wasn't feeling well." I hated lying, but I couldn't pull her into the mess I was in. "As great as soup sounds, I don't think us being alone together in my room is great for my chances at gold tomorrow or yours this weekend," I added and pressed send. I didn't care if it was forward. She knew how I felt about her. And I was pretty sure I knew how she felt about me. She was staring at me earlier like she wanted me to fuck her right in the train. But she needed to focus on winning her games so she could get the money she needed to take over for her grandmother. I wasn't going to stand in the way of making her dreams come true. Thinking about the way her face lit up when she talked about the bakery made me smile. She had to win gold. She just had to.

Besides, I had my own race to worry about. I needed to focus so that I wouldn't end up like Liam. Or worse...if they did something to Em. Just the thought made me actually feel like vomiting.

After I got this meeting out of the way, I'd try to get some sleep. I wasn't favored to win. Ervan Cook from Jamaica was supposed to win all of his races, including the one against me. But no one knew how hard I had been training. I wouldn't cheat to get my gold. And I knew I didn't have to. I could do this. For Em.

Isadora was waiting for me outside the north village exit, just as instructed. Part of me expected her to show up in thigh-high leather boots and a short leather skirt, but I was pleasantly surprised to see that she had instead worn a fairly normal outfit of jean shorts and a cut off Team Brazil tank top.

"Hi, Isadora," I said. "Thanks for agreeing to help me out."

"You decide to fuck me?" she asked.

"What? No. I really need your help."

"Oh," she replied with a small smile. And for the first time, I thought her smile might actually be genuine. "What do you need for me to do?"

"We can talk about that once we get inside. But first we need to figure out how to get you through security. I was thinking I could go through with my security pass, and then I could pass it to you through the fence. They might notice that the picture..."

"Are the guards all men?" asked Isadora.

"Uh, yeah, I think so."

"Then it is no problem. I show you." Isadora confidently walked over to the security checkpoint and put her bag on the scanner. The guard waved her through the metal detector and then put a hand up to stop her.

"ID please," he said.

Isadora reached into her pockets and came up empty. She feigned a confused look and then reached into her bra to pretend like she might have stashed it in there instead.

"I don't know where it went," she said, in an accent that didn't sound as thick. "I must have left it in my dorm."

The guard shook his head. "Sorry, no entry without an ID."

"What if you search me? I promise I'm not carrying any naughty weapons." Isadora bent over the conveyer belt and spread her legs. When the guard didn't immediately respond, she shook her ass a little.

"Are you trying to get me fired?" asked the guard. "I guess you can pass, but don't tell anyone."

Isadora stood up and smiled at him. "Thank you."

Damn, she's actually pretty good at this. This might work even better than I had hoped.

I went through next without any issues and then met up with Isadora again.

"How'd you know that would work?" I asked.

"Just because Rodrigo uses me for my body doesn't mean I don't have other talents too," she said in her normal accent. "Men are, what do you say," she paused for a second, searching for the word, "stupid."

"Do you not like Rodrigo?"

"My feeling does not matter. I belong to him."

"Have you ever tried to escape?"

"I've thought sometimes, but it's impossible. And I have nobody close in my life. I would have no money and nowhere to go."

"What if I told you I could help?"

She looked at me skeptically. "Why help me?"

"Rodrigo threatened to kill my sister. He threatens to take what's most important to me, I'll take what's most important to him."

"I'm not most important to him. That is money."

"That's why you're going to take his money too. Somewhere, he has a slip of paper that's going to be worth millions if I succeed in rigging the games for him. All you have to do is find it and steal it from him."

"Where would I go to?"

"Disappear. Go wherever you want. You'll have all the money you ever need."

"I will consider. Is that why you brought me here? For talking?"

"No, I also need you to help me with something else. Did you bring the sex toys?"

Isadora opened her bag and started pulling out toys. "Dildos, butt plugs, anal beads, vibrators, cock rings."

"Good."

"Strap ons, ping pong balls, a rubber chicken..."

Rubber chicken? What? "Okay, I get the idea. You came well prepared."

"So what are these for?"

"There's a table tennis player named Marco Kramer. He's staying in Room 712 of Dorm 9. I want you to go there and show him the time of his life."

Isadora frowned. "How will that sabotage? You think I'm unpleasant to be with? I'm good at the sex."

"No. I'm sure you are. Just make sure that by the time you're done with him, he has trouble walking."

"You want me to use the sex toys on the ass?"

"It sounds weird when you say it like that, but yes."

"That's easy. This one will work especially well for the ass." Isadora reached into her bag and pulled out a floppy black dildo that was easily a foot long.

Poor Marco. "I'd rather not know exactly how it goes down. Just get it done."

"Okay. Anything else you need of me?"

"That's all. Thanks for your help, Isadora. And good luck finding Rodrigo's ticket. I don't know what he did to your family, but we'll make him pay."

CHAPTER 22
Wednesday
ALINA

"Alright, that's enough film study for today," said Coach Hammond. "I think you girls are ready for Italy tomorrow."

I let out a sigh of relief. For the past 45 minutes I had been watching the clock counting down to when we were supposed to get out. I knew that getting out on schedule would give us time to get to the track to see Bryce's race, I just never thought Coach would actually not keep us late.

"There is one more thing though," continued Coach.

Damn it. Is she really going to make us run more stairs?

"The US ITA Committee sent me a memo today about the tiebreaker event. Apparently they think it's appropriate to waste our valuable practice time on something that is never even going to happen, but nonetheless, I have to talk to you about it. As you've probably heard, the USA and Brazil could potentially have the same medal count at the end of the games, so per the official ITA rulebook, they have to start planning for a tiebreaker event. For some reason, the geniuses making the rules thought it would be a good idea to let the host nation choose the event, which in this case means Brazil got to choose an event in which they believe they're superior to the USA."

I glanced up at the clock. *Come on. This is going to make me miss Bryce's race!*

"Brazil has chosen for the event to be a strip dance, which I guess in South America is considered a form of ballroom dance rather than something you'd see in a strip club. So I have to ask: are any of you interested in volunteering to perform for the USA?"

My teammates all laughed.

"Good, that's the reaction I was expecting. I'd hate for one of you girls to do it and lose focus on volleyball. Speaking of which, maybe this whole tiebreaker business does have a silver lining. Brazil's performer will be Gabriela Santos. And after the way she tore us apart in the group stage, her losing focus on volleyball isn't the worst thing to ever happen."

Of course Gabriela would want to do a strip dance. She probably works at a strip club as her side job anyway.

"Any questions?" asked Coach. She looked around the room, but no one had anything to say. "Okay then, I'll see you all tomorrow for the semi final against Italy. And don't let me hear any stories about any of you partying tonight."

The minute we were dismissed Kristen and I sprinted to the locker room, grabbed our stuff, and then rushed to the train station. We made it on the train thirty seconds before the conductor closed the doors.

After we caught our breath, Kristen turned to me. "I can't believe you didn't volunteer to go against Gabriela. This could be your chance to pay her back for all the shit she did to you."

"How would embarrassing myself by stripping in front of the whole world and losing to Gabriela be getting her back? That seems like just the kind of thing she would have tried to trick me into doing back in college. And how is the ITA even allowing a strip dance to be an event? They won't be able to show that on TV."

"Have you ever heard of that show Bailando por un Sueño?"

"No."

"It's the Argentinean version of Dancing with the Stars. They've had strip dances on there for a while and it was a big deal when one of the contestants actually stripped. Most of them just dance around in lingerie and occasionally take their bra off at the end while they're facing away from the audience. They never actually show anything. For the most part it's no more revealing than the outfits they wear on Dancing with the Stars."

"In that case, I'll totally do it."

"Really?!" Kristen's face lit up. I almost felt bad that I was joking.

"No way."

"Damn it, Alina. You could probably even get Bryce to do it with you. Imagine being up on the stage half naked with Bryce..."

"Tempting, but I'd much rather be fully naked with Bryce and have it be in private rather than on stage."

"At least watch a video of it before you decide."

I was going to tell Kristen that watching girls strip wasn't really my thing, but she somehow managed to bring up a video of it on YouTube before I could get a word out. I watched the video. It wasn't quite as tame as Kristen had made it sound, but it also wasn't just a naked girl pole dancing like I had imagined. Instead, the girl and guy started out fully clothed and danced provocatively, slowly stripping their clothes off until they were both in sparkly underwear.

"See, that's not so bad," said Kristen.

"Yeah, but it would still be embarrassing to do it, especially when I lose to Gabriela."

"Well if you aren't going to do it, then I'll do it for you."

"Are you sure?" I asked. "You'd really do that for me?"

"After what she did to you? Hell yes."

"Wow, you're the best."

Kristen shrugged. "I try. I'll email Coach now. Hopefully she won't be too pissed." She pulled out her phone and started typing. "Before I hit send, I do have one condition."

"Oh yeah?"

"You have to agree to be my understudy in case I get injured and can't perform."

"But..."

"Oh, come on. In all the years we've known each other, how many times have I been injured badly enough to not be able to play?"

I thought about it for a second. "None?"

"Exactly. And what are the odds that the medal counts are actually tied at the end of the games?"

"One percent? Less?"

"Basically zero. The event is never going to happen, but by signing up we send a message to Gabriela that we aren't afraid of her. And we get to hang out and probably learn a dance from a world class choreographer. It'll be fun."

"I don't know..."

"You really want to pass up the opportunity to watch me crush that stupid bitch in a dance-off? Come on, you know I've got the moves to beat her. Who else is going to do it? One of those twelve year olds on the gymnastics team? Or maybe a nice broad-shouldered swimmer? I don't think so."

Kristen was right. She was an incredible dancer. And watching her beat Gabriela would be amazing.

"Okay, I'll be your understudy," I said. *I can always back out if she actually does get injured.*

"Great!"

Oh God, what did I just agree to? Kristen had taken advantage of my hatred for Gabriela and somehow made me forget all about the fact that I was agreeing to be the understudy to her for a strip dance. A strip dance! "Actually, I think..."

"Nope, too late to change your mind. I already hit send."

"What? How did you even have time to add that to the email? I literally agreed to it 2 seconds ago."

"I'm just that good. Now...do you think we can get the guys to agree to be backup dancers for it? Or at least, get Tim to agree and have Bryce be his understudy?"

"Is that even a question? I'm pretty sure ballroom dancing is one of Tim's favorite hobbies."

"Really? I've never heard him mention it."

"Neither have I. But I'd be shocked if he didn't love it."

"Well, I hope you're right. We can talk to them about it after Bryce's race."

CHAPTER 23
Wednesday
BRYCE

Alex lifted up one of the earphones of my noise canceling headphones. "Your woman is here," he said and let the headphone slap back against my head.

I left DMX blasting in my ears as I scanned the crowd. His music took me right back to growing up, reminding me of why I ran in the first place. It was always about survival. *Today is no different.*

My eyes fell on a sign in the crowd. "If You Race Against Bryce, Be Prepared to Pay the Price...Of Losing."

I laughed. Alina had tied in the fact that I was all about the money. Well, the sign was accurate. There was only going to be one winner, and it was definitely going to be me.

Tim pulled off my headphones. "You're up, sweet cakes."

I shook my head. Why did he always call me that?

"Bring home our gold," Alex said and slapped my back. He had won a bronze earlier today and Tim had won a silver. All together we'd have a sweep. Not that I needed any more motivation.

"Done." I walked onto the track.

This was the most important race of my life. It was a race for my life. But I had always run for my life. Despite what I told myself, this race was different. Because it wasn't just about me, it was about Em too. Losing wasn't an option. I jumped up and down before leaning down and putting my feet in the starting blocks. I was on the inside track. Ervan Cook was directly to my right. *Eat my dust, Cook.*

"Runners on your marks!" The announcer said.

I looked down the track. I had no backup plan. All I was relying on was my own speed. I had briefly thought of tackling Cook at the last second if I needed to. But that would just result in me getting disqualified. Rodrigo said I had to win. Winning was the only option. I took a deep breath and pressed my fingertips into the track. I could almost hear my blood bumping.

The horn sounded, signaling the start of the race. My feet flew off the starting blocks. That's how I always liked to think. I wasn't running. I was fucking flying. And never in my life had I flown this fast.

I didn't look toward my right. I focused on the finish line and the cheers in the crowd. Cheers for me. The hot Brazilian breeze rushed past me, somehow heightening the roar from the stands, somehow making me feel even more alive.

I could see Cook in my peripheral vision. Only Cook. I knew why he was favored to win. He was damn fast. I had studied his tapes. And I knew exactly how to beat him. He was used to winning. He was used to always being ahead. He didn't know how to come from behind, because he never had to. And there was no way in hell I was letting him pass me.

It felt like my feet were barely touching the ground as I ran through the finish. I didn't bother reducing my speed slowly. I skidded to a stop and turned back to the stands. Alina was screaming, jumping up and down, waving the sign in the air. The next moment, Alex, Tim, and a bunch of my teammates were lifting me in the air, carrying me toward the podium where they were going to hand out the medals.

I did it. I fucking did it. This was everything I had ever worked toward. And more. This medal meant so much more. I wasn't ashamed of the tears that ran down my cheeks. I beat Ervan Cook, the fastest sprinter in the world. Which meant I was the fastest sprinter in the world. At least the fastest at the 100 meter dash.

The next few minutes were a blur. I stood on the top tier of the podium and bent my head as the gold medal was placed around my neck. I put my hand on my chest as they played the national anthem. My eyes teared up again. I was safe. Em was safe. I knew that I still had more to do in order to get us out of this mess. But I wasn't going to think about that right now. Right now, I had just won gold and that was all that fucking mattered.

"You're fast as lightening, man," Cook said in a very Jamaican accent. He was sporting the silver medal. He had already won several golds in other events. I shook hands with Cook and the guy who won bronze.

All the while, my eyes scanned the crowd. There was only one thing I wanted. And then I saw her, running toward the crowd that had formed in front of the podium.

CHAPTER 24
Wednesday
ALINA

He won! I was running down the stands and toward the medalist podium before I even realized my feet were moving.

"Alina, wait up!" Kristen yelled from somewhere behind me.

I didn't know why I was running. I didn't know what I was going to do once I reached him. I just wanted him to know how amazing he was. And sweet, and funny, and sexy, and perfect. He was so perfect. I needed to tell him.

His eyes locked with mine as he hopped off the podium. He pushed his way through the crowd easily.

As soon as I reached him I jumped into his arms. Or maybe I tackled him. But he gracefully caught me as I wrapped my legs around his waist and clasped my hands behind his neck. "Bryce, I..."

He silenced me with a kiss. But not just any kiss. A kiss that seemed to reverberate in every nerve in my body. The kind of kiss you read about in stories. The kind that stops time. Where nothing else in the world matters but this moment. I ran my fingers through his hair as his tongue explored mine. I loved the taste of him. I loved how his strong shoulders felt under my hands. I was in so deep that it felt like my head was spinning.

His hands slid to my ass and I moaned into his mouth, tangling my fingers in his hair. My whole body felt alive. I wanted him. All of him.

When he pulled back, his chest was rising and falling fast. And I knew I was panting so loudly that he could probably hear me.

"That kiss was better than gold." His voice sounded husky with desire.

"I doubt that, but I love that you said it." *Love. There I go again.* "I mean..."

He kissed me again. Softer. Slower. More passionate. Even more mind blowing. I grabbed the back of his neck, deepening the kiss.

I was very aware that his hands were sill on my ass. He seemed to pull me even closer to him, holding me firmly against him. *Oh God.* I moaned again.

He pulled back again. His smile made my skin tingle. The way he was staring into my eyes made me blush.

"You were amazing, Bryce. You're so amazing."

His hands slid up my back as he set me back down on my feet. Luckily he was still holding onto me, because my knees felt weak.

"I wasn't lying," he said. "So much better than gold."

I wanted to stay in this moment forever. This was what every athlete dreamed of. Gold. And he had ran to me. He wanted to share this moment with me. His moment. His victory. I pressed the side of my face against his chest and listened to his steady heartbeat. It suddenly felt like I already had what I wanted. Bryce's arms around me. I hadn't felt this happy in such a long time. Maybe he was right about the kiss being better than gold. His arms around me surely had to feel better than a medal around my neck.

"I got a bronze," Alex said from behind me. "Where's my kiss?"

Bryce kept his hand firmly planted on my back. "Don't look at me," he said to Alex.

Alex laughed. "I was talking to Alina."

"You should ask Tim for one instead."

"Ew," Tim said. "But surely a silver deserves a kiss, m'lady?"

I turned around to see Kristen peck him on the cheek.

Tim fanned himself. I feel like he didn't mean for it to be funny. He just liked acting like every woman from every black and white movie ever.

"Okay, let me get another picture of the two of you together," Kristen said.

"Another?" Had Kristen seriously taken a picture of us making out?

"You think I didn't capture you tackling him earlier? You don't know me very well. Pics or it didn't happen, remember? That's what you said."

"I thought you were very graceful," Bryce whispered in my ear as he smiled for the camera. His hand was still wrapped around my waist. I hoped he'd never let go.

"It's time to celebrate!" Alex said. "Who's ready to not remember the rest of the night?"

Bryce laughed. "You can count me out of that. What do you want to do tonight, Alina?"

"Oh, no. You should go out with your friends to celebrate."

"I'd rather hang out with you."

That's what Chris should have said. But Bryce wasn't Chris. He was so much better. "Okay, how about we all go out for a little bit and get dinner? And then maybe catch a movie or something?"

"That sounds perfect."

"I'm in for dinner. But I'm skipping the movie. To-night I'm finding myself a prostitute," Alex said.

Kristen laughed. "You're going to get so many diseas-es."

"Maybe I should just sleep with you instead then."

Tim slapped him across the face.

"Dude, what the hell? You know that I hate when you slap me!"

"Don't disrespect this beautiful specimen."

Kristen linked her arm in Tim's. "You're such a gen-tleman," she said and kissed his cheek again. This time he didn't fan himself. He kind of had a smug look on his face. For a second I thought that maybe he wasn't gay at all. Maybe he was just the best player I had ever seen. Because Kristen was definitely crushing on him. I quickly dismissed the thought. *No way.*

***

"There are officially no strippers in Brazil. All the liter-ature was wrong." Alex took another shot and slammed the glass on the table.

Tim laughed. "You probably just have to leave the ath-letes' village to find them."

"Right. Like I'm going to leave the athletes' village when people are being murdered on the other side of the gates? I don't think so."

Bryce's arm seemed to tense around me.

I put my hand on his thigh and looked up at him.

He immediately grabbed my hand, removing it from his thigh. But he kept his fingers interlaced with mine.

Maybe sex wasn't on his mind. I knew it shouldn't be on mine either, but I couldn't help it. I felt like all I had been doing since we met was resisting him. I didn't want to resist him anymore. Indulging on every inch of him was probably the most accurate description of what I wanted to be doing right now.

"Maybe you have a super slutty volleyball friend for me?" Alex asked.

Kristen laughed. "Even if we did, we're on a sex ban. One of our teammates broke it and got benched for the first four games here. No one else is going to risk missing out on playing for gold."

"Well, maybe after you guys win. Who's up for that movie?"

"I thought you didn't want to watch a movie?" Bryce said. He was rubbing his thumb against my palm like he had on the train.

Was he actually trying to get me alone? My heart raced at the thought.

"What the heck else am I going to do? Our room is probably a little bigger since it's for three instead of two. How about we all go back to our place and rent something?"

"I hope I folded my laundry this morning after ironing. That would be embarrassing," Tim said and laughed. He looked truly concerned.

What had he been ironing? Jock straps?

"I'm going to go close the tab," Alex said.

Bryce only had one beer. Instead of celebrating hard like everyone else seemed to be doing here, he was snuggled up next to me in our booth. I rested my head on his shoulder. I had never felt this comfortable around anyone before.

"Are you sure you don't want to dance before we go?" Tim asked. "I'd love to show you my moves."

Kristen laughed. "Not tonight. But speaking of danc-ing, Alina and I volunteered to be dancers in the tiebreaker. Not that it's ever going to come to that."

"Oh my God. That's fabulous," Tim said.

"And we need backup dancers..."

"Say no more," Tim said. "I can take over from here. I'll be your choreographer. We can have auditions for proper backup dancers tomorrow after your game. I'll be a dancer too, obviously. But Bryce and Alex will have to be understudies. They don't have the proper balance and grace required for this type of dance. Which one of you is the leading lady?"

"Kristen," I said. "I'm just the understudy." I looked up at Bryce. "It would be awesome if you'd be my fellow understudy."

"If it means hanging out with you, then absolutely. But like Tim said, I don't have the proper balance and grace required for that type of dance. So hopefully it doesn't come to that." He winked at me.

"Alex!" Tim yelled when Alex got back to the table. "We get to dance in front of the entire world!"

"Umm...what?"

Tim filled in Alex as we all walked back to their dorm and began talking strategy with Kristen. I tuned them out. I didn't care what their strategy was. There was no way I was ever going to be a part of that dance.

"Didn't Gabriela Santos volunteer for Brazil?" Bryce asked.

"Yeah."

"So you want to completely annihilate her in your vol-leyball game and in the tiebreaker?" He smiled at me.

"That doesn't sound so bad. But I'm just going to beat her in volleyball. I'm not actually going to dance in the tiebreaker. Besides, there isn't going to be a tiebreaker."

"Well, it was brave to volunteer."

I never considered myself brave. "Kristen kind of tricked me into it."

"Still."

The way he was looking at me made my face flush. I had worn the dress to dinner that I thought was too sexy for our first date. The sparkly one that Kristen had deemed appropriate and I had deemed inappropriate. But tonight I wanted to look sexy. If Bryce made a pass at me, I wasn't going to deny him. Hell. Having sex tonight would probably help me focus better in the game on Saturday. Because recently sex was on my mind a lot more than volleyball. All I could think about since Bryce won gold was how his lips felt on mine and how his hands felt on my ass.

We walked up the stairs to their room.

"I'm sorry it's such a mess," Tim said immediately after he flicked the light on in their room. He ran over to his perfectly made bed and plumped the pillows. And then he removed his athletic shorts from the ironing board and put them in a drawer.

Who irons athletic shorts? In fact, the label on them probably specified "do no iron." Or maybe it didn't, because no one in their right mind would do it anyway.

Alex turned the TV on and flopped down on the only couch.

Bryce adjusted the pillows on his bed to lean against the headboard so that we could sit up. "Is this okay?"

I was already kicking my shoes off. "It's great." I slid onto his bed and pulled the sheets up to my waist.

His Adam's apple rose and fell as he watched me climb into his bed. He shoved his hands into his pockets and turned toward the TV.

For a moment he seemed engrossed in the news report about some table tennis player losing.

"He was walking around like he had something up his ass," Tim said.

Bryce shook his head. He was probably wondering why Tim knew what that looked like.

"What movie should we watch?" Alex asked. He was scrolling through the list of titles available on demand.

Bryce walked over to the other side of the bed. He hesitated for a second before sliding under the sheets beside me. He put his arm around me and I rested my head against his shoulder. I felt like I fit perfectly in his arms. His cologne completely engulfed me. I had that fleeting thought again that I wanted to lick his skin. *Calm down.*

"How about that new movie based on the latest Nicholas Sparks book?" suggested Kristen. "I heard it's just as good as The Notebook."

"Nah," Alex said, cutting Kristen off. "Let me check out the adult movies."

"Stop degrading women!" Tim threw a pillow at Alex's head.

Bryce laughed. "This is basically every night with these two. Why don't we just watch that new comedy with Owen Wilson?"

"I've been dying to see that!" I said. And we liked the same kind of movies? If I had to watch one more stupid action movie with Chris I probably would have killed myself.

"Me too."

Everyone else agreed that it looked good and Alex turned it on.

Owen Wilson was as funny as Owen Harris was hot. My school girl crush on Owen Harris didn't seem nearly as strong as when I was around Bryce though. And Bryce was in my fantasies way more than Owen Harris ever had been.

I put my hand on Bryce's stomach. His abs immediately tensed. *God.* I could feel his muscles through his shirt. But I wanted to run my fingers through the lines of his six pack. I had been dreaming of doing that ever since I had run into him in the locker room. I moved my hand to the buttons of his dress shirt. I slowly undid one button and then another. His body seemed to stiffen even more. Before he could protest, I slipped my hand into his shirt. *Fuck.* It was even better than I had imagined. His skin was so soft. And he had at least an eight pack, if not more.

I moved my thigh on top of his legs. I didn't care that it pushed the hem of my dress up. I wanted his hands on my bare ass. If there was no one else in the room I would have straddled him and moved his hands to my ass for him. I would have unhinged his belt in a heartbeat. I so badly wanted to taste him. Just the thought was making me wet.

Instead, I undid another button and slid my hand even lower down his torso.

His breathing hitched. He ran his hand down my back and stopped at the hem of my dress.

Touch me. I lifted my thigh a little higher, making the hem of my dress rise even more.

His fingertips slipped onto my ass. He groaned. It was so quiet and low that I wouldn't have heard it if I wasn't right next to him.

He slid his hand a little lower, cupping my bare ass cheek. His touch was scorching.

I slid my hand down farther trailing my fingers through his happy trail.

"Alina." His voice sounded so seductive. Just like it had after our kiss.

"Bryce." I hoped my voice sounded alluring and sexy. I traced the waistline of his pants.

He grabbed my hand to stop me from exploring further. "Are you trying to make this impossible?" he whispered.

"No." My heart was beating so loudly that I thought he could probably hear it. "I want to celebrate your victory."

He pulled the hem of my dress down and sat up a little straighter. "Not tonight."

I hadn't thought about him turning me down. He probably thought I was such a slut. I removed my leg from his and sat up straighter too. I bit my lip and turned my attention back to the movie. I was so embarrassed. I could feel his eyes on me, watching my reaction. Was this just a game to him? To see how much I'd embarrass myself because of this stupid sex ban? I folded my arms across my chest.

The bed sagged slightly, but I didn't look toward him. I was so mortified. I squeezed my eyes shut. For some reason I wanted to cry.

"You have no idea how much I want you, Alina," he whispered in my ear.

His words and his warm breath against my skin made me swallow hard.

"You're all that I can think about." He kissed the side of my neck. "I want to kiss every inch of you. I want to taste you. I want to hear you scream my name." He lightly bit my earlobe.

Holy shit. I pressed my thighs together.

He grabbed my chin and tilted my face toward his. "I just meant that we can celebrate together after you get your gold. I don't want to jeopardize your chances of winning."

I got completely lost in his blue eyes. "Kiss me."

He smiled. "Yeah, I can do that." His hand slipped to the back of my neck as he pulled me closer to him. He was such a good kisser. But I could also feel his restraint. He wanted to rip my dress off just as badly as I wanted to rip all his clothes off. He seemed to pull back way too soon.

"I can't wait until Saturday night," I said. I nestled my head onto his chest. In just a few days I'd have gold around my neck and Bryce on top of me. And I couldn't deny the fact that I was more excited about the second one.

CHAPTER 25

Thursday

BRYCE

It was hard to get out of bed. Not because I was depressed, but because everything was so perfect. I had won my race, and more importantly, I had kissed Alina. And it had taken every ounce of restraint in me not to take it further. All I wanted to do was pin her to the mattress last night and have her. I didn't even care that there were other people in the room. It was like I needed her. And she had kissed me like I was the air she needed to breathe. She definitely felt the same way about me that I did about her. Life was good. I wanted to stay in bed as long as possible so that nothing could make that feeling go away.

"Dude, come look at this," said Tim. He was on his laptop at this desk. Alex wasn't anywhere to be seen. Alina and Kristen had left last night after the movie.

I had wanted to ask Alina to stay. I wanted to hold her all night. Hell, I wanted to do a lot more than hold her. Saturday couldn't come fast enough. "Do I have to?" I groaned. "I thought I was going to be able to sleep in now that my race is over."

"Sleep in a different day. I need your help."

"Alright, one second." I rubbed my eyes, rolled out of bed, and pulled on a pair of athletic shorts. I didn't feel comfortable wearing boxers around Tim after he wanted me to check out that dude in the showers the other day.

"So what am I looking at here?" As far as I could tell, it was just a team photo of the USA diving team.

"I think I might have found Python!"

"Who?"

"Python. The guy with the giant penis. See." He pointed at the crotch of one of the divers. "Doesn't it look like he has a huge bulge?"

I couldn't help but laugh. "Please tell me you're joking."

"Oh, you think it's not big enough? Hmm...I guess you're right."

"No, I meant that you're joking about trying to track him down."

"Would the CEO of the Guinness Book of World Records pass an eight foot tall man on the street and not measure him? I don't think so."

"What does that have to do with this?" I asked. "Are you the CEO of a company that keeps track of records for the world's largest penis?"

"No, I just want to ask him how he does it. Please just tell me if you think this might be him."

"I don't know. Instead of looking at his package, why not look at some of his other features that would actually be visible in the photo."

"I didn't look at his face. All I know is that he had a huge penis, great abs, and skin the color of velvety milk chocolate."

"So he's black. Do you remember what hairstyle he had?" *Am I really having this conversation right now?*

Tim stroked his chin. "No, I don't think I saw that. Just his huge penis."

"I dunno how you're going to find him then. Maybe you should just give up and pray that I never tell anyone about this conversation."

"What? Why? We should tell more people so that they can help us find him. Not telling anyone would be like the police classifying an amber alert as top secret."

Tim mentioning an amber alert made me think of Em, which immediately made me think of Rodrigo and that stupid burner phone. If Tim showing me pictures of well endowed black men hadn't completely ruined my state of bliss, the thought of Rodrigo certainly did. *Hopefully there aren't any new missions for today.*

Tim was so focused on his hunt for Python that I didn't even have to be discrete about checking the phone. I just grabbed it out of my drawer and opened the drafts folder:

Good work yesterday. I'm sure your sister appreciates it. One final mission: Make sure the USA wins the tiebreaker event.

At first I thought it was an easy assignment because the tiebreaker was so unlikely to happen, but when I reread it I realized that it was worded in such a way that made it seem like Rodrigo was certain it would happen. The only explanation was that Rodrigo had other operatives working to ensure that the USA and Brazil tied in overall medal count.

I deleted the draft and put the phone back in my drawer.

"Hey Tim, how confident are you that you'll be able to choreograph a dance that will win Kristen gold in the tiebreaker? If it happens."

Tim spun around in his chair. "Uh, I dunno. Maybe fifty-fifty. I mean, my choreography will obviously be the best, but I found a video of Gabriela doing the samba and she's pretty freaking good at it. And our backup dancers are another variable that could tilt the odds against us."

"Could you do anything to get those odds a little higher?"

"I guess I could research the judges to see what they like, but that's bordering on violating the integrity of the ballroom. And you know I would never do anything to jeopardize such a beautiful, noble sport."

"What if someone's life depended on it?"

"I know that it's easy to get sucked into the cut-throat world of competitive dance, Bryce, but don't you think you're being a little dramatic?"

Did Tim seriously just accuse me of being dramatic? I think I might kill myself.

"Bryce? Is everything okay?"

I took a deep breath. It was clear Tim wasn't going to do anything to improve our odds unless I told him about Rodrigo and his threats against Em. And fifty-fifty odds of the USA losing and Em getting killed were way too risky for my liking. I had to tell him. "If I tell you something, do you promise to never tell anyone else about it?"

"You're the love of my life, Bryce. You know you can tell me your secrets."

"I'm what? No, Tim. How many times do we have to go over this? This is the same as the difference between being *in love* with someone and loving them like a brother."

Tim shrugged. "Still don't see the difference."

"The love of your life is the girl that you want to be with forever, not something...never mind. It's not worth explaining."

"Whatever you say. Now what was that secret?"

"Remember the other night when the Uber driver drove off with me?"

"Yeah. He made you carsick."

"No." I lowered my voice just to be sure no one would hear us. "He kidnapped me and took me to some strip club where this asshole threatened to kill Em if I didn't help them rig certain events."

Tim looked concerned for a second and then started laughing. "You had me for a second there. But you're going to have to do better than that if you want to trick me."

"Tim, I'm serious. Look, he even gave me a burner phone where he tells me what to do through drafts. He's trying to rig the games so he gets a huge payout on some bet he made." I pulled the phone out of the drawer and tossed it to Tim.

"Wow, you're serious? Why don't you take this to Coach?"

"Because he has Em. He's not messing around. He even showed me a live video feed of Em sitting in her dorm."

"Shit, really?"

"Yes."

"So what are you gonna do then?"

"I have a plan to take him down, but for now I have to play along. He wants me to ensure that the USA wins the tiebreaker event."

"And he'll kill Em if the USA loses?"

"Yes."

"Shit. Fuck the integrity of the ballroom. I'll do whatever it takes to win this thing for you."

"What did you have in mind?"

"Just let me work my magic. Em's going to be okay." He slapped my shoulder reassuringly and went back to his computer.

CHAPTER 26
Thursday
ALINA

This is it. I bounced the ball in front of me and took a deep breath. Just me and the ball. I tossed the ball up and made perfect contact with my hand. My serve sailed over the net.

The libero from Italy's team dove for the ball and hit it short to the setter. The setter ran toward it and bumped it toward the net.

I ran back onto the court, ready to dig the inside hitter's spike. But the hitter spiked it right into the net.

Oh my God.

"Ahhhh!" Kristen yelled and threw her arms around me. Soon my whole team surrounded me. The crowd chanted "USA, USA, USA!"

"We're going to the finals!" Coach Hammond yelled.

We had just secured at least a silver. We formed a circle around Coach Hammond, our arms interlaced. Half the girls were crying. I looked toward the stands. Bryce was folding up his sign. I just wanted to kiss him.

"Brazil plays the Dominican Republic in a few hours. So we'll know who we're up against by tonight. Tomorrow we'll watch all the footage of whoever wins that game. We're not taking any chances. We're going for gold here, ladies. No parties. No celebrating. Get a good night sleep tonight and drink a lot of water. Practice starts at 9 a.m. sharp tomorrow."

We all put our hands into the middle of the circle and yelled, "USA!"

As soon as we disbanded, I searched for where Bryce had gone. I found him standing by the exit with Tim. I ran over to him and threw my arms around his neck.

He laughed and lifted me off the ground, spinning me in the air before placing a kiss against my lips. Just when I was thinking how nice it would be if he pushed my back against the wall, he pulled back.

"Congratulations, Alina. You were amazing."

"One more game."

Bryce raised his eyebrow. "One more game till what? Gold?"

I bit my lip and shook my head back and forth. "I mean, yes, but..."

He tucked a loose strand of hair behind my ear. "Of course I know what you're talking about. I actually can't stop thinking about it. One more game."

I was glad the same thing was on his mind.

"Okay, wrap it up," Tim said. "We have to get going. People will be arriving to the tryouts in half an hour."

"I can't wait. This is going to be so much fun," Kristen said.

"Congrats on the win, gorgeous." Tim kissed her cheek and put his arm around her shoulders.

Whoa, when did that happen?

"Maybe you're the ones that need to wrap it up," Bryce said.

Tim laughed. "Unlike you two, we're extremely good at multitasking. Isn't that right?" He winked at Kristen and she immediately blushed.

How did I not know what was going on right now?

"Chop, chop!" Tim said. "We need to go scrutinize some sexy male dancers."

I was seriously concerned about Kristen's mental state.

***

"Wow," said Bryce. "Come look at this."

I walked over to the door and peered out into the hallway. The hallway was filled with guys auditioning to be backup dancers.

"Holy shit," I said. "I thought we'd be lucky to get five guys. This is insane."

"Where's my first dancer?" called Tim from behind the judging table we had set up on the far wall of the dance studio.

"Sorry, I'm calling him," said Bryce. He called in the first guy and then we both took a seat at the judging table.

Tim opened a binder and clicked a pen open. "Name?"

"Artie Williams."

"Thank you, Artie," said Tim. "Just a few questions and then I'll want you to perform a few moves. Let's see...okay, what experience do you have with dance?"

"No formal training, but my hips don't lie."

"You think this is a joke? Get the hell out." Tim pointed at the door.

"For real?" Artie looked shocked.

"Next."

"Can't I show you some moves?"

"Not interested. Next."

"Fuck you, man," muttered Artie as he left the dance studio.

"That was kind of harsh," said Kristen.

"Not really. I only want dancers who will take this as seriously as I do. Let's hope the next one is better."

Bryce brought the next dancer in, a guy named Lucas. Tim greeted him in the same way he had with Artie, starting with a question about his experience.

"I've been practicing ballet since grade school," said Lucas. "My friends made fun of me, but it really helped me take my game to the next level."

Tim scribbled down some notes. "Good, good. Have you ever performed competitively?"

"A few times."

"How do you feel about being nude on stage?"

What? "What does that have to do with anything?" I whispered.

"Just trying to keep him on his feet. Part of dance is being able to improvise. The stage can be a dangerous mistress for an inflexible performer."

"I've never had to be nude for ballet, but I'm willing to do whatever the performance requires of me," said Lucas.

Tim nodded approvingly. "What are your thoughts on devil's threesomes?"

Oh my God. He's just trying to get a third for him and Kristen. I started to tune out Tim's super inappropriate questions and Lucas's answers. Instead I started to think about all the places in the dance studio where Bryce and I could have sex. Definitely pressed up against the mirrors. Maybe he could do me from behind with my hands against the stack of workout mats. The ballet barre would give us some great angles to explore. The possibilities with that were pretty endless...

"Have you practiced the dance piece from the website?" Tim asked, drawing me out of my fantasies.

I was slowly losing my mind. All I could think about was sex.

"Yes."

"Then let's see what you've got." Tim hit play on his phone and a Spanish sounding song started playing.

I didn't know what the dance was supposed to look like, but from what I could tell, Lucas did awesome. All of his movements were crisp and on beat. *Is this the actual dance?* There were more hip thrusts than would generally be appropriate, but I guess it was a strip dance. And maybe I was just imagining it because I was so freaking horny.

Tim hit stop on his phone. "Great, thank you, Lucas. I'll email you later tonight to tell you if you made it or not."

"Thank you for the opportunity." Lucas turned and left the room.

When the door was closed, Tim turned to us. "So what'd you guys think?"

"I thought he did great," I said.

"Yeah, he seemed good," agreed Bryce.

Tim nodded. "I agree. My only concern were his looks. I thought he looked a little weird."

"I thought he was cute," said Kristen.

"Alright then, I guess that's a yes for him. Kristen has a great eye for the attractiveness of male features. Let's get the next..."

The door opening interrupted Tim. A woman with a measuring tape around her neck walked into the studio.

"Can I help you?" asked Tim.

"Hi, I'm Annie. I'm the stylist."

"Ah, excellent. Is what I sketched out going to work?"

"Yes, I think so. I just need to measure the girls and then I'll be able to get to work. It's going to be a rush, but I can make it happen."

"Great. Girls, will you please go with Annie to get measured?"

I kind of wanted to sit here and keep daydreaming. There was no point in me getting measured. There wouldn't be a tiebreaker. And if there was, Kristen would do it. "Sure," I said instead and followed Kristen and Annie into an adjacent room.

"Strip down to your panties and bras," Annie said as soon as the door was closed.

I glanced at Kristen. But she didn't hesitate at all. She pulled off her jersey and slid off her spandex shorts. *Okay.* I stripped down to my underwear and sports bra too.

Annie was a master with a measuring tape. She expertly wrapped it around us, writing down measurements in her notebook. I was a little suspicious of some of the measurements. Like the one that ended an inch under my ass. And the one that just ran from right under my breasts to right above my underwear line. Whatever outfit Tim had sketched must have been as miniscule as possible. But it was a strip dance. The outfits had to be sexy.

"I hope you girls like sparkles," Annie said as she wrote down a few more things in her notebook.

Kristen laughed. "Perfect, that's what I requested. Tim is really doing a good job, don't you think?"

"Yeah," I said.

"I'll be right back," Annie said. "I'm going to go grab a few fabric options."

As soon as Annie left, I turned to Kristen. "About Tim...what's going on between you two?"

Kristen shrugged. "What do you mean? He's such a gentleman, don't you think?"

"Mhm. But did something happen between you two?"

Kristen laughed. "Of course. He won a silver medal yesterday. I had to congratulate him."

"What does that mean?"

She raised her eyebrow. "I gave him a hand job during the movie."

"Kristen!"

"What? It doesn't violate our sex ban. I just pleased him. I'm still horny as hell. And don't pretend that you and Bryce weren't fooling around under the sheets."

I wish. "Nothing happened. We're waiting until Saturday night."

"Ugh, Saturday night can't come soon enough. Tim's penis is huge."

"Oh my God."

"What? I'm so horny. If I don't have sex with Tim I'm going to hop on whatever stranger I see right after our game. At least Tim is a gentleman. And sexy. He's so freaking sexy."

I laughed. "But aren't you worried that he's gay?"

"What are you talking about? All he does is flirt with me."

"Right." *Does she not hear the same things I hear?*

Kristen laughed. "You're so ridiculous. Your gaydar is officially broken. Tim is definitely straight. Trust me."

"Yeah, I guess so." *But probably not.*

Annie walked back in holding a few swatches with varying degrees of sparkle. Kristen picked out the shiniest one. If it did come down to a tiebreaker, everyone's eyes were definitely going to be glued to Kristen.

We both walked back out into the dance studio.

The guy dancing had his shirt off and was doing the weird thrusting moves that Lucas had done.

"Brilliant!" Tim shouted. He stood up and started clapping. "We'll be in touch. But between you and me, you're a shoo-in."

The guy shook Tim's hand and then left the room.

"Having fun, guys?" I asked and sat back down next to Bryce.

"Tim is having the time of his life."

"I'm passionate about everything I do." He glanced over at Kristen.

I guess he'd be doing her on Saturday night. *So weird.*

"I truly am enjoying this, but I'd be lying if I said I wasn't bummed that Python hasn't shown up yet," Tim said. "I was hoping to lure him out of hiding."

"Um...what now?" I asked.

"You do not want to know," Bryce said and put his hand on my thigh.

All of my attention was now drawn to his hand.

"Well you have to tell us now," Kristen said. "You can't just throw that out there and not tell us."

"He's magnificent. He has skin the color of creamy milk chocolate and a penis the size of a baseball bat."

"Oh God," Bryce said. "Please stop talking."

"No, this is great. Now they can join our mission to find him."

"You're a part of this mission?" I asked Bryce.

"Kill me," he whispered.

I laughed.

"He sounds like a great third," Kristen said with a laugh.

"My kinky woman," Tim said and kissed her cheek.

Kristen's phone started buzzing in her bag. She pulled it out. "Shit." She looked at me.

I knew what she was going to say before she even said it.

"Brazil beat the Dominican Republic," she said.

I thought I'd be upset. But I wasn't. I wanted to play against Brazil for the gold. I wanted to beat Gabriela Santos once and for all. "It's okay. We're going to crush them."

Kristen smiled. "That's my girl."

Bryce put his arm around my shoulders. "You're definitely going to crush her."

I was glad he'd be cheering me on instead of making out with Gabriela. *God.* I hated that Chris had just popped into my head. *Stupid asshole.* He'd be making out with a loser after Saturday night. Because despite what he had said, Gabriela Santos was not better than me at anything. Well, maybe strip dancing. But that's just because she was a whore.

Tim called in the next dancer and I let my mind wander back to all the things I wished I was doing with Bryce. Which first involved him slowly tracing his hand up my thigh. Yup, I was officially a sex addict.

CHAPTER 27
Friday
BRYCE

I put my hands on Alina's hips again. We were the only two understudies, so we were fooling around in the back of the dance studio, half paying attention, half trying to avoid our primal urges. *One more day.*

"Is this right?" Alina asked. She bent down low, pressing her ass against me.

Fuck yes. "Yeah, that seems right."

I pulled her waist so that we'd be pressed even closer together.

Alina laughed and stood up. "I'm pretty sure Lucas isn't doing that to Kristen."

"I think we're doing it right."

"Mhm. Sure. Here, let me try to do that two step thing again." She grabbed my hands and did something that involved shimmying. I was having trouble not staring at her breasts. She turned to the side and I dipped her low.

"No, no, no!" Tim yelled from the front of the room. "Everyone stop! The thrusting needs to be more forceful. You have to make the judges believe that you wish you were naked. It's the heat of the moment people! I need to feel the romance!"

"I'm pretty sure Tim has lost it," Alina whispered to me.

I laughed.

"Bryce!" Tim yelled. "Get up here. I need to show them what I mean."

"Oh God," I mumbled. I made my way up to the front of the room.

"Lucas," Tim said. "Grab Kristen's waist like this. Lean over," he whispered to me.

"Okay." I felt like I knew where this was going. But he was taking this so seriously to help me. I'd do whatever he needed me to do in order for us to win this thing.

Tim grabbed my hips and thrust hard against my ass.

Alina was laughing in the back of the room. If I didn't love hearing her laugh so much I might have considered punching Tim in the face. Instead I just did what he said.

"Harder, Lucas! Thrust harder!" Tim thrust against my ass again.

And I couldn't help laughing.

"Let's take five," Tim said and let go of me. "Kristen, Alina, come here."

"You seemed to enjoy that," I said to Alina when she reached us at the front of the room. She was still laughing as I wrapped my arms around her.

"I'm pretty sure that was sexual abuse."

Tim cleared his throat and handed Kristen and Alina each a shoebox. "Now that we have the general movements down, you should probably start breaking these in."

Alina lifted the box to reveal sparkly blue stilettos. I was starting to wish she's actually be the one in the dance. Tim had shown me the sketch of the outfits and Alina would look amazing.

"How are we supposed to dance in these?" Alina asked. "They're so high."

"Practice makes perfect." Tim clapped his hands together. "Get to it."

Kristen was already putting them on. "I would have preferred flats, but these shoes are amazing. Great choice, Tim."

"I knew you'd love them. Alina, come on." He snapped his fingers. "Time is of the essence."

Alina put on the shoes. She was about six inches taller in them, but still a lot shorter than me. They made her legs and ass look even more amazing. *One more day.*

"Back of the room, you two. Okay, Kristen, let's do it from the top. Bump and grind, people!"

The music started blaring again.

I literally had no idea what I was doing. But Alina was doing a pretty good job following Kristen's lead. And my favorite part was coming up again. Alina twirled around and bent low, pressing her ass against me again. It hit me in just the right spot now. I tried to think of something depressing so I wouldn't get a boner. My athletic shorts certainly weren't going to hide anything. *Puppies dying. Rodrigo. Shit.* I let go of her waist and ran my fingers through my hair.

She turned around. "Are you okay?"

"I'm good. You can do that move for as long as you want."

She laughed. "So, I've been thinking. You said you were going to be able to visit Em more if you won gold. Does that mean you'll be coming to the east coast a lot now?"

I smiled. Was she really worried that once the ITAs were over we'd never see each other again? Couldn't she tell how much I liked her? I could see a future with her. This wasn't just some meaningless fling. "I was already motivated to visit more. And now that I've met you?" I grabbed her waist and pulled her in close. "I'm probably going to be there all the time." I leaned down and kissed her. Her hands immediately wrapped around my neck, drawing me closer to her. Kissing her made my head spin.

"Understudy love birds!" Tim yelled. "Pay attention or I'll make you run laps!"

Alina laughed and turned around again, picking up the dance right where the song was. She leaned down and flipped her head back, whipping her hair through the air.

But now I was having trouble focusing. For some reason it had just hit me. There weren't that many events left. Brazil was down by one gold. If that stayed the same until tomorrow night, it was going to come down to the last event of the ITAs, the women's volleyball final. Brazil and the USA were both guaranteed to get a silver or gold out of it, so I assumed one of Rodrigo's other operatives would be in play to rig the game in favor of the games going to a tiebreaker. If Brazil was up by one silver and down by one gold, the game would be rigged against the US. Alina would lose. She wouldn't get enough money to save her bakery. And I couldn't do anything about it.

CHAPTER 28
Saturday
ALINA

The spectators were already filing into the stands. We had passed by the line outside the volleyball arena. It was going to be absolutely packed. This was the last game of the ITAs. And we were definitely going to win. We were going to bring home the last gold for the USA. I closed my eyes and took a deep breath.

"Alina, are you okay?" Kristen asked and sat down next to me.

I opened my eyes. "I'm great." And I meant it. I was hyper focused. There wasn't a doubt in my mind about what was about to happen on that court. I'd finally beat Gabriela once and for all.

"You should probably get dressed. The game starts in 20 minutes." Kristen already had red, white, and blue Kinesio tape wrapped up and down her arms and legs and lots of the other girls were already doing their pregame rituals.

I nodded and stood up. I pulled my hair into a ponytail and opened up my locker. As soon as my locker door opened, photos fell out, spreading all over the floor.

"What the hell?" I bent down to pick them up and froze. *Oh God.* I could feel the tears coming to my eyes. Chris banging Gabriela. Tons of photos of Chris fucking Gabriela against a wall in Club Blue. It was obvious because there was a neon blue sign above their fucking heads that said Club Blue. I flipped one over. It was dated from the night Chris had won his gold. *He lied to me. I knew he lied to me!*

"Alina?" Kristen's voice sounded miles away. I saw her crouch down next to me and before I knew it, she had grabbed all the photos. "Alina?"

I sat down on the locker room floor. It shouldn't hurt like this. Chris and I had broken up. I liked Bryce. Why did it hurt so much?

"Alina?" Kristen put her hands on my shoulders. "Gabriela's just trying to get in your head. Don't let her win."

That's why it hurt. It wasn't that Chris had cheated on me. I knew he was a dick. It was the fact that Gabriela had won him over. She always beat me. She always took everything away from me.

"Alina, say something."

Instead I burst into tears.

"Shit," Kristen mumbled. She wrapped her arms around me. "Alina, you can beat her today in the one thing that matters the most to her. In front of the whole world."

But I didn't feel like facing her. I felt like admitting defeat. All I wanted to do was crawl into my bed and pull the sheets over my head.

"It's time to kick her ass once and for all."

***

I knew my eyes were still puffy as I made my way out of the locker room. The pep talks from Kristen helped.

The pregame warm-ups went by in a blur. All I knew was that way too many of my practice serves hit the net. *Focus!*

When it was time to shake the other teams' hands, I knew exactly what I was going to say to her. I was going to look her in the eyes and say, "Nice try." And then I was going to annihilate her in the game. When I got to Gabriela, she locked eyes with me and smiled, just like always.

She grabbed my hand under the net. Before I could say what I wanted, she said, "I'll make sure to tell Chris you said hi." She winked at me and released my hand.

I was going to kill her.

Kristen put her hand on my back and pushed me forward to shake the next player's hand. "I hope you're enjoying Alina's sloppy seconds," she said to Gabriela.

Gabriela scoffed.

Why didn't I say something clever like that? Why didn't I say anything at all?

I took my place on the court. I scanned the crowd looking for Bryce. That's what I needed. To see him cheering me on. To know that one person was on my side. I saw him smiling, holding his sign. Tim and Alex were on either side of him. Alex had a sign of his own: "I heard gold wasn't even the best thing you ladies are getting tonight." There was a winky face at the end.

Oh my God. I laughed out loud. I shook my head and looked across the court. There was no way Gabriela fucking Santos was beating me again.

And she didn't. We won the first game by three points, despite the fact that the refs were making awful calls. Coach Hammond's face was bright red from yelling so much.

As we switched sides, Gabriela walked by me. "Looks like your boyfriend's here," she said with a huge smile on her face.

Again, I couldn't think of anything witty to say to her. We had just beat her in the first game, and she was still the one crawling under my skin. Was she trying to have sex with Bryce too or something? I looked up at the stands to see what Bryce was doing. Instead, I saw Chris taking a seat a few rows in front of Bryce. He was wearing a Team Brazil T-shirt. He had a bouquet of flowers in his hand, like he already knew Gabriela was going to win.

Are you fucking kidding me? Traitor!

My first serve of the game went right into the net. The rest of the game wasn't much better. None of my bumps seemed to hit the mark. And every single one of Kristen's spikes went right at Gabriela's face. The only problem was that Gabriela was good, and all she had to do was take one step back and bump it perfectly to their setter.

"That was in!" Coach Hammond yelled at one of the refs. "Do you need fucking glasses?!"

We lost by 10 points.

"What the hell was that?" Coach Hammond said as we made our way off the court. "I knew practicing for that stupid tiebreaker would throw you two off your game," she said, directly at me and Kristen. "And if you two would get your heads in the game, you wouldn't even need the tie-breaker. Focus on the game. All of you!"

I had never seen her this upset before. I ran back onto the court. Coach Hammond's wrath was enough to make me focus. It was exactly what I needed. Gabriela and Chris were both awful people. Who cared what they did together? I liked Bryce. I really liked Bryce. I took a deep breath. And I needed this money. I needed to win gold. Coach Hammond was right. Now my head was officially in the game.

But even with me playing better, it didn't seem to matter. It was almost like the game was rigged. The line judges were blowing easy calls, all in Brazil's favor.

"It was like a foot in!" Nina yelled after her serve was called out. "What are you talking about?"

The ref lifted out a yellow card from his pocket.

"This is such bullshit," she mumbled. The ref gave her a warning look. One more wrong move and she'd be ejected from the game.

We started hitting all our shots directly into the middle of the court to avoid bad calls. And eventually we got up by two points to win the third game. We were leading the match, two games to one.

I took a huge sip of water. All we needed to do was win one more game. Then gold was ours. Coach Hammond was having a heated discussion with the refs instead of lecturing us. Which probably meant she thought they deserved her wrath more than we did.

I closed my eyes for a second and just listened to the crowd. This might be the last volleyball game I ever played. At least at this level. I wasn't sure I could ever give it up completely. The crowd's excitement was electric. It revved me up even more. *We're going to win.*

The ref blew the whistle and I ran back onto the court.

"Ow!"

I snapped my head around. Jess, our inside hitter was on the ground holding her elbow.

Coach Hammond was already kneeling next to her. "They spilled water over here!" she screamed, pointing at the other side of the court.

The coach from Brazil walked over and put her hand on her hip. "None of my girls did that."

The closest ref came over to evaluate the situation. "One of your own players could have spilled that," he said.

Meanwhile, Jess started sobbing. She was clearly in a lot of pain. An athletic trainer knelt down next to her. Jess winced when she lifted her arm.

"This is a delay of game," the ref said.

What the hell? One of our best players had just gotten hurt. And maybe sabotaged. And we were the ones delaying the game?

Coach Hammond shook her head. "Fine." She motioned for Jess's backup to get on the court. Unfortunately Jess's backup wasn't nearly as good. All of us seemed a little shaken. I was still probably the most off my game. The game was close again, but this time Brazil pulled off the win.

I shook my head as I walked off the court. We were tied two to two. It all came down to one last game.

"Girls," Coach Hammond said. "You all know what this game means. It's not just a gold for you. It's a gold for Team USA. It brings us out on top. And we are not the ones that are going to lose bragging rights for the USA. Not on my watch. The refs clearly favor Brazil. So we hit every ball toward the center. Do it for Jess. Do it for yourselves. Do it for whoever you want, just get it done."

We all nodded and put our hands in. "Team USA!" we yelled at the top of our lungs. I ran back onto the court.

The cheers from the crowd reverberated through me. My heart seemed to beat to the rhythm of the cheers. I looked up at Bryce in the stands. He was on his feet waving his sign in the air, cheering. I smiled and got ready for the first serve.

Bump, set, spike...perfection. After several minutes, we were up by three points. I looked over at Gabriela and smiled, hopefully mimicking that fake smile that she always gave me.

She locked eyes with me and smiled back. And then she winked at me.

Why the fuck is she winking at me? She's just messing with me. She's just trying to get in my head.

I dove and missed my next dig. *Fuck.*

The next play, I was able to get it to the setter. Nina spiked the ball from behind the middle of the net, perfectly toward the back corner. It skimmed the Brazilian player's arm before landing outside the lines.

Kristen high-fived Nina.

The ref pulled his arms to his shoulders, signaling that the ball was out.

"Come on!" Nina yelled and tapped her right hand against her left wrist. "She touched it! It only went out because she touched it!" She pointed toward the player who had clearly touched it. The girl shrugged her shoulders innocently.

The ref pulled out his red card and blew the whistle.

"This is bullshit!" Nina yelled. "Coach, do something!"

But there was nothing that Coach Hammond could do. She called for a time out. "I told you to hit it toward the center!" she yelled at Nina.

"It was a perfect shot, and you know it." Nina grabbed her water bottle off the bench. "This game is fucking rigged!" Nina shouted. She was quickly escorted back to the locker room.

Is was one thing to lose Jess, but Nina was our best server and it was her turn to serve next. Which meant a backup was going to take her place. Nina would have brought us the rest of the way. She would have served us to victory.

"Kelsey, get over here," Coach Hammond said. Kelsey got off the bench. "You're taking Nina's place."

"But I'm not a middle hitter."

"Yeah, but you're the best backup server we have."

"But I play in the back row." She looked so nervous.

"You'll be fine."

Except it wasn't fine. I ended up having to dig twice as many balls without Nina there to help block at the net. But eventually we got the ball back.

Kelsey's first serve went straight into the net.

"It's okay." I gave her a high five anyway. I needed to help calm her jitters or we were going to lose this thing. Besides, I had lost a serve in one of the games today too.

I didn't even realize that it was Gabriela's turn to serve. I took a deep breath. We just needed to get the ball back and tie it up again. I bumped the ball almost perfectly to our setter, but Jess's backup spiked it out of bounds.

Shit. Gabriela served the ball again. I stepped to the left, but stopped. It was going out.

The ref put his hands forward, signaling that the ball was in.

"What the hell?!" Coach Hammond screamed "That was out!"

Luckily she was the one yelling. I bit my tongue. The last thing I needed was to be ejected. I glanced up at the scoreboard. I hadn't realized that Brazil was one point away from winning. I swallowed hard. *You got this.*

Gabriela served the ball and time seemed to slow. If Jess had still been in, she would have stepped back and gotten the ball. But her backup stayed glued to the net.

No. I dove forward, my stomach sliding against the floor. The ball landed an inch in front of my hand.

The crowd erupted in cheers. For Brazil.

Everything suddenly felt cold. I tried to stand up, but my legs gave out. I collapsed on the court, tears streaming down my cheeks. I lost. It was my fault that we lost.

I heard Coach Hammond throw her clipboard on the floor. I felt Kristen wrap her arms around me. She was sobbing almost as loudly as me.

The roar of the crowd was suddenly deafening. Everyone seemed to be cheering for their home team. The sound echoed around in my head.

This is all my fault.

The next thing I knew, our whole team was standing on the podium, getting our silver medals. But I couldn't seem to stop crying. I didn't want silver. Silver wasn't enough money for the bakery. Silver wasn't enough to beat Gabriela. Silver wasn't good enough. It wasn't gold.

They started playing the Brazilian national anthem. The medal was heavy around my neck. I felt like I couldn't breathe. I needed to get out of there.

Seeing Gabriela on the gold medal podium just made it worse. She towered above me. She was always towering above me.

As soon as the music stopped, Gabriela jumped down to the silver podium and gave me an apologetic hug. "How does it feel to always come in second place?" she whispered.

I just stood there, frozen, thinking about how badly I wanted to punch Gabriela in the face.

"I'm guessing not good?" she continued. "I wouldn't really know. I'll have to take your word for it. I've never lost something so important before." She let go of me, winked, and turned back to her teammates.

My throat felt dry. I wanted to have some great comeback, but I didn't have anything to say. It was worse than not good. It felt awful. It felt like I was drowning. I needed air. I couldn't breathe. I stumbled off the back of the platform and ran around the crowd toward the exit.

And I ran straight into Bryce.

His arms immediately wrapped around me. I pressed my face against his chest and breathed in his familiar scent. It was better than fresh air.

Bryce didn't say anything. There wasn't anything to say. We both knew there was nothing that could make this better. Instead, he just held me in his arms, his chin resting on top of my head. He held me as I sobbed ugly tears. He held me until I had left a huge wet spot on his shirt from my tears. He held me until I couldn't cry anymore. And then he just kept holding me as the stadium slowly emptied out around us.

CHAPTER 29

Saturday

ALINA

Bryce and I had talked about what we were going to do after the game. It was all I had been able to think about for days. But I didn't want our first time to be like this. We were supposed to be celebrating. I didn't want pity sex. Luckily he wasn't making any moves. He was just sitting on the couch holding me, letting me rest my head on his shoulder. He seemed to understand my dismal state of mind. Probably because he had been trying to cheer me up for a few hours already.

I wanted him to know why I was so upset. I didn't want to hold anything back from him. "It's my fault," I whispered into his shirt. I bit my lip.

"Alina." He shifted so that he could look directly at me. "It wasn't your fault. The refs were clearly..."

"No." I sat up. I tucked my bangs behind my ear. "Gabriela knows how to crawl under my skin."

He stared at me for a second. "Did she do something?"

"When I opened up my locker this morning, these pictures fell out. Of her and Chris... having sex." *Oh God.* "From the night he swore they only kissed. I knew he was lying. And I know that Gabriela put those pictures in my locker to throw me off my game. I hate that she knows how to manipulate me. She knew how much that would mess with my head."

Bryce lowered his eyebrows.

"Not because I still have feelings for Chris." I grabbed Bryce's hand. "I don't care about that, I just..." my voice trailed off. "She always wins. She always beats me." It felt like I was going to start crying again, but I didn't think I had any more tears in me. "I thought I could win this time. I thought this time would be different."

"It was. They cheated."

I shook my head. "It doesn't matter. I still missed the last shot."

"It kind of looked like the girl in front of you could have easily stepped back and gotten it."

"But she didn't. And I reacted too slowly. And I missed a serve. I played badly the whole time because Gabriela is better than me."

"I don't think she's better than you."

I lifted the silver medal off my neck. I didn't even know why I was still wearing the stupid thing. "This says otherwise."

"An ITA silver medal is a huge accomplishment."

"Ugh." I tossed it on the bed.

Bryce laughed.

"We were supposed to be celebrating tonight. Not...this." I was still in my sweaty jersey. I probably smelled. But Bryce hadn't complained at all. He was the sweetest guy I had ever met. "You have no idea how much I was looking forward to...that. To being with you." I felt my cheeks flushing.

He smiled and ran his thumb across my palm. "I don't mind waiting."

"But you're flying back to Pasadena on Monday. And I'm going to Wilmington." I wanted to freeze time. I'd live in this moment of pain as long as it meant I'd have more time with him.

He smiled. "I wouldn't mind having a super long layover in Philly."

"Super long?"

"Let's just say everything I'm planning on doing to you is going to take awhile."

I gulped.

"Are you hungry?"

I searched his face. He didn't look disappointed about not having sex. He looked a little relieved that I was finally talking. I wanted him to come home with me. Maybe I'd kidnap him like I had thought that Uber driver had. "I'm starving."

"How about I go get some pizza?"

"Pizza sounds perfect."

He stood up. "And I'll get some fancy new dessert to try." He leaned down and kissed me before heading out the door.

My stomach twisted into knots. *Dessert.* I wasn't going to be able to afford to fix up the bakery with the money from a silver medal. I'd barely even be able to cover rent for a few months. I needed to call home. I needed to tell them I'd get the money another way. They couldn't sell it yet.

I pulled out my phone and called my mom. After a few rings she answered.

"Hi, sweetie." I could tell that she knew. Of course she knew. She had been watching all of my games.

"Mom." My voice caught in my throat. I didn't think I had it in me, but I started crying again. The realization that I wouldn't be able to take over the bakery seemed to hit me in a rush. Gabriela had taken everything from me.

"It's okay," my mom said in her naturally soothing voice. "It's going to be okay, sweetie."

"No. Mom, it's not enough. Dad's going to sell it. I need more time."

"Shhh. It's okay. I'll talk to him. He's not going to sell it before you come home."

I put my face in my hands.

"Alina, they showed the crowd on the TV. We saw Chris."

Oh God.

"He was wearing a Team Brazil T-shirt. Is everything okay   with..."

"We broke up. He cheated on me with Gabriela Santos." I lifted up my head. I had talked to my mom a few times this week, but I hadn't mentioned Chris at all. I just didn't want to think about him.

My mom didn't say anything for a long time. "What an asshole."

"Mom!" My mother never cursed. I had never heard her say something like that in my life.

She laughed. "Well, that's the only way to describe him."

I couldn't help but laugh. It sounded weird in my throat. Like I had forgotten what feeling happy was like. I ended up coughing instead of laughing.

The door of my room opened. I thought it would be Bryce, but Kristen walked in. She looked a little happier. "Where's Bryce?" she asked.

I put my hand over my phone. "He went to get pizza."

"Is that your mom?"

I nodded.

"Tell her I say hi."

I lifted the phone back to my ear. "Kristen says hello."

My mom was super polite. I thought she'd immediately say, "say hello to Kristen for me." Instead, she said, "He went to get pizza? If you're not with Chris, who is the he that Kristen if referring to?"

The smile that came to my face didn't feel weird like my laugh did. "His name is Bryce. He's on the track team. We've been hanging out a lot."

"Talking about him has seemed to cheer you right up."

I didn't say anything. She was right. Maybe tonight could turn around. I couldn't change what had happened earlier. A silver was still damn good. I shouldn't be moping around my last few days in Brazil. Screw Gabriela. I just wanted to focus on Bryce.

"Isn't it a little fast though? You've only been there for two weeks. I don't know when you broke up with Chris, but..."

"Bryce is a really good guy, Mom. It's not like it was with Chris." I looked over at Kristen. She was staring at me, but she quickly looked away and pretended to fold some clothes when we made eye contact. "He actually hears me, you know? We have so much in common. He's so easy to talk to. He's supportive and sweet and really handsome. And even though he lives in Pasadena, his sister lives in Philly. So he'll be around a lot." *I hope.* I pulled my knees to my chest. *Oh my God, I'm falling in love with him.* "I really, really like him," I said instead.

"Just be careful, sweetie. When I saw you fall to your knees after the game, I..." her voice trailed off. "It's so hard to see you upset. You'll understand when you're a mother. It kills me to see you hurting."

"I know, Mom."

"But if he makes you happy, hold on to him."

The door opened again and Bryce walked in.

"He does. He actually just came back with food, so I have to go."

"Okay. I love you so much. Enjoy your last few days there."

"I love you too, Mom. See you soon."

Bryce smiled and walked over to me. "Hey, Kristen," he said. "Want some pizza?"

"Absolutely."

I couldn't take my eyes off him. I knew it was fast. But I was falling for him. My heart actually hurt at the thought of saying goodbye on Monday night. But if he was serious about making a stop on the east coast, then I didn't have to worry about a goodbye yet. Eventually he'd have to go home though. Maybe I'd go to Pasadena with him. I could save up more money and start a new bakery. I wanted to tell him how I was feeling. I didn't want to take things slow. For once in my life, I didn't want to play it safe.

"What?" he asked with a smile. He took a big bite of pizza.

I'm falling in love with you. I shook my head. "Nothing." I grabbed a slice.

"We have to eat fast," he said.

"Why?"

"Apparently Tim booked us a spa day."

"Us? Does that mean you too?"

"Um...yeah. Tim was rather insistent about it." He shrugged. "He said it was like massages and stuff. To make sure we're all ready for the dance tomorrow."

"Oh, no, the dance tomorrow," I said with a mouth full of pizza. I hadn't even been thinking about the stupid tiebreaker.

Bryce laughed. "It's our chance to beat Gabriela. Well, Kristen's chance I guess."

"I am definitely going to win this dance off. It's time to finally show that bitch her place." Kristen opened up the container with a delicious looking piece of chocolate cake. "And a spa day sounds perfect," Kristen said. "That's just what we need, right, Alina?"

Right now all I needed was for Bryce's arms to be around me. And for us to celebrate the way we had originally planned. I cleared my throat. "Absolutely."

CHAPTER 30

Saturday

BRYCE

The spa was on the third floor of Dorm 22, which from the outside looked suspiciously like a five star hotel. The rumor was that all of the highest profile athletes were staying there and that after the games it would be converted into an actual five star hotel.

I immediately felt relaxed just walking into the place. The walls were lined with waterfalls that produced a constant, soothing background noise that nearly put me to sleep when combined with the vanilla fragrance they were pumping into the room.

A middle aged woman greeted us at the front desk. "Welcome to the Athletes' Spa. Can I have your name please?" she asked.

"Tim Wood, and this is Kristen, Alina, and Bryce."

"Let's see..." She scanned her computer screen. "Ah, there you are. Would you prefer a male or female massage therapist?"

"We'll take a male," said Kristen immediately.

"We will too," agreed Tim.

"Wait, what?" I said. *Damn it. I should have known Tim would want a man.*

Alina and Kristen started laughing. It was the first time Alina had smiled since losing her match. I didn't want that smile to go away again, so I decided to keep the joke rolling.

"You know what?" I said. "Send us the biggest, strongest men you've got."

Alina laughed even more.

Tim raised his hand for a high five. "My man. I underestimated you."

"Hey, what if we want the biggest, strongest men they've got?" said Kristen. "That doesn't seem fair."

Tim shook his head. "I'm sorry my dear, but the spa is like a street fight. The early bird gets the hunk."

"I don't see how that phrase applies to a street fight..." I said.

At this point, Alina was laughing hysterically. God, I loved her laugh.

The woman at the desk looked concerned. "I should actually point out that the spa has fairly strict rules of etiquette and is nothing like a street fight. For example, any requests for sexual favors from your massage therapist will lead to early termination of your massage." She pointed at a sign behind her titled Spa Etiquette.

"Don't worry," I said. "I'll make sure he doesn't try any funny business with the masseur."

"Good. We should be ready for you in about a half hour. While you wait, you're welcome to relax in the sauna or hot tub. Your massage therapists will come get you when they're ready. The men's locker room is to your left, the women's is to your right."

"Have fun with your hunky men," said Alina.

"How could we not?" asked Tim.

I glanced back at Alina as we walked towards the locker room. *This spa would be so much better if the facilities were co-ed.*

Tim and I changed into towels and then I followed him to the sauna. The hot, humid air blasted us as soon as we opened the door. There were a few guys sitting on the wooden benches, but there was still plenty of room for Tim and me.

I sat back and tried to relax, but it was hard not to focus on the tiebreaker event tomorrow. If all went according to plan, Em would be safe, Alina would be happy to see Gabriela lose, and Isadora would take down Rodrigo. *But if it doesn't go according to plan...* I shook the thought from my head.

"So what do you think our odds are for tomorrow?" I asked. "Still fifty-fifty?"

Tim shook his head. "Have faith, Bryce. I can't control for all the variables, but I'd say we have at least a 90% chance of winning."

"Really? You're that confident?"

"I wouldn't joke about competitive dance."

"What makes you so sure? Practice was good, but not that good."

"I have a few cards up my sleeve," said Tim.

"Like what?"

Tim glanced around at the other guys in the sauna. "You really want me to tell you?"

Good point. Better not to discuss it here. "No, I'll trust you."

"As you should. Just sit back and relax."

I leaned back against the wall and closed my eyes. I tried to focus on my breathing instead of the tiebreaker.

It worked for about two minutes until Tim nudged me.

"Dude, did you see that?" he asked.

"What? No, I had my eyes closed."

"Follow me." He hopped up and ran out of the sauna.

Against my better judgment, I got up and ran after him. He was standing in the middle of the hall looking both directions when I caught up to him.

"What's going on?" I asked.

"I think I saw Python."

"What? Not this again."

"I think he was that guy sitting next to us. When he got up to leave someone hit him with the door and his towel fell off for a second. It was definitely him. Man, I should have known that such a majestic creature would be found in the spa. I wonder if there's a treatment he does to make his penis so big."

"Well, he's not here. The hallway is empty."

"He's not in the hallway, but he must be near. Let's split up and look before the trail goes cold."

"I think that spying on spa-goers violates spa etiquette."

"This is bigger than spa etiquette."

Was that a pun about the size of his penis? I decided to pretend like it didn't happen. "Well, I'm going back in the sauna. Good luck."

"Come on, Bryce. Please help me," pleaded Tim. "It's important."

"Mr. Wood and Mr. Walker?" said a man who had just entered the hallway.

"That's us," said Tim.

Thank God. They couldn't have come at a better time.

"Hi, I'm Brad, and this is Jimmy. We'll be your massage therapists today." They stuck out their hands to shake ours.

As we shook hands with them, Tim turned to me and whispered, "Brad has the grip of a full grown grizzly bear. We're in for a treat."

Ew.

We followed the men down the hall to our massage room. They waited outside while we took our towels off and lay face-down on the massage tables.

Jimmy started massaging my back. It really did feel good, although it took a little while for me to forget about the fact that it was a man doing it. He started at my shoulders and worked down to my lower back, and then he poured some sort of hot oil on me. I thought he was going to keep massaging, but instead he just patted the area.

"Fuck!" I screamed as a sharp pain shot up my back. "What was that?"

"First time getting waxed?" asked Jimmy.

I turned to look at Tim. "What the hell, Tim? Did you sign us up for a wax?"

"No, just you. I always keep my body baby-smooth."

"Well what if I don't want to be baby-smooth?" I asked as Jimmy applied another layer of wax to a different spot on my back.

"It's part of the agreement you signed when you agreed to participate as an understudy in the dance. We can't have any stray hairs poking through your costume. Those suits are tight and HD catches everything."

Jimmy pulled on the wax and it felt like a layer of my skin came with it. I gritted my teeth and tried not to scream again.

"See, it's not so bad," said Tim. "The only bad part is when he does your package, but I'm sure Jimmy will be gentle. It's worth it for the results though. Alina will love it."

"Nope, I'm not doing this."

"You're really not going to do this after all I've done to help you with this tiebreaker? Not cool, Bryce. Not cool at all."

Tim was right. I had asked an awful lot from him for this tiebreaker and he hadn't even flinched. And now he was just asking me for this one thing. Even if it was a full body wax, I couldn't say no.

"Alright, fine," I said. "But after this we're even."

"Deal. Gentlemen, will you please excuse me for a minute? I need to use the restroom." Tim got up, wrapped his towel around himself, and left the room, leaving me to endure the pain of a full body wax by myself.

CHAPTER 31

Saturday

ALINA

The heat in the sauna was super relaxing. Tim really did know just what we needed after losing. *Stupid Gabriela.*

"You're falling for him, aren't you?" Kristen asked.

I opened my eyes and smiled. "I am."

"Did you two bang this afternoon?"

I laughed. "No. I was too busy crying hysterically."

"I figured."

"What about you and Tim?"

Kristen sighed. "It was weird. I was being super seductive. It was like he didn't understand any of my cues. God I'm so horny."

I wasn't at all surprised that Tim didn't understand a woman's cues for wanting sex. "Weird."

"I think he's doing a self-inflicted sex ban so we both perform well tomorrow or something. That's the only explanation I can think of."

Or he's gay? "That makes sense. He's super into the performance. I was thinking after we're done at the spa I might try to take things to the next level with Bryce."

"Well, good luck with that. If Tim has a sex ban, I'm sure he's put it on his understudy too."

"Geez. The only good part about having a silver medal is that it means the games are over and we can have sex again." I sighed and rested my head against the wall behind me. "I feel like I'm going to internally combust."

"So I'm not the only one."

"Having sex with Bryce is literally all I can think about right now."

"Good. I'm glad you're not thinking about the game. Besides, we still have another shot at crushing her and Brazil. So really, we should just pretend the game never happened."

"You mean you have another shot at crushing her and Brazil," I said.

"Right. But it'll be a victory for both of us."

"It is going to be fantastic seeing her face when you win."

"Mhm. And after we get gold this time, then we get to have sex with our sexy new studs."

"Is it tomorrow night yet?"

Kristen laughed. "I think those are our masseurs." She gestured at the two strong men that had come into the room. "If Tim and Bryce got the biggest, strongest men here, I'm glad we didn't. These two looked plenty strong. The men working on them must be terrifying."

I laughed.

We followed the two masseurs into the massage room. They left as Kristen and I got onto the table.

"How does this work exactly?" I asked and climbed onto the table. "Do we put our towels around our waists?"

"Just drape it over your ass and lay face down. They won't be able to see anything."

It was good she was here. I felt like I always did the wrong thing. I probably would have just laid down naked on the table and shocked them if Kristen hadn't been there. I didn't want to offend the Brazilian culture.

I had never had a professional massage before, but as soon as his hands touched my back, I knew why people got them. It felt amazing. I closed my eyes as the masseur's hands ran down my back. *Shit.* I was so wound up that this was making me incredibly horny.

"Oh, God that feels so good," Kristen moaned.

Apparently I wasn't the only one feeling that way. I was very aware of exactly where the man's fingers were.

"Is there anywhere in particular you want me to focus?" he asked.

Yes, between my legs. "Umm..my lower back."

He pushed with just the right amount of pressure. I bit my lip so I wouldn't moan embarrassingly. His fingers went slightly beneath my towel, massaging just above my ass. *Holy shit.*

"Oh yeah, right there," Kristen moaned.

If was official. We had both somehow become sex addicts during our training. It was hard to find the massage relaxing when I was so horny. When it was done, I was ready to leave. I was going to get Bryce to come back to my room. If we even made it to the room. Maybe we could just find an empty room here.

"Your spray tans will start in 15 minutes," one of the masseurs said before leaving the room.

"Spray tans? Screw that," Kristen said as she wrapped her towel around herself. "I think we should go find the guys." It was like she was reading my mind.

I laughed. "We can't go wandering around the spa."

"We have 15 minutes to do whatever we want. And I don't know about you, but I have been dying to see Tim naked. I can't even think straight. I'm going insane."

"Okay, fine. But we have to be back here before they come looking for us."

"We better run then."

I stepped into my slippers and ran out of the massage room with her.

Kristen opened up the first door we came to in the hallway. She peered inside and quickly closed it. "Definitely not them." She giggled.

I shook my head. "We just became peeping Toms."

"No. Peeping Tom-ets. Which, let's be honest, is a lot less creepy."

"Is it though?"

"Do you want to see Bryce naked or not?"

Of course I do. "Why would they be naked? We weren't naked during our massages."

"I don't know. If we catch them off guard maybe they'll stand up really quickly and their towels will slip. You're good at getting Bryce to drop his towel. Come on." She grabbed my arm and pulled me to the next door. Bryce and Tim weren't behind door number two either. We tried several other doors, opening them slowly and peering inside, hoping no one would hear us.

"This is going to take forever," I whispered.

"But the payout is soooo worth it."

"I wonder if Coach Hammond knows she turned us into sex addicts?"

Kristen laughed. "Oh geez, you're right. We're acting crazy, aren't we?"

We both looked at the unopened door in front of us.

"How about one more door?" I said.

"Deal. And then we stop our man hunt."

I nodded.

Just when Kristen touched the doorknob, the door opened and Tim walked out with a huge smile on his face. He looked so happy that I wouldn't have been at all surprised if he had just received a happy ending from his masseur. Kristen's jaw visibly dropped at the sight of him with just a towel wrapped around his waist. He certainly had muscles in all the right place.

Tim cleared his throat. "Ladies, what are you doing out here? Your spray tans should be starting any minute."

"I know, but I was thinking..." Kristen put her hand on the knot at the top of his towel.

Tim grabbed her hand and pulled it to his lips. "Trust me, darling, it'll be so much better if we wait until tomorrow. I have a huge surprise for you." He kissed her knuckles. "I'm going to make all your fantasies come true."

Darling? All her fantasies? Huge surprise? I started laughing. Was he seriously talking about his dick? "Is Bryce in there?" I asked. Kristen had gotten to see Tim in just a towel. Now it was my turn.

"No, he's not. And you ladies need to take this seriously," Tim said. "Spray tans. Now." He pointed down the hall to the tanning room.

Kristen made a pouty face. "Fine."

I felt two hands wrap around me before I had a chance to turn around. "I like you in just a towel," Bryce whispered in my ear.

I giggled.

He turned me around so I could looked up at him. I immediately ran my hands down his strong chest and abs.

"You're so sexy," I whispered. "And...hairless?" I remembered him having a happy trail when I had tried to seduce him the other night.

Bryce laughed uneasily. "Yeah, apparently having no body hair is important for the dance tomorrow."

I laughed. "Seriously?"

He smiled. "You certainly seem like you're in a better mood."

"There is one thing that would put me in an even better mood." My fingers stopped at the knot in his towel. But he didn't look like he wanted to stop me at all. His

Adam's apple rose and fell. It was almost like he was daring me to keep going.

Tim cleared his throat. "That's quite enough, you two. No sex until after we win gold tomorrow."

"But we're not even performing," Bryce said.

He wants me right now just as much as I want him.

"I don't care. Get your hands off her, Bryce. Now."

Bryce sighed and let go of my waist. It took every ounce of restraint to not jump on top of him.

"Are you sure that sex ban should apply to us?" I asked.

Bryce was smiling down at me. God he was so sexy. We were only a few inches away from each other and his cologne had completely engulfed me.

"Understudies are essential for the success of a show. You two will not jeopardize the integrity of everything we've worked for. Do you know how hard it's been to arrange this whole thing?"

"Tim's right," Bryce said.

What?

He leaned in closer to me. "Besides, the longer we wait, the more explosive it's going to be," he whispered in my ear. "I promise it'll be worth the wait." He lightly bit my earlobe.

Oh my God. I pressed my thighs together. I wished I was still wearing underwear.

"Now, ladies, please make your way to room 17 for your spray tans," Tim said.

"Fine." Kristen linked her arm in mine. "Later, boys." As soon as we were out of their earshot, she said, "What did he say to you? Your face is so red."

I smiled. "That it would be worth the wait."

"Swoon worthy much?"

I pressed my lips together. Definitely swoon worthy. I looked over my shoulder before we entered the room. Bryce was staring so intently at me that it made me gulp. Tomorrow night was certainly going to be explosive.

The lady at the spray tan counter greeted us and described how everything worked. Before I knew it, I was putting on goggles and a little thing that pinched my nose. I got in and closed my eyes. After a few minutes a buzzer went off and I stepped back out. My body didn't seem to look any different.

"Is it supposed to show up right away?" I asked Kristen.

"I think it might take a few hours or something," she called from behind her door. "We can ask Tim when we're done."

Of course Tim will know.

***

My back was pressed against the wall outside my room and I was panting embarrassingly loud. Bryce kept his hands on the wall on either side of my face as he caught his breath. That kiss was just...*wow.* I knew our sexual chemistry was out of this world. But it wasn't just that. He understood me. He respected me.

"I really, really like you, Bryce."

"I really, really like you, Alina." His smile made my knees feel weak.

"Thank you for today. I can't even explain how much that meant to me...you being there."

"There was nowhere else in the world I'd rather be."

I looked up into his blue eyes. We hadn't even known each other for a week. But it felt like I had known him for years. "I want you to come inside."

He leaned forward and pressed his forehead against mine. "Ask me again tomorrow night."

I sighed. "I'm making it seem like all I care about is sex, but that's not it. I just feel so close to you already. It's more than just physical for me."

"It's more for me too." He put his hand on the side of my face and placed a soft kiss on my lips. "I'm..." he shook his head and pressed his lips together. "Alina, you've completely consumed me."

That was exactly what I was feeling. He was all I could think about. Like I lived and dreamed Bryce. I wasn't even sure if I was falling in love with him, or if I had already crossed the line into love. But I couldn't tell him that. It was way too soon. I didn't want to freak him out. Instead I stood up on my tiptoes and kissed him.

He immediately pushed my back against the wall, pressing himself against me again. When he pulled back I was completely out of breath.

"You should get some sleep," he said. "We have a big day tomorrow."

I wasn't even sure if he was talking about the dance against Brazil or all the sex we were going to have afterwards. All I knew was that I didn't want to say goodnight like this, with me not saying anything back to him after he had just opened up to me. "If you do have a layover in Philly, I don't think I'm going to be able to let you get back on that plane," I blurted out. It was the first thing I could think of that wasn't, "I'm in love with you, Bryce."

He smiled. "That's good, because I'm not going to want to get on it anyway."

CHAPTER 32

Sunday

ALINA

Kristen and I arrived at the arena a few minutes before her scheduled rehearsal time on stage. Practicing in the studio was one thing, but getting a feel for the actual stage before the performance was key. Or at least, that's what Tim told us.

A security guard kept us away from the stage while the clock ticked down to our fifteen minute time slot. They didn't want us interrupting or getting a peek at another girl's dance before the actual event.

"Your turn," said the security guard. He opened the door and stepped aside.

Gabriela walked out. Her lips turned into a cruel smile when she saw us. "Losing to me twice isn't enough for you girls?" Then she paused and waited for Chris to come through the door too. "Actually, I guess it's three times now. He was your boyfriend, right?"

Seeing them together made me lightheaded. All the blood must have been rushing to my balled fists.

"Fuck you," said Kristen. "Chris, you're a cheating asshole. And Gabriela, you're a stupid bitch. You two are perfect for each other."

"We're also both gold medalists. Something you two know nothing about."

"Just wait a few hours when you're looking up at me on the gold medal podium. Then we'll see who's laughing."

Kristen pushed past Gabriela and Chris, bumping both of them with her shoulders. I followed and the security guard closed the door behind us.

"God, I fucking hate both of them," I said. "Thank you so much for volunteering to do this. Seeing you beat her is going to be the best moment of my life. Well...until the after party with Bryce." Just the thought of it sent chills down my spine.

"Believe me, I'll enjoy beating that bitch just as much as you. Now, lets..." Kristen stopped dead in her tracks when we pulled back the curtain to look at the stage. "Holy shit."

"Holy shit is right," I muttered. For some reason I had expected the arena to be the size of my high school auditorium. It was about thirty times as big.

Pyrotechnics guys and stage hands worked feverishly on various curtains and flags and contraptions while camera crews were testing the HD cameras around the perimeter of the stage. The front of the stage was curved outwards, and then there was a catwalk that led to a circular platform with a few steps up to a raised portion. From the brief practice I had, I knew that the raised part could rotate. We made sure to incorporate that into the routine. The judges table was directly in front of that. Beyond that, there were thousands of rows of tiered seating. I could barely see up to the back row, but the huge flat screens above the stage and on the walls ensured all the spectators would have a perfect view of the performances.

"This is going to be awesome," said Kristen.

Or terrifying. "Ready to do your rehearsal?"

"Yup, let's do it." Kristen pulled out the pair of sparkly blue heels Tim had picked out for the dance and put them on. I had a matching pair, and based on our practicing in them to break them in, I knew they weren't going to be easy to dance in.

I pulled my phone out of my bag and waited for Kristen to get her shoes on and take her starting position behind the curtains. She stuck her hand through to give me a thumbs up and I hit play. The songs that Tim had spliced together started playing. It probably would have been better if all the backup dancers had been here too, but Tim said wardrobe needed them all morning to get their outfits just so.

Kristen burst through the curtains with so much confidence and rocked the first few moves. *Gabriela doesn't stand a chance.*

I sat back and enjoyed the performance. It was flawless.

And then she went to dismount the rotating platform.

"Shit!" she screamed as her ankle twisted under her. She collapsed to the stage.

"Kristen! Are you okay?" I ran over and put my hand on her shoulder.

Kristen scrunched her face up in pain. "Yeah, I think I'm okay. Give me a second."

"What happened?"

"I just landed funny in these damn shoes. I knew Tim should have let us wear flats. Alright, help me up."

I reached out and helped Kristen to her feet. She winced when she tried to put weight on her right foot.

"Are you sure you're okay?" I asked.

"No. Damn it, I think I sprained my ankle." She was standing on one leg and using me for balance.

"Should I try to find a trainer?"

"I'll find one later. But right now, we shouldn't be worried about me. This is your dance now."

"Oh my God..." I had been so concerned about Kristen being hurt that it hadn't hit me until just then. I was the understudy. And now that Kristen was hurt, I was going to have to perform the dance. On this stage. I looked around at the cameras, the thousands of empty seats in the audience. My head started to spin. "Nope. No. This can't be happening. We need to find someone else to do this."

"Who else? You were the only other girl in all of our dance practices."

"Right. Okay, well, maybe your ankle just needs some tape?"

Kristen laughed a little. "Alina, tape isn't going to fix this. The dance is in less than three hours and I can't even put pressure on it."

"I really don't think I can do it. What if the guys just all go out there without us?"

"I wouldn't mind watching that, but I don't think it's allowed. I'm pretty sure this is a women's event, so without a woman, we'd be disqualified. Alina, you can do this. I saw you in practice. You know it just as well as I do."

"Yeah, I can do the moves in the studio. But in front of all these people? And what if I lose? I'll have to kill myself if Gabriela beats me again."

"You know you can't think like that. If you were that afraid of losing, you'd never have gotten this far in volleyball. We go out on that court every day thinking that we're going to win. This is no different. Just picture the look on Gabriela's face when she's looking up at you on that gold medal podium. That'll be priceless."

"You really think I can beat her?" I asked.

"I know you can. But first you need to do a rehearsal run. We only have a few more minutes before we get kicked off the stage."

"Should I wear my shoes?"

"Do you have an understudy?"

"No."

"Then hell no. You're wearing sneakers until five seconds before you perform. We can't have you spraining your ankle too."

***

The music stopped and I looked over at Kristen. *Please tell me I wasn't awful.*

"Alright, I'd say you're ready," said Kristen. "My only advice would be to not shy away from the sexy parts. Arch your back more. Really get into it. It's supposed to be a sexy dance, so be sexy. You haven't had a problem being sexy with Bryce during practice, that's for damn sure."

"But this is in front of millions of people."

Kristen shook her head. "The lights on stage will be so bright that you won't be able to see any of that. While you're dancing you can just pretend like it's you and Bryce, but in the end, you're going to do such an awesome job that you'll be happy all those people are there to see it."

"Is Bryce even gonna be out there with me? He's Tim's understudy, so unless Tim was practicing in high heels this morning and tweaked his ankle like you, he's not going to be out there." *Actually, Tim practicing in high heels wouldn't really surprise me that much.*

"I'll go to the guys' locker room and convince him that you need Bryce out there. But first let's go to our changing room and find me some crutches."

I helped Kristen to her feet. She draped her arm around me and hopped on one foot towards our changing room.

Our changing room was marked with a gold star with "Kristen - USA" printed in the middle. I held it open and let Kristen hobble through. There were three women inside. One was pulling a ridiculous amount of makeup out of a duffel bag and setting it on a counter in front of one of those fancy mirrors with all the light bulbs on the side. Another had at least three different curlers and flat irons plugged in and was cleaning off a comb. And the third was our wardrobe designer, Annie, who had just hung up Kristen's dress and was making a few last minute measurements with a tape measure.

All three of them turned to look at us.

"Hi, girls," said Annie. "I'm just putting a few finishing touches..." She paused and looked at Kristen. "Are you okay? Why are you hopping on one foot like that?"

"I sprained my ankle during the rehearsal. Alina is going to have to dance for me."

Annie shook her head. "That's why we have understudies."

"Do you think you can find me some crutches?" asked Kristen.

"Sure, I'll be right back." Annie looped her tape measure over Kristen's dress and hurried out of the changing room.

The girl with the curling iron took a step towards us. "Hi, I'm Judy, and I'll be doing your hair. Cindy will do your makeup. We're gonna make sure you look amazing."

"Hi, thanks," I said. "Is it okay if I shower first? I got all sweaty during the rehearsal."

Judy smiled. "Of course. There's a bathroom right through there." She gestured to a door on the opposite side of the room. "I put a few products in there for you to use."

"There's a towel and robe waiting in there for you," added Cindy.

"Okay, great. Thanks," I said. *At least I'm getting pampered before humiliating myself in front of millions of people.*

"Did you want me to wait until Annie gets back?" I asked Kristen.

"Kristen hopped over to the makeup chair and sat down. "That's okay. I'm comfy here. You should go shower. This is your big day now."

She was taking her injury surprisingly well. I thought she had been so excited to perform, but now that she couldn't, she didn't seem the least bit upset. In fact, she didn't even really seem to be in that much pain. *Oh my God, is she faking her injury just to get me to perform? She was the one who demanded I be her understudy.*

"Are you sure your ankle isn't feeling any better?" I asked.

Kristen lowered her foot to the ground and winced. "Ow, damn."

Okay, definitely not faking. I guess it was wishful thinking that she'd be faking and actually be able to perform.

"Go, take your shower," said Kristen. "The sooner you shower the sooner Cindy and Judy can start working their magic."

"Thanks for being so supportive. I know you really wanted to do this dance."

"As long as we win gold and wipe that smug look off Gabriela's face, I don't give a damn which one of us is out there."

I gave Kristen a smile and walked into the bathroom. As promised, a fluffy towel and robe were hanging up on the wall and the shelf in the shower was lined with bottles of shampoo, conditioner, and lotion that had super expensive sounding brand names. I turned the water on, stripped off my sweaty clothes, and stepped inside.

When I was a kid, showering was one of my favorite parts of my daily routine. I remember waking up on cold winter mornings. The sun would still be hidden below the horizon. I'd be so cold when I got out of bed, but I'd run right into the bathroom and take a nice, hot shower. And for those fifteen minutes, I was warm and at peace. Whatever tests I had coming up, whatever boy problems or drama with my friends, none of it mattered while I was in the shower. All that I would focus on was the sound of the water hitting the tiles. There were times when I wished I could just stay in the shower forever.

This was one of those times.

I took extra long rubbing the shampoo in, then I told myself that I should let the conditioner sit for a little longer before rinsing it. I even soaped myself up twice. But it was all just prolonging the inevitable. Eventually, the shower came to an end.

I turned the water off and stepped out. The steam from the shower had filled the entire room, so the air was pretty warm. *Maybe I should crack a window. Or escape.*

The thought lingered in my mind as I walked over the window and opened it. I was on the ground floor. I could easily just hop out and catch an Uber to somewhere far away from here. It was so very tempting, but I couldn't stand the thought of letting Gabriela win. I had to at least try to beat that bitch.

I guess this is really happening. I'm going to do a strip dance in front of the entire world.

CHAPTER 33

Sunday

BRYCE

I didn't know how early Tim had left for the arena that morning, but when I got to the locker room, it became clear he had been there for hours. He had folded each backup dancer's outfit in front of their locker and left a hand written note of encouragement on top.

"Hey, Bryce," said a voice behind me.

I turned around and nearly screamed. Tim was dressed from head to toe in a super tight American flag morph suit. I couldn't see any of him, just his silhouette covered in an American flag.

"What do you think?" he asked. The tone of his voice told me he was probably grinning like an idiot under the morph suit.

"I think it's creepy as hell. Why didn't you just pick some normal pants and a button down or something?"

"All the backup dancers being silhouettes will shine a spotlight on Kristen's beauty. I think they turned out awesome."

"If you say so. Are you still feeling confident?"

Tim put a hand on my shoulder. "Bryce, trust me. Kristen is going to win gold and Em is going to be fine."

"I hope you're right."

"I am. Kristen knows all the moves and the dance is choreographed especially for the judges. It's going to be perfect."

I heard the door to the locker room swing open. Tim looked at the clock.

"The other dancers are even arriving early. I knew I was teaching them well, but..." Tim stopped dead in the middle of his sentence.

I turned to see why. Kristen was standing behind me. Using crutches.

"Guys, I can't perform. I sprained my ankle," said Kristen.

Tim laughed. "Nice try, Kristen, but I'm not falling for that."

Kristen shook her head. "I wish I was joking, but I'm not. I twisted my ankle during the rehearsal this morning."

"This is a disaster," Tim said. He looked a little pale.

"Alina knows the dance," Kristen said. "She's going to kill it."

"No, it's not that. I'm sure she'll do great." He stared at me for a second. "It's just...I think I'm gonna be sick," muttered Tim. He started to unzip his morph suit as he ran towards the bathroom.

"Oh God, I hope he gets that thing off in time," said Kristen. "And by the way, what the hell is he wearing?"

"That, unfortunately, is what the backup dancers will all be wearing," I said.

Kristen scrunched up her face. "Weird."

"So you really can't perform?"

"Nope. I can't put any weight on my ankle. Alina's going to do awesome though."

"You think she's ready for it? I'm just worried about her going against Gabriela so soon after that bullshit yesterday. Those fucking refs..."

"God, don't even talk about that shit." Kristen shook her head. "I think she's ready though. She just killed it in rehearsal. As long as you're out there to give her encouragement, I think she'll do great."

"But I'm not going to be out there. Not unless one of the other backup dancers gets hurt or doesn't show."

"Yes you are," said Tim. He had unzipped his morph suit and pulled the top down around his waist.

Kristen leaned on one of her crutches and fanned herself with her hand. "Now that's what the backup dancers should wear."

"Tim, I can't let you do that," I said. "I know how much doing this dance means to you. You're the better dancer, you should be out there."

Tim waved his hand dismissively. "No way. Trust me, you need to do this now. You being out there to support Alina gives us the best shot to bring home the gold."

"You sure?"

"Yes." Tim picked up the morph suit in front of my locker and tossed it to me. "Now suit up."

CHAPTER 34

Sunday

ALINA

"It's starting," said Kristen. She turned up the volume on the TV mounted on the wall of our changing room.

It was a good thing I was scheduled to dance last, because Judy and Cindy were still working on my hair and makeup and I was still wearing my bathrobe. I turned my attention to the TV.

The cameras panned over the thousands of people in the audience cheering as Owen Harris walked out onto the stage. He was dressed in a tux rather than the suits he usually wore in the studio.

"Ladies and gentlemen," began Owen, "welcome to our final event here at the 2017 International Tournament of Athletes. Incredibly, after two weeks and over 900 medals, Brazil and the United States are both even with 41 gold, 27 silver, and 29 bronze. It would be against the spirit of the games to end with a tie, so we have the pleasure of seeing one final event: the strip dance."

Owen stopped and repeated everything he had just said in Portuguese before continuing.

"To ensure a proper level of competition, athletes from the five countries with the most medals will be competing. The order has been predetermined based on a random draw. Germany will go first, followed by Russia, China, Brazil, and the United States. The scoring will be determined by our panel of five esteemed judges. Each judge will give the performances two scores on a scale of one to ten. The first score will be for technical aspects and the difficulty of the dance routine. The second score will be for creativity and sensuality. The top and bottom scores for each category will be discarded, and then the total score will be the sum of the remaining scores. The maximum possible score is 60. In the event of a tie, all scores will be taken into account, including the highest and lowest in each category."

Owen again stopped to translate his speech to Portuguese and then the camera zoomed in on the first judge.

"At the judging table, we have Mi-sook Park from South Korea, famed instructor at the Seoul University of Performing Arts." Mi-sook Park nodded her head curtly.

"Next we have Dean Smith from South Africa, award winning choreographer for countless movies and music videos." Dean gave a toothy grin and turned around in his seat to wave to the crowd. He seemed a hell of a lot more fun than Mi-sook.

The final three judges were Leon Green, a Jamaican performer, Lucas Ramos, a TV personality on a Chilean dancing show, and Corinne Bellerose, editor-in-chief at a hoity-toity sounding French dance magazine.

"Done!" said Cindy, spinning my chair away from the TV so I could look in the mirror.

"Holy shit," I muttered. I barely recognized myself. My hair had been curled, but in a way that made it look a million times better than when I do it. And somehow Cindy had done my makeup to accentuate all my best features and make my imperfections disappear. She had turned my eyes into mini American flags by applying sparkly blue eye shadow and adding red and white striped eyelash extensions. She also made my lips appear way more full than they ever had before. My upper lip was blue with white stars, and my bottom lip was striped red and white.

"Wow, you look incredible," said Kristen.

"Can you guys always follow me around and do my hair and makeup all the time?" I asked.

My stylists smiled. "We're glad you like it."

"Ready to get dressed?" asked Annie.

"Yeah," I said. I got up and walked over to a raised platform in the center of the room. It seemed so fancy, like I was at one of those boutiques on the shows where girls try on $10,000 bridal gowns.

Annie untied my robe and hung it up on a hanger, leaving my completely naked. I didn't know if I should cover myself or not. *Is it rude to have my tits everywhere? Or will it make everyone uncomfortable if I act like it's a big deal and cover myself?*

Before I could come to a conclusion, Annie handed me a lacy blue thong. It didn't cover much, but it was better than me standing here completely naked.

Then Annie grabbed two sparkly blue stars about two inches wide and peeled some white paper off the back of them.

"Are those pasties?" I asked.

"Yup."

"If you think I'm going to prance around stage wearing pasties, you're crazy. Taking my bra off isn't part of the dance."

Annie laughed. "Well that would certainly get the judges attention. But no, that's not what they're for. They're more of an insurance policy against any unfortunate accidents. Things can move around when you're dancing. Wouldn't you rather everyone get a peak at one of these blue stars than at your nipples?"

Oh God. I was already nervous enough about this performance. Now I had to add a nip slip to my list of horrible things that might happen. "Yeah, I guess so."

Annie positioned the stars on my nipples, somehow without actually touching my breasts. "Hold those there for twenty seconds."

I reached up and pressed the stars onto my nipples. It felt so strange having them there. While I held them in place, Annie pulled a lacy blue push up bra off of a hanger and brought it over to me.

"Arms out," she said.

I put my arms out and she slid the bra onto me. Then she went around and hooked it in the back. Next came the red and white striped garter belt and stockings. One of the stockings was red and the other was white.

Annie took a step back and admired her handy work. She tilted her head and tapped her finger against her lips. "Can you pull your garter belt down a bit on the left? And adjust your breasts."

"You mean push them up?" I thought I knew what she was talking about, but I didn't want to be awkward and grab my boobs unless that was what she wanted me to do.

She nodded.

I tugged on my garter belt and then reached into each of my cups and pulled my breasts up. I hadn't looked in a mirror yet, but just from looking down I could tell that this was the best pushup bra ever. My cleavage had never looked this good before.

"Perfect," said Annie. "Alright, Cindy, time to work your magic."

"Huh?" I asked. "I thought my makeup was already done?"

Cindy walked over and put a few makeup containers and brushes on the floor next to me. "Your face is done, but you still need a little body makeup. Believe me, you'll like how it looks."

"Body makeup? That's a thing?" I looked at Kristen. She shrugged.

"I'm just going to add some foundation and highlight a few areas," said Cindy as she brushed make-up onto my legs and ass. Then she added a few strokes with a different brush around my ass and blended the lines with some sort of sponge thing. The next area she focused on was my cleavage. When I looked down a second later, my boobs looked even bigger.

"Whoa," said Kristen. "Can you teach me how to do that?"

Cindy smiled. "It's pretty simple. It's like face contouring, only for your body. I'm sure you can find a tutorial on YouTube."

"Alright, ready to put your dress on?" asked Annie. She had already taken it off the hanger.

"Wait, this is what I'm stripping down to?" I twisted my neck to look back at my ass. The thong covered nothing. *Oh my God. No.*

"Yup," said Annie.

"You look freaking hot," said Kristen.

"But...my ass is everywhere. Are you sure I'm not supposed to wear some boy shorts instead? This seems wildly inappropriate."

"Asses aren't a big deal in Brazil," said Annie. "Thongs are just the norm for bikinis down here. Anyway, I'm just following Tim's orders."

I turned to Kristen. "You need to have a talk with your man. Why did he want to show your ass to everyone?"

"He's just doing his best to make us win. You really think Gabriela isn't going to be strutting around in a thong? Hell, we'll be lucky if she keeps her underwear on."

"Fuck my life." As much as I hated to admit it, Kristen was right. We needed to go all out to beat Gabriela, because Gabriela would sure as hell do whatever it takes to beat us. *Like bribing the refs in the final. So many shitty calls...*

"For what it's worth, your ass looks beautiful," said Kristen. "Cindy did an awesome job. Go look in the mirror."

"Do I have to?"

"Yes. Go look."

I stepped off the platform and got between the mirrors. "Damn," I said. Somehow, Cindy had made all of the stretch marks on my ass disappear. I still wasn't comfortable mooning millions of people, but at least it would be slightly less mortifying than I anticipated.

I got back on the platform and Annie helped me slip into my dress. Then she helped me strap my blue stilettos on, slid some red, white, and blue bracelets on my wrists, and put dangly earrings in each of my earlobes.

"All done," said Annie with a smile.

I carefully stepped off the platform and walked back to the mirror. I didn't want to twist my ankle like Kristen had. *Or maybe I should to get out of this horrible performance.* The thought was tempting, but I couldn't do it. I had to beat Gabriela.

I looked in the mirror and twirled around. The blue dress was covered in sparkles, had a super deep V neckline, and had slits practically up to my hips. If I wasn't going to strip it off anyway, I would have been horrified at how revealing it was.

"You have to admit," said Kristen, "Tim has a great eye for fashion."

"His eye for fashion was never what was in question."
I turned to my three stylists. "Thank you so much for all the magic you three just pulled off. I've never felt so pretty in my entire life."

"You look beautiful," said Cindy. Judy nodded in agreement.

"You're going to do awesome," agreed Annie.

Kristen smiled at me. "Time to go win gold."

CHAPTER 35
Sunday
ALINA

"By the way, there's a high probability that you'll be totally freaked out by Bryce's outfit," said Kristen as we approached the door to go backstage.

"Oh God. Did Tim put all the backup dancers in man thongs?" A picture of Bryce wearing a man thong flashed through my head. "Actually, maybe that wouldn't be so bad."

"Uh, not quite."

I held the door open for Kristen and then went through. I immediately saw what she was talking about. In the corner, Tim was leading a group of men in American flag morph suits doing jumping jacks.

"Please tell me that's not them," I said.

"Who else would it be?"

"Fair enough. How do I know which one's Bryce?"

"Just look for whichever one gets a boner first when they see you. Those suits don't exactly provide much coverage down there."

My eyes immediately gravitated to their crotches. Kristen was right - I could see a pretty clear outline of all their packages. *So that's why Tim chose these suits.*

One of them turned to look at me. "Hey, eyes up here," he said.

"I'm sure she would say the same thing to you if she could see where your eyes were looking under that creepy mask," said Kristen.

The guy shrugged. "Alina, you look stunning."

"I hope you're Bryce," I said.

He laughed. "Of course I'm Bryce. How could you not recognize me?" He gestured toward his morph suit.

"Maybe because all I can see is the outline of your penis?"

"Then after the dance we need to get you more familiar with that part of me." Bryce didn't bother to hide the fact that he was looking me up and down.

"Just because I'm dressed like a whore doesn't mean you're going to get lucky," I said and touched his arm. I would never get tired of feeling his biceps. Despite my playful banter, Bryce was 100 percent getting lucky tonight.

"How else would we celebrate you crushing Gabriela?" He put his hand on the side of my face.

I wished I could see his eyes. They always seemed to comfort me. And I was so nervous. "Good point. Did her scores come in yet?"

"No, I think she's still dancing. Let's take a peek." Bryce pulled me towards the curtain and pushed it aside the tiniest bit to give us a look out on stage.

We were on the side of the stage rather than the back, so I couldn't see the audience, but I had a perfect view of Gabriela dancing around like a slut with a bunch of shirtless, oiled up men. Shockingly, she still had her skirt and her bra on, but it took all of three seconds for her to go to center stage and rip her skirt off. Her thong was just as revealing as mine, but she made it way worse by immediately turning around and doing some samba move that made her ass jiggle all over the place. As much as I hated to admit it, she was a great dancer.

"Ew," I said. *Shit, does Bryce like watching this?* "You better not have a boner right now."

"If he doesn't now, he definitely will after he sees your lingerie," said Kristen.

I turned around and looked at Bryce's package. He put his hands up to prove that he wasn't getting turned on. "Don't worry, Gabriela's disgusting."

I smiled at him. "Good boy."

"Kristen's right though," said Bryce. "I'm not sure how long I'll be able to contain myself when you're out there dancing."

"Are you sure you're okay with me doing this? I'm basically going to show the entire world my ass."

"I want you to do whatever it takes to beat Gabriela, even if it means showing the entire world your ass. They can look all they want, but as soon as the performance is over, it's all mine."

I swallowed hard. "How soon after the performance?" I asked with a wink.

He shrugged. "I dunno. I might not be able to wait for you to get off stage." He put his hands on my hips.

Oh my God. Is he serious? He seems kind of serious.

"Alright you two," said Kristen. "Keep it in your pants for another five minutes. I think Gabriela's performance is almost over."

I looked back out through the curtains just in time to see Gabriela unclip her bra and throw it into the audience. She shimmied for a second and then turned back around to walk back to center stage. I was happy to see that she was at least wearing pasties and hadn't just completely flashed the judges. No one seemed to care, but it was pretty obvious that her tits were fake. Just like everything about her.

She danced around a little more and then finished by making out with one of her dancers.

"I hope that guy realizes he just contracted AIDS," said Kristen.

As soon as the music stopped, Gabriela put her arm over her chest and laughed like she was actually embarrassed to be half naked on stage. Owen Harris came out and was about to start talking when a hand on my shoulder pulled me away from the curtain.

"What are you three doing?!" asked Tim. He looked exasperated. "I've failed as a teacher if you don't know that you should never watch the performance right before yours. You should have been meditating."

"Sorry, I just wanted to see the competition," I said. "Do you know what scores the other girls got?"

"China forgot about the whole strip part of the dance and ended up with a score in the low twenties. Germany got a 37 and Russia got a 41. Those are good scores, but they're both beatable with the routine we have planned."

"Good, because there's no way I'm walking away with anything less than gold."

"That's the spirit. Okay, one quick thing before we begin. You know how we practiced ripping shirts open for that one part?"

"Yes."

"Well, instead of that, during that part you're going to pull these tabs." Tim felt around on Bryce's morph suit until he located a little piece of fabric sticking out. "Got it?"

I reached out and felt the tab Tim was talking about. "Yeah, okay."

"Great. Kristen, take Alina to the curtain behind center stage. Bryce, follow me. I have a last minute change I want to go over with you."

"What's the last minute..." I started, but Tim had already pulled Bryce away. Not only was I curious about the last minute change, but I had hoped for a few final words of encouragement from Bryce.

I walked with Kristen around the perimeter of curtains until we were on the spot marked as center stage. I peered through the curtain to look for Gabriela's scores on the jumbotron, and... *Holy fucking shit.* The auditorium had been intimidating when it was empty, but now that it was completely full, it was a million times worse. Kristen was right that I couldn't see the faces of the audience, but I could still tell that they were there. The cameras were just as intimidating. Not only were they showing HD close-ups on massive TV screens mounted on the wall, but they were broadcasting those same images to millions of people around the world. My knees started to feel weak and I grabbed onto Kristen, nearly knocking her over.

"Oh God," I said.

"What's wrong? Shit, did she get a perfect score?"

"What? No. I didn't see her score. I just saw the crowd. Kristen, that's so many people. How am I going to do this?"

"Alina, you're going to be amazing. Just focus on hitting your first few moves and you'll be fine. Now, let's figure out what scores Gabriela got so you know what you have to beat."

Kristen and I looked out through the curtains again and located her scores on the jumbotron. It wasn't broken down by judge, but it was split into the two categories. She scored 28 out of 30 for technical difficulty, and only 15 out of 30 for creativity and sensuality.

"Damn," said Kristen. "Only 15 for sensuality after she pulled her tits out and made out with someone?"

I shrugged and scanned the other scores. Gabriela had scored the highest of anyone for sensuality. The Chinese girl had only scored a 4 in that category, and the other girls both had sensuality scores in the low teens. "It looks like that's the best score yet in that category though. And overall she's winning with 43 out of 60 total points."

"That's great. That means she'll be on the silver medal podium to watch you get gold. You ready to crush this bitch?"

"Yeah, let's do this," I said as confidently as I could muster. *Or maybe I should pull a fire alarm.*

I moved the curtain again to see the spotlight focus on Owen Harris. *Oh my God, I'm going to be performing a strip dance in front of Owen Harris.* I wasn't sure why I hadn't realized it before. My heart started beating even faster. This was going to be absolutely mortifying. "I can't do this with Owen Harris watching. I'm going to embarrass myself."

"Whatever," Kristen said. "He's no Professor Hunter."

I laughed. I remembered Professor Hunter's marketing class at the University of New Castle. Kristen had always been so nervous whenever he called on her. I looked back at the stage. Kristen was right to a certain extent. But I wasn't thinking about Professor Hunter. I was thinking about Bryce. And one thing was damn sure. Owen Harris was no Bryce Walker.

Owen Harris raised the mic to his mouth. "Ladies and gentlemen, Alina Smith performing for the USA!" The crowd cheered as Owen Harris left the stage. The spotlight dimmed to black. In the darkness, my backup dancers rushed on stage and formed two lines from the front of the stage back to the curtain. One by one, blue spotlights focused on each of them as they stood up and pointed towards me behind the curtain.

"Go show Gabriela how to dance," said Kristen as the dance track started playing over the loud speakers. "I'm going to go watch from the audience to get a better view. You got this, Alina. Make that bitch wish she never fucked with you. "

It's time.

I didn't have time to think. I just had to burst onto stage. The crowd erupted in cheers as I strutted towards the front of the stage. Hearing that applause and not falling on my face within the first three seconds of my dance was a huge confidence boost. In fact, the applause was electric. And unlike volleyball where people were cheering for the entire team, this applause was just for me.

My confidence grew with every move I hit. For a second I even tricked myself into thinking that it wasn't going to be bad at all, but then I remembered that Tim had choreographed it so that the start was fairly tame. I tried not to think about what was coming.

Grinding was the first sexy thing I had to do, but luckily it was with Bryce.

"You're doing awesome," he said as I dipped low and then pushed up on him. It felt like he was starting to get that erection he had promised me. I wasn't sure if I could do this without him here for support. *Or without his hands on my waist.*

My mind started to wander to what I would do with his erection after this dance. God, I was so horny. *Focus, Alina!*

CHAPTER 36
Sunday
BRYCE

Alina looked so fucking hot dancing around in her dress, with the high slits giving glimpses of her lingerie and the low cut neckline exposing her cleavage. Part of my brain was focused on my dance moves, but the majority of my concentration went into not getting an erection. My tight American flag morph suit showed the outline of my penis even when I was flaccid, so I could only imagine what would happen if I got a full on boner. It would turn my crotch into an extremely patriotic teepee.

Two of my fellow dancers stepped forward so that they were standing on either side of Alina as she gyrated her hips. One of them grabbed her arm and pulled her against his body. She ran her hands through his hair and grinded on him for a second before the other guy snatched her away and received the same treatment. Jealousy shot through me. It was tough watching her dressed the way she was and dancing on those guys. I just kept telling myself that this was just a performance. She was mine, and after the dance, I was going to show her exactly what that meant.

When Alina spun away from the two guys, the one she had been grinding on kept hold of her dress, causing her to spin right out of it.

Wow. I had to blink to make sure I wasn't dreaming. Alina was now dancing around wearing nothing but red, white, and blue lingerie. Her garter belt squeezed her tiny waist to accentuate her perfect figure, but my favorite part was the way the straps holding her stockings up framed her magnificent ass. I already thought it was the greatest ass I had ever seen when I watched her play volleyball in her spandex shorts, but seeing her dance around in her thong and heels took it to an entirely different level.

All of the hard work I had done earlier to not get an erection was immediately wasted. The fabric of the morph suit felt strange as it pressed against my growing erection.

Fuck. It was like every ten year old boy's worst fear coming true: having a boner with nothing to hide behind. When I was in grade school, I had this irrational fear of having to stand up in class while I had a boner. I would always get so nervous every time I had a boner, and by some cruel twist of fate, thinking about having a boner just made it even worse. During those terrifying moments, my mind would race and come up with ridiculous plans for how I could hide my erection if my worst fear came true and I had to stand up for something. One plan involved stalling to stand up while I discretely tucked it into the waist band of my pants. Another was to stand up close enough to the desk so that my boner would be pinned down. I even made sure that I always had a book easily accessible in my desk so that I could hide my junk behind it in a dire situation.

Those were all great plans for hiding a classroom boner, but they were worthless on stage. And thinking about it was just making it worse. Visions flashed through my head of "boner guy" becoming an internet sensation, much like "left shark" did after Katy Perry's half time performance.

Then I realized something. Even though the morph suit made my boner ridiculously visible, it also covered my face. I could let my boner go crazy, and no one except for those familiar with the choreography would know it was me.

CHAPTER 37

Sunday

ALINA

Since finding out that I would be dancing in Kristen's place, I had been mortified by the thought of getting my dress ripped off on stage. It's just like wearing a bikini, I had told myself, but it really wasn't. For starters, I was wearing a thong rather than a bikini that actually covered my ass. But the biggest difference was that I was dancing provocatively in front of thousands of spectators rather than happily playing in waves while no one paid any attention to me besides for a few perverts hoping my tits would pop out when a wave hit me.

For a second, it was every bit as mortifying as I thought it would be. But then the thunderous applause swept over me. Nothing could have made me feel totally okay with dancing around in this lingerie, but the enthusiasm of the crowd at least gave me enough confidence to keep me from running off the stage.

I began to wonder what Bryce was thinking about all of this. I had never been this scantily clothed in front of him before. I spun around, trying to search for him, but it was hard to tell which was him with all of the backup dancers faces covered. Hopefully he was enjoying this just as much as the crowd. It was almost like I was doing a strip tease for him. Because if he didn't pull me off this stage and bang me immediately after this was over, I was going to lose my fucking mind. Every touch by one of the dancers seemed to turn me on even more. Were they all being extra handsy because I was in my lingerie or was I imagining it?

I decided it was best to focus on my dance rather than my lack of clothing. The only thing worse than stripping in front of the whole world would have been stripping in front of the whole world and losing to Gabriela. I did a few moves, thankfully ones that kept me facing forward so I wasn't mooning the audience, and then put my arms out and allowed two of my backup dancers to carry me over to a turn table on the side of the stage. They lifted me onto the table and then all eight dancers spread out around it.

Since this type of strip dance was most popular in South America, Tim had choreographed this part of the dance to be me doing the samba while my dancers rotated the platform. Kristen had put hours into practicing the samba and just about mastered it. I hadn't.

I started to do the moves, but rather than looking like the samba, I was pretty sure I was just twerking. Chris had somehow convinced me to learn how to twerk a year or so ago, so I was actually pretty good at it. I cringed as the platform rotated to reveal my jiggling ass to the audience, but there was no going back now. I put my hands on my knees, arched my back more, and moved to the beat. If I was lucky, the judges would just think I meant to be twerking rather than doing the samba.

To my surprise, a guy in a morph suit suddenly ran across the stage doing back flips and hand springs. It wasn't part of the routine, but maybe Tim had recruited an extra backup dancer to fly across stage doing crazy acrobatics to distract the judges whenever I was screwing shit up. If that really was his plan, Tim was a genius.

When the acrobat disappeared, my backup dancers all formed a group so that I could fall backwards into their arms. *Oh God, their hands are all over me. Focus, Alina!* They carried me back to center stage, and for the dismount, they flipped me over two dancers who had crouched in front of us. The crowd cheered when I stuck the landing. Or maybe they were just excited about the view of my ass I had given them during my flip.

I took a deep breath as all eight of my dancers formed a line across the front of the stage, all with their hands on their hips. I walked behind the first dancer in line and slid my hands under his arms and around to his stomach. I was supposed to be feeling for a tab to pull, but I was distracted by his muscles. My fingers caressed the ridges of his abs, like a buggy riding over sand dunes. Sexy, rock hard sand dunes. *Is this Bryce?* I felt around for a little longer than I should have before pulling the tab to rip his American flag body suit open.

The crowd and judges gasped as his suit tore open. *I guess his abs look as nice as they feel.*

I moved to the next man and repeated the process. Unfortunately the tab on his suit was easier to find now that I had some practice, but I still let my fingers wander for a bit. I didn't remember what order the guys were in for this, so it was possible that this was Bryce.

CHAPTER 38
Sunday
BRYCE

I kept my arms on my hips and stared out into the crowd as Alina went down the line, slowly ripping our morph suits open to show off our abs. After watching Alina twerk on that platform, my boner had grown even more. Thick jeans wouldn't have even been able to hide it, much less this paper-thin spandex. Not that I was checking out their junk, but I had noticed that most of the dancers were enjoying Alina's performance as much as I was.

I heard a rip next to me and then felt Alina's hands slide around my waist onto my stomach. She traced the contours of my abs with her fingers and even let them wander to my pecs for a second before pulling the tab. *Did she do that with all the dancers?*

The rush of air against my skin was extremely refreshing after dancing around in an outfit with so little ventilation. I would have thought I would only feel the air against my abs where the fabric had been pulled away, but I felt the breeze all down the front of me. Not only that, but the uncomfortably tight fabric now felt much looser. It almost felt like...

Oh shit.

I looked down and confirmed my suspicions. Rather than a small part of the fabric tearing away to reveal my abs like it was designed to do, the entire front of my suit had broken at the seams, leaving my erection waving freely in the air. In front of thousands of people.

Fuck! Did my boner combined with Alina pulling the tab really make my suit explode? Or did someone tamper with my suit like I had done to poor Yao Kai? Why the fuck did I let Tim convince me to go commando under the morph suit?

My first instinct was to put my hands over my junk, but I quickly decided that wasn't an option. This was a choreographed dance, but the audience didn't know *what* we had been choreographed to do. As a result, all we had to do was make it look like everything was planned. And that meant not covering my junk. As far as the audience and judges knew, male nudity was just part of the routine.

I glanced to the side to see if I was the only one suffering a wardrobe malfunction. Part of me assumed that my dick was the biggest and therefore most likely to rip my suit open, but it turned out that wasn't the case. Well, actually, my penis was definitely the biggest, but that didn't mean that my suit was the only one to rip open. We were all standing in a row, erections pointed right at the judges.

I tried to get a read on how the judges felt about our collective wardrobe malfunction. The Asian lady had her lips tightly pursed, clearly not impressed. But the French lady looked amused, and I was sure the three male judges were enjoying Alina's dance. If we were lucky, eight guys whipping their dicks out would boost the creativity portion of Alina's score.

After unleashing the penis of the eighth and final backup dancer, Alina spun around and lay on the stage. Then she got on all fours and began crawling in front of us. If I didn't already have a boner, watching her arch her back and crawl across the stage definitely would have given me one. It was impossible not to picture myself walking up behind her, ripping her thong off, and fucking her right there on stage. God, her ass was a thing of beauty.

The only problem was that every other guy in the world watching her performance, including the seven men standing next to me, were likely thinking the same thing. *Whatever.* They could look and want all they wanted, but at the end of the day, she was mine. *Hell, in less than five minutes she'll be mine.*

As Alina crawled in front of us, the dancer to my left began tearing the remnants of his suit off, leaving only his head covered. It was probably a good idea, because if we didn't take them off, the torn suits could have been a tripping hazard during the end of the routine. One of the other dancers followed his lead, and then another. Soon we were all tearing our suits off.

CHAPTER 39
Sunday
ALINA

Tim really did a wonderful job of choreographing this dance to make it as awkward as possible for someone wearing a thong. Sure, any dance would be uncomfortable to perform in a thong, but this one especially so. Every other move I had done since losing my dress required me to bend over or arch my back. I looked at the jumbotron where they were showing video from the HD cameras positioned around the stage. Unsurprisingly, the current feed was a close-up of my ass.

Seeing the video made me feel even more self conscious than I already did, so I turned my head to look at my backup dancers instead. Not only would it give me an opportunity to be sexy and whip my hair around, but I also hadn't gotten to enjoy the view of my backup dancers' abs.

Whoa! What the fuck is happening? I expected to see a line of beautiful six packs, but instead I found myself staring at eight throbbing erections, one of which was the most enormous penis I had ever seen. *Oh my God, that must be Python!* For once in his life, Tim had not been exaggerating. Python's erection was actually terrifying.

It took a second for me to process how it had happened, but it appeared that the seams on the morph suits had all busted when I pulled the tabs that should have only torn away a small portion of the fabric. The men all began tearing the fabric away from the neck down, leaving only their faces covered.

As the men finished stripping, more cheers erupted from the audience, mainly from women. And I could see why. Just as an artist spends countless hours perfecting a painting or sculpture, so too did these men. Only their works of art were their bodies, with every muscle sculpted to perfection. It's natural for humans to identify each other by their facial features, partially because usually our faces are exposed and our bodies are covered, but here on this stage, the script was flipped. Their faces were still covered by the American flag morph suits, but their bodies were exposed in all their glory. And each of their bodies told a story. Some had woven a tale of years in the gym, adding bulk to specific muscles. Others had spent more time running, whittling away body fat to leave every fiber and ripple of their muscles just visible below the skin. Despite the differences, their stories all had the same ending: a throbbing erection. *For me. God, I'm so fucking horny. Focus.*

I wondered which one was Bryce. When I had fooled around with him in the dorm, he had a happy trail that I could probably identify. But Tim had made him get waxed at the spa. And he must have had all the other backup dancers get waxed too, because they were all completely hairless. I focused on the abs next. All of them were shredded, and at least half, maybe more, looked like they could belong to a runner. And all of them had impressive erections.

Wait, did I really make all of these men that excited? The thought was exhilarating. My ass had been the focal point of the dance thus far, and I had been expecting everyone to find it repulsive. But instead, the opposite had happened. Just looking at my body had given all eight of my dancers full erections. Then a crazy thought came to me:

From my sample size of eight men, I had given all of them erections. Did I have the same effect on the millions of men watching around the world? *Oh my God. Why the hell am I thinking about this? Why the hell am I checking all of them out?*

At the end of my crawl, I was supposed to climb up the final man in line like a sexy cat. I would have been fine with doing it with Bryce, but instead, it was Python. *Fuck my life.* I reached up and grabbed his naked thighs, feeling his smooth skin and tight muscles. As I continued my climb, I had to dodge to the side to avoid his massive black cock slapping me in the face. But there was no avoiding it bouncing against my cleavage and poking into my stomach. I tried to ignore the excitement caused by coming into contact with his hard cock, but despite my best efforts, my heart beat accelerated and my body tingled with desire.

"Sorry," I muttered. *Awkward.*

"I don't mind at all," said Python. "In fact, I like slapping you with my cock."

Did he really just say that? I spun away from him, and as I did, I caught a glimpse of Gabriela standing backstage, laughing at me.

That fucking bitch! She sabotaged my dancers' costumes to try to throw me off!

I started my weird samba/twerk combo dance again while my backup dancers fanned out to form a circle around me. I couldn't believe it, but the dance was almost over. It really had gone by in a flash. Probably not for the guys though. I could only imagine how mortified they were that they had accidentally gotten nude in front of thousands of people.

The only problem was that I didn't know if I had done enough to win gold. I wasn't the best dancer and the wardrobe malfunction may have hurt us more than helped us.

The next move involved me going to the front of the stage, which gave me an opportunity to look at the judges' faces. They all looked moderately entertained, but their expressions weren't enough to make me feel super confident that I was going to win gold. *Fuck.* I had to do something. Time was running out.

Should I take my bra off like Gabriela did? I pushed the thought out of my mind as quickly as it had come. But when I turned around and saw all my backup dancers standing there with their cocks out, I knew I had to do it. They hadn't even flinched when it had happened to them. If they were willing to do that, I could certainly take my bra off. *Thank God for these pasties.*

I unhooked my bra and covered myself with one arm as I turned back towards the crowd. The crowd cheered as I threw my bra off the stage. And they cheered even louder when I moved my other hand off my breasts.

I kept my arms up for a few seconds before two of the guys came around and held an American flag in front of me.

From practice, I knew that Bryce would be to my left. I couldn't help myself from glancing down to see which erection belonged to him. I was not at all disappointed.

"Did you guys mean to whip your cocks out?" I said to Bryce. I felt like I had to yell to talk to him over the cheer of the crowd.

"No. I think someone sabotaged them," he replied.

"Gabriela. That bitch!" I looked over to the side stage. Gabriela was standing there in her thong and pasties with a stupid smirk on her face. First she stole my boyfriend to mess with my head before our volleyball match, and now she sabotaged the costumes for my dance. *I can't let this bitch win gold.*

The music cut out and the crowd cheered. But they weren't cheering nearly as loud as they did for Gabriela. It was obvious that she was going to get the gold and Brazil was going to win the medal count, and it was all my fault.

"Think I did enough to win?" I asked.

"You did incredible, Alina. But honestly, no. I mean, Gabriela made out with someone at the end of her dance and only got a 15 for sensuality."

"Shit, we should have put a kiss in."

"There's still time."

"Okay, take your mask off."

"That's too complicated. And anyway, you're going to have to outdo Gabriela in order to beat her." He glanced down at his erection.

What?! "You want me to give you a blowjob in front of thousands of people?" *Shit, maybe he wasn't joking about not waiting to get off stage before fucking me.*

He shrugged. "They'll just be able to see the shadow behind the flag. If anyone asks, you can just say you didn't actually do it."

"No way, Bryce."

"Alright. I guess silver is pretty good."

I looked over at Gabriela again. Chris was standing next to her and she was saying something to him. My blood started to boil. I couldn't imagine Gabriela up on that gold podium looking down at me with my silver. Again.

My eyes returned to Bryce's cock. If I had been thinking clearly, I would have told him he was crazy. But I wasn't thinking clearly. My desire to beat Gabriela combined with my starved sex drive overpowered my rationale with surprising ease. *Fuck it.* "This better get me the gold."

Before I could change my mind, I dropped to my knees and grabbed his erection. It was huge. I could have easily fit both hands on it. But this wasn't a handjob. This was a fucking blowjob. I pumped my hand down his length as I swirled my tongue around the tip. I looked up to see the look on his face as I took him into my mouth, but all I could see was his creepy American flag morph suit covering his face.

Cheers and some gasps erupted from the crowd when they saw the silhouette of what I was doing behind the flag. My dance track started pumping through the speakers again.

God, this was so hot. After all this waiting, I was finally able to have him. With the cheers as encouragement, I brought my hand up to meet my mouth and then slid my hand and my lips down his shaft in unison. Bryce moaned loudly. I pulled back and started bobbing up and down to the beat of the music.

His fingers intertwined in my hair as he began guiding me. "That feels so fucking good, baby."

I tightened my lips even more. I loved making him feel good. And as soon as we were off the stage, we'd be doing more than this. I was already wet. Thinking about having him just made it even worse. I didn't care that people could see our silhouette behind the flag. I didn't care about winning gold. In this moment, I just cared about him. This felt right. Our chemistry was so scorching. I wanted him to rip all my lingerie off and have me right in the middle of the stage. I had completely lost my mind. It was just me and Bryce. And God, it felt so right.

"By the way, why do you keep calling me Bryce?" he asked.

I pulled his cock out of my mouth and looked up at him. "What!?" It felt like my heart had stopped.

"Yeah, I'm not Bryce. That's Bryce." He pointed to the guy holding the other side of the flag.

"Shit, are you serious?" It felt like my whole world was collapsing. This perfect moment was actually the worst moment of my life. I tried to think back to practice. I could have sworn Tim was always standing on this side of the flag, which meant Bryce should have been there in his place. Maybe I switched the sides in my head though. *Fuck*.

He nodded.

I turned to the actual Bryce. "Oh my God, Bryce." I put my hand over my mouth. "I'm so sorry. I thought that was you."

"It's my fault," he said, shaking his head. "I went to the wrong side of the flag."

"Why didn't you stop me?!" I swallowed hard. What the hell had I just done?

"I just wanted you to win gold, Alina. I know how much it means to you."

With me still on my knees, his erection was only a few inches away from my face. I didn't know if he would ever forgive me for blowing some other guy, but the only thing my irrational, oversexed mind could come up with to make it up to him was to blow him too.

I grabbed his cock and went right to sucking, trying to do better than I had done on the fake Bryce to show him how sorry I was.

"Fuck, Alina, I forgive you. Just don't stop. Don't stop, baby." Now Bryce's fingers intertwined in my hair.

The crowd cheered even louder than before. And they cheered even louder when the guys dropped the flag.

Holy. Shit. Having everyone see the silhouette of me giving head behind the American flag was one thing. I could have said it was an illusion, that I didn't really do it. But now, with the flag on the ground, everyone could clearly see that it was no illusion. I was on my knees, on stage, in front of thousands of live spectators and millions more on TV, with my lips wrapped around Bryce's penis.

CHAPTER 40
Sunday
BRYCE

FIVE MINUTES EARLIER

The spotlights followed Alina and two of the backup dancers walking to the front of the stage, effectively making the rest of us on the stage invisible. As the dancers pulled an American flag in front of Alina and the music cut out, I ducked off stage. I had to get to my phone so I would be ready to send Em a warning if Alina didn't win gold. Although at this point, I thought she had a pretty good shot. She had gone all out to win, even taking her bra off. It made me incredibly jealous that everyone got to see her beautiful breasts, but if her taking her bra off got her closer to the gold and Em closer to safety, I wasn't going to argue. And I certainly didn't mind the view of her spectacular tits, so perky and full. I hoped I would see more of them, not covered by pasties, later that night.

I got a few funny looks from stage hands as I sprinted over to the bag I had hidden behind some props. If they hadn't been watching the performance, I could see why they'd be shocked to see a nude, fully erect man running around backstage. *Oh well.* Covering myself was of secondary importance to making sure I had a way of contacting Em. I fumbled around in the bag until my hand hit my phone.

Someone patting me on the back startled me.

"Dude, that was great!" said Tim.

Of course it's Tim. Who else would pat a naked man on the back? "Think it was enough to win gold?" I asked as I pulled Em's contact info up on my phone.

"Maybe. Alina did a kickass job, especially with only a few days of practice. And you did great not freaking out when your suit tore open."

"Man, I couldn't believe when that happened. Do you think Gabriela sabotaged the suits to fuck with Alina's performance? Or is Yao Kai getting us back?"

"Neither."

"Huh? Why do you say neither?"

"Because I designed the suits to make that happen."

"Why the hell would you do that?" I asked.

Tim grinned at me. "You said to make sure the USA won this event at all costs, so that's what I did."

"How is a bunch of naked guys going to sway a judges panel made up of a majority of men?" *Why the hell did I trust Tim with this task? Now my sister is going to get fucking killed. Fuck!*

Tim laughed. "The male nudity wasn't for the judges, it was just phase 1 of my master plan."

"What?"

"When I looked into the judges' backgrounds, I found a few interviews where some of them commented positively on Luciana Acosta's performance in Chile's version of Dancing with the Stars where she took her top off and didn't have any pasties on. The translation was slightly ambiguous, but it seemed like at least one of the judges on today's panel would have liked to see her take things even further."

Further?

"So further is exactly what I decided to give them."

"How so?"

"Okay, so you know how we always practiced with me holding one side of the flag at the end?"

"Yes..."

"And then how right before the dance I told you to switch spots with one of the guys in the background so you could make a quick exit?"

"Yes."

"Well, that was actually so that Alina would think it was you holding the flag at the end. Since you all had your faces covered, she wouldn't realize it wasn't you."

"And?"

"I told the guy to pretend to be you and suggest that she give him a blowjob to boost her sensuality score."

"Dude, she's not going to fall for that shit. Wait, weren't you planning all this for Kristen rather than Alina? I thought you liked her, why would you want to trick her into blowing some other guy?"

"Because there's more. I had a friend hack into a few of the judges' computers to see what they were into. What he found was tons of porn featuring girls with multiple partners. So the plan was for the guy on the other side of the flag to pretend to be you after Alina blows the first guy for a few seconds. I figured she'd be so mortified about blowing the wrong guy that she'd easily agree to blow the second guy too, and then they'd drop the flag."

"Tim, that's the worst plan I've ever heard."

"Why? I'm like 50% sure the judges will love it, and I know Alina will. I went through a lot of effort to only choose men with larger than average penises and also to screen them to make sure they were disease free. It's all about the attention to detail."

"Well, it might have worked on Kristen, but it's not going to work on Alina. I sure as hell hope her dance was enough to win the gold even without your shitty plan. Let's go see her scores." I started to type Em's number into my phone as we walked over to the curtains to see the scores come in.

I was surprised to see Owen Harris still behind stage peeping out through the curtain. He should have been out there with Alina getting her scores. *And why is the music still going?*

Owen Harris pushed on his ear piece and leaned down towards the microphone on his label, speaking way faster than I had ever heard him speak on air. "I don't know what the hell to do! Should I try to stop it?"

Shit. He could only be talking about one thing.

I found a break in the curtains and peered through. The naked dancers were all still standing in a line. Alina was on her knees in front of the man she thought was me, her red, white, and blue lips wrapped around his cock as she bobbed up and down on his length.

Fuck! I pushed the curtain back and started to run out on stage, but Tim grabbed my hand to stop me.

"Dude, just wait a second," said Tim. "Any minute now he's going to tell her that he's not you and she'll stop blowing him. You going out there and making a scene will just ruin her shot at gold."

I pushed him off of me. "So I'm just supposed to sit here and watch while Alina sucks some other guy's cock?"

"Yeah, what's the big deal? I told you that the guys are disease free and all have nice big penises. Just sit back and enjoy the show, and afterwards she'll really owe you something good."

"Why is them having big penises a good thing? And you totally would have been okay with this if it was Kristen?"

"Of course. Women have needs, and watching them get those needs fulfilled is a beautiful thing. You like porn, don't you?"

"Not really, and especially not when it's Alina and some other guy!"

"Relax, dude. She doesn't even know who those guys are. She just thinks she's blowing you right now. God, men can be so possessive sometimes. You should just think of it as a performance."

How is this happening right now? I thought Alina was super into me. Then I remembered what I had said to her right before the performance. *"I want you to do whatever it takes to beat Gabriela, even if it means showing the entire world your ass."* There was no way that she could have taken that to mean that she should blow one of backup dancers, right? *Shit.* I also said I might not be able to wait for her to get off stage before having sex with her. *Fuck!*

"Look at what Alina wishes she was doing to you right now," Tim said and slapped me on the back. "You're a lucky man."

"What is wrong with you?!"

"What do you mean? It's going really well. Kristen has been super horny because of their sex ban, so I figured Alina would be too. Apparently I was right. Everything is going according to plan."

I didn't know what to do. I couldn't mess up the dance. Em's life depended on it. But I also couldn't just stand here and let a guy that Alina thought was me take advantage of her. "I can't watch her suck another man's dick, Tim."

"Don't worry, that's not the plan."

"What do you mean?"

"She'll stop soon. The man on the other side of the flag is about to pretend he's actually you. This is going to be so great. There's no way she's not going to get a perfect sensuality score."

I looked back over at Alina. The guy who she thought was me had his hands in her hair and was guiding his cock in and out of her mouth. *Jesus.*

"Fuck this, I have to stop him," I said. I reached to take my mask off.

"You can't go out there. I forgot to replace my name with yours on the final roster, so if you show your face, Alina could be disqualified. You have to just let my plan take course."

Shit. I had to do something, and fast. It was so very tempting to pull off my mask, but then she'd be disqualified and all of this would have been for absolutely nothing. *Shit, shit, shit.*

Tim smiled and gave me the thumbs up.

No! Thumbs up is not the proper response to this situation. Even though Tim obviously thought this was awesome and didn't understand why I didn't enjoy watching Alina giving a blowjob to another guy, he was the one who concocted this whole thing in the first place, so maybe he would have an idea of how to stop it.

"Tim, we have to stop this." I pulled my mask off and threw it on the ground.

"Why? Alina is going to really thank you for this." Tim clapped his hand on my back.

"Alright, I know you don't understand this, but I really am not enjoying this. You have exactly ten seconds to come up with a way to stop this without Alina getting disqualified or I'm going to knock you the fuck out and stop it myself."

Tim looked around and then up, and then shook his head. "I would say pull the curtain, but she'd still be in front of it. But Owen Harris is standing over there. Maybe as host he could put a stop to it?"

"This better fucking work," I said.

I put my hands over my junk as we walked over to Owen.

"Owen?" said Tim.

He turned and looked at both of us, clearly making a concerted effort to keep from accidently looking at my penis. "Tim Wood, right?" he asked. "The choreographer for all this?"

"That's me!" said Tim.

"This is insane. Was this choreographed into the performance?"

"Let's just call it a wardrobe malfunction," Tim said with a wink.

"Well, you better hope the judges like it as much as the public does. This thing is blowing up on social media."

"Wait, are you actually broadcasting it?" I asked. *There's no way...*

"No. God, no," said Owen. "The FCC would sue us into oblivion if we did. We just blurred it out when you guys got naked, and then cut the feed when we realized what she was doing behind the American flag. I think they caught it fast enough so that no one at home even saw her start to give head. We've just been showing highlights from earlier and saying we're having technical difficulties."

Thank God.

"But #ITAblowjob has set a record for the most used hashtag over a one minute span in the history of Twitter."

"How does anyone on Twitter know about it if you cut the feed?"

"Cell phones in the audience, and some news stations around the world didn't censor it as quickly as we did." Owen pulled out his cell phone and scrolled through the

Twitter feed for #ITAblowjob. Most of the tweets were grainy cell phone images of Alina blowing the guy behind the flag or comments about how hot and/or how much of a slut she was, depending on if the poster was male or female. Owen clicked the button to bring up more recent tweets, and suddenly the grainy images were replaced with HD shots of a silhouette of Alina clearly sucking a random guys dick behind the American flag.

"What the hell?" I asked. "How are people getting these images in HD?"

Owen pointed to the logo in the bottom of the images. "I think that's the logo for some sketchy news station in Croatia. They must have decided to post the official feed to their website to get five minutes of fame."

"But how are they getting that feed from your cameras?" asked Tim.

"Our contract to broadcast the ITAs in the US requires us to send all the uncut footage to other stations around the world that purchased the rights for their countries. That station in Croatia..."

I stopped listening when a gif popped up on the Twitter feed of Alina bobbing her head up and down. *Fuck! This has to stop.* "Owen, you have to stop this. She must be over her allotted time or something."

Owen pointed to his ear piece that he used to communicate with the producers back in New York. "I thought for sure they'd have me stop it, but they told me the official rules don't permit me to enter the stage until it's clear the performance is over."

"How the fuck does no one at the ITAs want this to stop?!" I yelled.

"I'm as shocked as you are that they haven't stopped it. But until they do, my hands are tied. If you want to stop it, maybe you could try to cut the lights or something." Owen shrugged and looked back out at stage.

I grabbed a random towel to cover up my junk as Tim and I sprinted into the hallway.

"What the hell?" asked the guard. Apparently he didn't know what was happening on stage, because if he did, my lack of pants would hardly be shocking.

"Long story," I said. "Where's the control room?"

"Why?"

"There's a uh...lighting malfunction. We need to check it out."

"Oh, okay. Down the hall to the right. Room 107."

We took off in that direction. Tim stopped me as we rounded the corner and saw there was another security guard standing outside the control room.

"Let me handle this," said Tim. "I feel like your current outfit hurts our credibility slightly."

"Okay. But hurry."

Tim calmly walked up to the security guard and said a few things. Rather than going inside, he turned around and came back to me.

"No luck," said Tim, shaking his head. "He said no one gets in without proper clearance."

"Then we only have one choice."

"Are you going to threaten to flash him?"

"Just watch." I sprinted down the hall. I didn't even bother to slow down as I approached the security guard, I just wound up and put the full momentum of my run into the punch. He hit the ground like a bag of bricks. I had knocked him out cold.

God, it felt so good to hit someone again. I wasn't sure if I had ever been this angry in my life.

"Holy shit," said Tim. He had run down the hall as soon as he saw me land the punch. "Are you trying to get us sent to Brazilian prison!?"

"No. Although going to Brazilian prison might help you realize how Alina's probably feeling right now on stage."

"They have dance competitions in Brazilian prison? Hmm...maybe I would fare better than I previously thought."

"God damn it, Tim. Just help me open this door so we can turn those lights off."

Tim grabbed the key ring off the unconscious guard's belt and started trying different keys in the lock. A second later, a bearded guy wearing headphones and a black T-shirt opened the door.

"Tommy?" said Tim. "Shit, of course it's you in here."

"I'm confused," I said. "Who's Tommy and why do you know him?"

"He's the stage manager. I've been working with him the past few days to get the lighting and sound squared away for the performance."

"Am I doing okay?" asked Tommy.

"Yeah, you're doing great," Tim said.

"Guys! Focus! We have to cut the lights."

"Why?" asked Tommy. "The crowd is loving it. Check this out." He waved us into the control room and sat down at a desk in front of 12 computer screens. Each one showed a different angle of Alina sucking cock. But now it was the guy on the opposite end of the flag.

"Fuck," I said.

"I knew she'd feel bad when the first guy said he wasn't you. Now she thinks that's you. Everything is going according to plan."

"What the hell is wrong with you, Tim?!"

"Actually, I'm glad you guys came," said Tommy, totally ignoring me. "I was having trouble deciding which view to put up on the jumbotron. "We have the classic side view which is pretty awesome, but I also positioned the sky cam to get a perfect overhead view of him ramming his cock in her mouth. And then of course we could always go for the face shot. Man, you can just tell she's loving it by the faces she's making. I was thinking about doing a split screen..."

"Tommy, cut the god damn lights."

"What do you mean?" he asked. "I felt like I was doing a decent job with the lighting. That reminds me, I was toying with this awesome idea. I have some backup fireworks from Russia's performance that I was thinking would be awesome to sync up if he gives her a cumshot to the face, like a grand finale sort of deal."

"God damn it! That's my girlfriend up there. Cut the fucking lights!"

"Wow," Tim said. "I didn't realize you two were at that level. Congrats, man. Geez, if I had known, I would have asked you if it was okay for those guys to do that."

Seriously? I had a sinking feeling in my stomach. If I had just asked Alina to be my girlfriend would she be out on that stage right now with those guys? I was trying not to rush her. She had just broken up with Chris. All I wanted was for her to be my girlfriend. I really liked her. Fuck, I more than liked her. If I didn't, I wouldn't be feeling the way I was right now. Like I wanted to kill everyone that was touching her. I knew I didn't want to be her rebound. But if I had known that this catastrophe would be the rebound she needed, I would have fucked her days ago to prevent this.

I felt like I was going to be sick. This had to end now. "Cut the fucking lights," I said again, more forcefully. I took a step toward Tommy.

Tommy put his hands up. "Chill out, man. I'm just trying to do my job here."

"I don't care what the fuck you're trying to do, because if you don't cut the lights in five seconds..."

"Okay, okay. I don't have access to the safety lighting in the auditorium, but I can blink the lights on stage if you want. You know, like how they do at the theater to tell people to take their seats. Or like the music at the Oscars when someone is rambling for way too long in their speech. That would probably give them the signal to wrap it up."

"Do it," I demanded. "And tell me where I can go to turn the lights off for real."

Tommy started hitting buttons just as the two assholes that were pretending to be me dropped the flag, showing the whole world Alina on her knees with a cock in her mouth. Camera lights immediately started flashing in the crowd right before the stage went black.

CHAPTER 41
Sunday
ALINA

I immediately pulled back. "What the hell, Bryce?"

"If you're upset about that, you're probably going to be even more upset when I tell you that I'm not Bryce either."

Fuck my life! "Are you serious?" *Oh my God, what the fuck did I just do?* I was kneeling on a stage looking up at a man who wasn't Bryce. And I had sucked two cocks, neither of which were Bryce's. I stood up and tried to run off the stage, but fake Bryce grabbed my wrist just as all the lights in the auditorium went out.

"What was that?" I asked. All I could see was flashes from the crowd, capturing the worst moment of my life.

"I dunno," he said. "Don't they flash the lights to signal that a performance should end soon? Better make sure you win now." As the lights came back on, he grabbed the side of my thong and tugged, tearing the thin fabric. At the same time, the other fake Bryce ripped off my pasties.

And just like that, besides for my garter belt, stockings, and high heels, I was completely naked in front of the entire stadium. And probably the millions of viewers at home. I immediately covered myself up with my hands the best I could. The music stopped and the crowd roared with approval.

Tears streamed down my face. I turned to run off the stage and ran right into Owen Harris.

He smiled at me and for a second his eyes wandered to my breasts. *Oh my God, Owen Harris just checked me out.* I put one arm in front of my breasts and my other hand between my legs.

"Wow, Alina," said Owen. "That was uh...quite the performance."

All I could do was stand there, covering my body. I had done plenty of post-game interviews in volleyball, but never a post-blowjob interview. I thought I'd be interviewed for the first time by Owen Harris after winning gold in volleyball. Not after having danced naked in front of him.

"Do you think the judges will react favorably?" he asked.

Reality started to sink in. I was supposed to perform a strip dance, and instead I had ended up blowing two guys I didn't know and getting completely naked. In front of the whole world. *Oh my God.* "Please tell me that wasn't being broadcast."

"Not by UBC, no. But you are quite popular on Twitter. Let's see if we can put that up on the jumbotron for you."

A second later the Twitter feed for #ITAblowjob appeared on the jumbotron. Whoever was controlling it slowly started scrolling. I expected to read a bunch of 140 character posts about me, but instead the feed was filled with HD pictures and gifs of me giving head and standing stunned and naked.

"Oh my God..." I was absolutely mortified. "Please tell me this is a dream." I knew my face was bright red.

Owen winced. "I'm afraid not. We were required to send the unedited footage to all the international broadcasts with rights to show the ITAs. One of them chose to air it."

Fuck! Fuck, fuck, fuck! "So the entire, unedited segment is available online?"

"Yes."

I gave a mortified laugh. It was all I could to do to keep from running off the stage in embarrassment. Thoughts of all the people who I didn't want to see me giving a blowjob flooded into my head. My mom, my dad, my grandma...really everyone in the world. And where was Bryce during all of this? Why hadn't he stopped me? I turned around, but all my backup dancers had exited the stage.

Owen put his finger to his ear piece. "Alright, I'm hearing that the judges have just about come to a decision, so let's get all the girls back out here."

"Can I please have a towel?" I asked.

The other contestants walked onto the stage, all wearing the lingerie they ended up in at the end of their performance. Compared to the cheers I got for having sex, the applause for the other contestants was lukewarm at best.

I was certain I would win gold if the audience were the one's voting, but they weren't. The judges were, and I had no idea what they were thinking.

The girls lined up next to me, with Gabriela right by me.

"Congrats on getting another silver, slut," said Gabriela.

Her words seemed to echo in my head and my tears started falling again. I was a slut. There was no other word to describe the kind of person who would do what I had just done. Oh my God, what the fuck had I just done? Her smug smile was suddenly all I could see. She had sabotaged my backup dancers' uniforms. And now she was going to win Gold again. I had ruined my reputation for nothing.

My life was over. I turned around to get off the stage, but Owen was standing there with a towel. I quickly grabbed it and wrapped it around myself as I wiped away my tears. I took a deep breath. There was no way I was going to run off the stage and give her that satisfaction. I was done letting her make me feel awful about myself. *Screw her.*

"You're getting second place this time, Gabriela. Fuck you, and fuck you for sabotaging my dancers' uniforms," I said.

"That wasn't me, honey." She rolled her eyes and looked toward the crowd. She waved her hand as if she knew they were cheering for her.

Huh? Who was it then? Wow, did Tim and Bryce really plan this whole thing? What the fuck is wrong with them?

Owen cleared his throat. "Okay, let me recap the situation before we hear from the judges. Gabriela, for Brazil, is currently in first place with a technical score of 28 and a creativity score of 15, for a total of 43 out of a possible 60. So to win gold for the US, Alina will need to have a total score of 44 or more, with the highest and lowest scores in each category being dropped. Judges?"

"Ms. Smith," said Mi-sook Park, the South Korean lady. "I thought your performance was a disgrace to the sport of dance and to these games. If it were up to me, you'd be disqualified. However, if I'm forced to score you, I give you a one in both categories."

It wasn't a great start, but I also wasn't surprised. I could kind of tell she was going to give me a horrible score based on the judgy way she had looked at me when I was twerking. I'm glad I couldn't see her reaction when I had been behind the flag. Luckily, my lowest scores in each category get dropped, so both of those ones would be thrown out and getting gold was still within reach.

"Ouch," said Gabriela with a smug look on her face. I tried to ignore her.

The next judge leaned forward. He was tall, dark and handsome. I was pretty sure he was the one who hosted some Chilean dancing show.

"Alina," he said with a smile. "Before I start, can I borrow that towel? I got all sweaty over here watching you perform."

"This towel?" I asked, pointing at the one wrapped around my body.

"Yup. Just toss it to me."

"No." I swallowed hard. He thought I was a slut too. Everyone in the world thinks I'm a slut! Despite what they had seen me do, none of these people were ever going to see me naked again. I gripped my towel even tighter.

The judge laughed. "At first I thought that everything that just happened was an accident. You're clearly a modest girl when you're not performing. So sweet and innocent." He gave me a sly smile. "Oh, I guess I'm supposed to score you? That's easy. Ten for both categories. I've seen countless strip dances on my show over the past eight years, but none of them even come close to that."

Yes!

"Wow, that's quite the difference of opinions between the first two judges," said Owen. "Alina can't get higher or lower scores in either category, so those will be dropped and every score from the final three judges will count. Dean Smith, what'd you think of Alina's dance?"

The third judge leaned into his mic. "Well, Alina," said Dean Smith, the choreographer from South Africa. "Overall I enjoyed the dance, but I felt the dance portion was a bit safe from a technical aspect. You didn't really attempt many difficult moves, and those that you did try left a bit to be desired. So for a technical score, I have to give you a four. However, I can't deny that the creativity and sensuality of your performance deserves a ten."

I wrapped my towel tighter around myself. Yes, I was happy about the score, but I was mortified that these judges were giving me ratings based on the horrible things I had just done. Or maybe they were just judging my naked body. *Fuck my life.*

The next judge, a slim black man with a bald head and bright white smile, immediately chimed in. "I have to agree with most of that, but I enjoyed the technical part of your performance more than Dean. The whole dance, even before the end, was very sensual, which is the most important part of a strip dance. So for that, I give you a technical score of six and a creativity score of nine."

Nine? Really? I was pretty sure Tim had choreographed the most creative strip dance in the history of the sport. *Giving head on stage?* I was going to kill him.

"Alright, that's 29 points so far," said Owen Harris. "It all comes down to our final judge, Corinne Bellerose. She needs to give you a score of at least 15 for you to take home the gold. Corinne, what'd you think?"

I took a deep breath. My heart was pounding out of my chest. I was so close to taking the gold from Gabriela. But it was all up to Madame Bellerose, an editor at a hoity-toity French dance magazine. She didn't look overtly disgusted like Mi-sook Park, but she also hadn't been grinning like a horny high-school boy like the three men at the judges' table had been.

"Miss Smith," she began in a heavy French accent. Her expression was still unreadable. "Your dance was mediocre. The strip parts were okay, but the dance moves were not so good. Some of them could have been much uh..." she fumbled for the word, "...crisper. So for your technical score, I give you a five."

Shit. That means I need a ten for creativity to win it.

"However, the end of your dance was incredible. A strip dance is so often focused on one woman removing her clothes, so the way you had your backup dancers strip as well was quite brilliant. But you even took it a step further. You teased us all by making us think the dance was over, and then you teased your dancers by giving them blowjobs, in front of each other. I could feel the passion and the desire and jealousy from the other dancers. Strip dances are all about building desire, and I think that dance made every man on the planet desire you. So for creativity, I give you a ten."

Ten? Did she really say ten? I looked at the jumbotron to check the scores. *Gabriela - 43. Alina - 44.*

Holy fuck! I really won!

"Congratulations, Alina," said Owen with a smile. "You just won gold."

I smiled and threw my arms around him.

He cleared his throat.

"Oh my God, I'm so sorry." Why did I just hug Owen Harris while wearing nothing but a towel?

"It's okay." He winked at me and lifted one of my hands in the air. And in that moment, all I could think about was that I won gold. I won gold and beat Gabriela.

The familiar sound of the crowd cheering for me filled the air. God, I loved that sound.

CHAPTER 42
Sunday
ISADORA

Sex, for many people, is when they feel most alive, connecting with another human on some base and animalistic level. Maybe I felt that way about sex at some point, before I was beaten and broken by Rodrigo and his customers, but now, only the ocean made me feel truly alive. It was the one bright spot in my life filled mainly with the darkness of drugs and prostitution. On the rare occasion that Rodrigo didn't demand my presence at the club, I would always go to the beach, and for a few hours, I'd smell the salty ocean breeze and feel the hot Brazilian sun beating down on my tan skin.

I took a deep breath, filling my lungs with the salty ocean air one more time before leaving the balcony to go back inside the penthouse suite of the Copacabana Palace. My best friend, Giovanna, was sitting on one of the four couches in the penthouse, while Rodrigo nursed a scotch at the bar in front of his laptop. I didn't have to see the screen to know that he was watching a live feed from Vitor of Bryce's sister, Emily. A similar video feed had been present on Rodrigo's laptop during every pivotal event, with the only variables being a different loved one based on which operative was supposed to be rigging the event. I didn't understand why he actually had to kill some innocent girl if Bryce failed. It would be smarter to just use the threat of her death to make Bryce do his bidding, especially since he would owe Vitor more money for actually carrying out the hit on the girl, but Rodrigo didn't see it that way. If someone crossed him, he took something they loved. It was brutal, but thus far in life, it appeared to have served him well.

That's going to change today.

"Is it back on?" asked Rodrigo in Portuguese.

"Not yet," said Giovanna. "The announcer is still claiming that they're having...technical difficulties." She looked down at her phone for a second and then held it up for Rodrigo and me to see. "But if you look at the Twitter..."

I looked at the screen. Someone in the audience had tweeted out a low quality ten-second video of the American girl giving head on stage to one of her backup dancers. It was behind an American flag, but it was definitely happening. There was no denying it. *Another life ruined by Rodrigo.*

"Holy shit," said Rodrigo. "That girl really knows how to give head."

"Hey," said Giovanna, pointing at the 80 inch TV on the wall. "I think it's coming back on."

I immediately turned my attention to the TV.

"We do apologize for the technical difficulties, but I'm hearing that everything is sorted out now. In just a second we'll take you back out to the tiebreaker. The announcer disappeared and was replaced with a live feed of all the participants on stage. Alina had a towel wrapped around herself and was wiping her face with part of it. Tears. The poor American girl was in tears. I shook my head. It just made my hatred for Rodrigo grow.

Rodrigo grabbed his laptop and brought it over to the couch. Giovanna scooted over to make room for him and

I slid into the seat beside him. All of our stares were glued to the TV, eagerly awaiting the scores of the judges.

***

"The fucking gringo did it!" shouted Rodrigo, jumping off the couch and pumping his fist in the air.

I couldn't help but smile. Maybe, just maybe, life was finally throwing me a bone.

"So the hit is off?" asked a cold voice from the laptop.

"Yes," said Rodrigo. "As always, your services are very much appreciated." With payment for the surveillance already having been completed, Vitor and Rodrigo's business was complete. The feed on the laptop went dark. "Girls, should we go collect on the ticket?"

"Soon," I said. "But first, we have a little something that will surprise you."

Giovanna and I stood and made our way to the bedroom of the suite. We closed the doors and quickly changed into the black leather cat suits we had packed. Rodrigo had a weakness for leather, and we planned to fully exploit that.

"Ready?" I asked, pulling on a pair of black thigh-high boots. My heart was pounding, partially from fear, but mainly from excitement. After all the shit Rodrigo had put me through, I was about to get my revenge.

"Ready," said Giovanna. I was pleased to not hear even a hint of uncertainty in Giovanna's voice. There would be no margin for error.

We pushed the doors to the bedroom open and walked over to Rodrigo. In an instant, he was on his feet. He reached for my ass, but I swatted his hand away. I waved my finger at him and bit my lip. "Not yet," I said.

"Fuck," muttered Rodrigo. "Where have you been hiding these outfits?" The growing bulge in his pants made his approval evident.

Men are so easy.

Giovanna and I each grabbed one of his hands and led him back into the bedroom, closing the doors behind us. I spun him around at the base of the bed and kissed him for a second before pushing on his chest to send him sprawling back onto the plush king sized bed.

Giovanna jumped on him, undoing his belt and dropping his pants in a fluid motion that could only come with years of experience in our profession. Within a second, his pants were at his ankles and Giovanna's tongue was pressed against his cock, licking it like a popsicle. Rodrigo went to grab her hair to force himself into her throat, but she pushed his arm away. "Not yet," she moaned. "I want to savor your big cock."

Big cock. Those words being used to describe Rodrigo's package almost made me laugh, because he really wasn't packing anything special. We just had to pretend like he was.

On the side of the bed, I traced my finger down my chest and tugged on the zipper. One little tug was all the help my breasts needed to free themselves of the tight fabric. I traced my finger around my aroused nipples.

"Fuck, get over here," demanded Rodrigo.

I crawled onto the bed and buried Rodrigo's face into my cleavage, pinning his hands above his head. With Rodrigo distracted, Giovanna took her mouth off of him and moved up to be next to me. In unison, we cuffed his hands to the headboard.

"What the hell?" said Rodrigo, his voice heavily muffled by my silicon breasts.

I pulled back and looked at him. "What's wrong? Did you want to touch these?" I pushed my breasts together and moaned. "Or maybe you'd rather touch these?" I reached over and unzipped Giovanna's suit.

"Damn, this is better than winning a bet," said Rodrigo.

I smiled and Giovanna and I made our way to the foot of the bed. Rodrigo's cock danced with excitement, probably anticipating a double blowjob, but we went right past his erection. We tore his shoes and pants off and then cuffed his ankles to the bed posts.

"So what do you want us to do to you?" I asked.

"You better fuck me."

"Hmmm..." I tapped my finger against my lips. "I think I can arrange the fucking of you. Giovanna, what do you think?"

"Yeah, let's fuck him," agreed Giovanna.

"How should we fuck him?"

"Cow girl?" suggested Giovanna.

"I had something else in mind. What if we take all his money?" I watched as his smug fucking smile changed into confusion.

Giovanna shrugged. "Okay."

"What?" asked Rodrigo. "What the fuck do you think you're doing?"

"We're fucking you, just like you wanted," I said, jumping onto the bed and frisking his pockets. He squirmed and twisted and tried to free himself from his bonds, but to no avail. I quickly found the betting ticket which was now worth millions.

"You fucking bitches," yelled Rodrigo. "I'll fucking kill you for this."

"I know," I said. "I've seen you nearly kill girls for sucking your tiny cock wrong, so I have no doubt you'd kill me for this that I am doing. But you know what? I'm fucking tired of your shit, Rodrigo. I'm tired of going to the club all the nights and doing whatever the fuck you want me to do. You act like you're the hot shit, but no one gives a shit about you and your filthy fucking club. Without this ticket," I waved the ticket in his face, "you are nothing."

Rage flashed across Rodrigo's face, but it quickly turned to a gentle smile. "Come on, girls. You really think I'd win this much money and not share a piece with you? You girls mean everything to me. I was going to make you both live like queens. And I still will if you let me out of these cuffs. We can pretend like this never happened."

I laughed. "Bullshit. The second I let you free, you'll kill the both of us."

"I would never hurt you," said Rodrigo.

"I wish that were true, but you've been hurting us ever since the day we met. Maybe it's time we returned the favor of the hurt." I pushed Rodrigo's sports coat to the side and unholstered his silenced pistol.

"What, now you're going to shoot me?" scoffed Rodrigo. "Come on, just untie me before you hurt yourself."

I slid off the bed and pressed the barrel of the gun against his penis. What was left of his erection from earlier immediately wilted under the cold sting of the metal barrel and the threat of his manhood being blown to bits. He tried to look confident, but I could see the fear on his face. I knew that look so well from all the times I had looked in the mirror at the club. The look only intensified as I took off the safety and put my finger on the trigger.

Rodrigo squirmed to try to get his penis to safety.

"Quit the movement or my finger might slip," I cautioned.

Rodrigo went still. "Don't do this, Isadora. Just take the ticket. Take the money. Just don't shoot me in the nuts."

I smiled. I wasn't a cruel person, but there was something so sweet about seeing the man who had tormented me for all these years being reduced to a groveling little bitch. "I'm going to ask a question for you, Rodrigo. I want you to think very carefully about your answer. If you get it wrong, you won't very much like the result. Understand?"

"Yes," he said.

"If our roles were the reverse, if someone had hurt you the way you hurt us, would you pull the gun trigger?"

Rodrigo hesitated for a second and then answered, "Yes."

I nodded and took my finger off the trigger. I knew I would never get a genuine apology out of him, but him admitting that he'd hurt us enough to deserve to be shot in the dick felt almost as good. "Let's go, Giovanna. We have a ticket to cash."

Rodrigo let out a sigh of relief as we zipped up our cat suits and walked towards the door.

If Rodrigo had only wronged me, I probably would have kept walking. But he hadn't. He left death and destruction in his wake wherever he went. Minutes ago, he had caused some poor girl to get gangbanged on stage and almost paid Vitor to carry out a hit on some random girl. If I walked out that door, it would only be a matter of time before some other girl took my place under his iron backhand. And I couldn't allow that to happen.

Before opening the door, I turned around, aimed the pistol, and redecorated the backboard of the bed with Rodrigo's brain. I was finally free.

CHAPTER 43

Sunday

ALINA

After I received my scores, the stage crew quickly set up the three-tiered medal podium while the girls who placed fourth and fifth were escorted off stage. A few guys in suits appeared on stage, as well as three women in traditional Brazilian outfits holding silver platters with the medals and flowers.

"Can I put on some clothes before we start?" I whispered to Owen.

He shook his head. "Sorry, we're already way behind on a tight schedule. The closing ceremonies can't begin until we're done here."

Oh well. I figured it was worth a try, but it really didn't matter that much. What mattered was that I was going to be standing on that gold podium, looking down at Gabriela. I held my towel firmly around myself.

"Ladies and gentlemen," announced Owen Harris. "Tonight, we've witnessed history being made as these women competed in the first ever tiebreaker event of these great games. Without further ado, let me present our medalists."

"Winning bronze, and representing Russia, Irina Alexandrov!"

Irina was greeted with warm applause as she stepped onto the lowest of the three podiums. One of the men in suits stepped forward along with the girl carrying the bronze medal tray. Dramatic music played as he put the medal around her neck and shook her hand. Another one of the suits approached and handed her the flowers on the tray.

Owen let her wave and enjoy the moment before moving on. "Winning silver, and representing Brazil, Gabriela Santos!"

The applause was louder for her, but the look on her face made it clear she didn't care. She was pissed that she didn't win gold. Her frowning face was a million times better than her smug smile.

She received her silver medal and flowers and then it was my turn. It felt like I couldn't breathe. *This is really happening.*

"And finally, winning gold for the United States of America, Alina Smith!"

I was met with thunderous applause as I waved to the audience and stepped onto the gold medal platform. I had imagined this moment a million times, but never quite like this. In my dreams, I was always fully clothed and surrounded by my volleyball team. But I had done it. I had won an ITA gold medal.

I bent down to allow the old guy in the suit to put the gold medal around my neck.

"Congratulations," he said, shaking my hand.

"Thank you," I said.

Another guy came up to give me flowers.

The suits walked away and the crowd cheered some more. I waved back at them and looked around, soaking in every detail of this moment. The crowd cheering, the American flag above my head, the pissy look on Gabriela's face. It was all perfect.

Except one thing. I thought about the first thing that Bryce had done when he had won his gold. He had run toward me. Would he want me to run toward him? After everything I had just done to win? I looked toward the side of the stage. A few of the backup dancers were standing there with towels around their waists. Their masks were off. But none of them were Bryce. Where was he?

"This is bullshit," Gabriela said, distracting me from my thoughts. "You should be disqualified."

"I would have thought a slut like you would have enjoyed my performance. Or has a guy never asked you to give him head before?" I wasn't even sure where my sudden confidence had come from. Maybe it was the gold medal around my neck. Or maybe it was just the fact that I was finally fed up with her bullshit. No matter what I had just done on stage, Gabriela wasn't better than me. And she never had been. She was a bully and a jerk.

"Fuck you." She looked like she was about to cry.

"Ladies and gentlemen," said Owen. "Please stand for the national anthem of the United States of America."

The Star-Spangled Banner started playing in the speakers. I put my hand over my heart. As I stood there listening to the music, the horrible realization of what I had just done hit me hard. *What the fuck did I just do?* Before the performance I had been horrified by the thought of stripping down to my underwear in front of the cameras. And then I had come out here and given blowjobs to two strangers and gotten naked in front of the entire world. Those things would forever be available on the internet for anyone to view, if they hadn't seen it already. Images flooded into my head of me introducing myself to someone and them saying, "Oh, I know you. You sure are good at deep-throating."

And what is Bryce going to think of me? He had to have been one of the guys standing behind me, but I didn't understand why he didn't try to stop me. I really thought the first guy was him. And then when it wasn't, my hormones willingly let me believe that the second guy was. Why the hell was I so gullible? Any normal person would have thought the second guy was lying too. Hell, any normal person wouldn't have sucked a guys cock behind a flag in the first place! I didn't even know if the man I loved had planned it, or had been horrified, or...

The national anthem ended and the crowd cheered again for me.

The man I love. I was in love with Bryce. But there was no way he'd want me now. Not after what I had just done.

I turned toward the side of the stage again. And there he was. He had a towel wrapped around his waist and his lips were set in a straight line. His arms were folded across his chest. He looked pissed. He looked so, so pissed at me. *Oh my God.* My chest started to hurt. It felt like I couldn't breathe. There was no way he had planned it. He looked so upset. He looked so hurt. And I was the one that had hurt him.

Bryce dropped my gaze and looked down at the ground.

Oh God.

All I could hear was this weird buzzing in my ears. I was numb to the cheers of the crowd. It felt like my heart had just broken into a million pieces. I needed air. I needed to not be standing on a stage in just a towel. And I couldn't look at Bryce being hurt. Knowing that it was my fault.

I felt the tears start to run down my cheeks. I jumped off the medal podium and ran in the opposite direction of Bryce.

I could have sworn I heard him yell my name. But clearly I didn't know his voice. Because Gabriela was right. I was a total slut.

I turned down a hallway, trying not to break my ankles in my heels. I stopped for a second and pulled them off so I could run even faster. When I reached my dressing room, I threw open the door and locked it behind me. Luckily my stylists weren't there. They had probably been watching the performance too. *Ugh.*

I immediately went into the bathroom and turned on the hot water. I felt so dirty after what I had done that all I wanted to do was take a shower. I imagined this was how it felt after a bad one night stand. But this wasn't dinner at Olive Garden followed by subpar sex with a selfish lover. This was blowjobs being broadcast around the world while Bryce watched in horror. Even though I could wash all the makeup and hairspray off, I could never wash away what had happened.

As I let my towel fall to the floor, I accidently caught a glimpse of myself in the mirror. *Oh my God.* I looked like such a whore. My eye makeup had run everywhere because of my crying, my stockings had runs in them, and the lace on my garter belt had been torn from when one of the fake Bryce's destroyed my thong.

Fuck! Could Bryce ever forgive me for what I had done? I didn't think so. I wouldn't if I was him.

More tears formed in my eyes and I looked away from the mirror. I couldn't look at myself. I wasn't sure I'd ever be able to look at myself again.

I stripped off my destroyed lingerie and got in the shower. The water was way hotter than it should have been, but I didn't adjust it. The hot water helped distract me from the shame of what I had just done.

I wasn't nearly done showering when I heard a loud knock on the door to the dressing room. Someone had been knocking earlier too, but I had ignored it. I wasn't ready to talk to anyone, not yet.

Go away.

Another knock. But this time, it was accompanied by someone with a Brazilian accent yelling, "Security, open up."

Security? Shit! I had been so focused on how much I hurt Bryce that I hadn't even thought about the legal implications of what I had just done. I had probably violated a dozen laws on public decency, and now they were coming to arrest me. *Will I spend the rest of my life in some Brazilian prison?*

"You have 5 seconds before we open the door ourselves," yelled the security guard.

Shit, shit, shit! I have to get out of here! I jumped out of the shower and ran out into the dressing room.

"Hold on," I said. "I'm not dressed." In a panic, I pushed the makeup chair under the door handle, threw on the clothes I had worn to the arena, and grabbed my purse. Thanks to my mini panic attack before the performance, I knew that the window in the bathroom was the perfect escape route. And I intended to make good use of it. Right before crawling out the window, I shoved my stupid gold medal in my purse and grabbed one of the luxurious towels to dry my hair on the go.

I got a few curious looks from the locals as I lowered myself onto the sidewalk. Usually I would have been concerned that they'd think I was weird, but after what I had just done, people seeing me jump out of a window was the least of my worries.

I ran a few blocks to put some distance between me and the security guards, and then I took a quick inventory of what I had in my purse. My cell phone, my wallet, some makeup, and most importantly, my passport. I wouldn't have usually carried it around, but it was required as photo

ID in order to board the train from the athletes' village to center city Rio.

While I waited for an Uber to arrive, I got on Expedia.com and searched for the next flight out of Rio. There was only one flight headed to the US with any empty seats left, and it was leaving in ninety minutes. Not nearly enough time to go back to the dorm and get my stuff. Kristen would have to just bring it home for me, if I ever went home. Assuming I made it out of Brazil without being arrested, which at this point seemed to have about a 50/50 chance of happening, I didn't think I could ever go home. I couldn't imagine how awkward it would be to see my parents. Actually, I could imagine it, and it was mortifying.

***

My heart was pounding the entire time I was in the customs line. Maybe I was just being paranoid, but it seemed like there were way more police officers than was normal for an airport. It didn't really matter how many officers there were, though. I was always going to have to show my passport to one of them to get through the line.

The bored looking officer at the desk said something in Portuguese and waved me over to his desk. I tried to avoid eye contact as I handed him my passport.

He flipped it and then held it up to compare me to the picture in the passport.

"Do you have valuables with you worth more than 10,000 Real?"

"No." At first I thought I didn't have anything with me at all, but then I realized I had my gold medal with me. "Well, actually..." *Shit, will showing him my medal make him realize who I am?* "Never mind. Nope. Nothing over 10,000 Real."

He gave me a funny look and then stamped my passport and handed it back to me. "Here you go."

I grabbed it and immediately walked away. I was just letting out a sigh of relief when the officer said, "Miss, wait." Another guard stepped in front of me and put his hand up.

Oh shit. I'm being arrested. Will they have to read me my rights, or will they just throw me in a prison to rot? Maybe I'll get one call to the embassy...

"You forgot this," said the officer.

I turned around and saw that I had left my purse on the counter. "Oh, thanks," I muttered.

"Are you okay?" asked the officer. "I didn't mean to scare you."

"Yeah," said the other officer. "Unless you're a fugitive or a smuggler, Gustavo is just a big teddy bear."

"Well I'm definitely not a smuggler," I said with a nervous laugh. "Or a fugitive. Nope. That's not me. I haven't done anything illegal at all. Nothing to fuge from." *Fuge? That's not even a word!* I turned to walk away and tripped over someone's luggage.

By some miracle, the officers just helped me to my feet and let me pass. I immediately found a souvenir shop and bought a Brazil hoodie and a pair of the biggest aviator style sunglasses they had available. Once I was suitably disguised, I followed the signs to my terminal.

Flight 786 - Nonstop to Miami - On Time - Boarding in 5 minutes.

Five minutes. If I could avoid arrest for another five minutes, I'd be home free. I'd still have to face the horrors of what I had done, but that was better than facing the inside of a Brazilian prison.

I glanced up at the TV to pass the time. It was the local Rio news, and the top story was of course about the ITA tiebreaker. I wanted to look away, but I couldn't bring myself to do it. I was too curious to see if they'd show my...performance. I was relieved when they just cut right to the medal ceremony. It didn't make it all worth it, not even close, but seeing Gabriela up on the silver medal podium looking so pissed did make me smile for a second. *I had finally beaten her.* Or had I? Sure, I had won gold. But at the same time, I had sacrificed everything I loved. I had lost Bryce, I had lost my dignity, and I could never speak to my Dad again, so I surely had lost the bakery. At best, it was a pyrrhic victory. At worst, it was the stupidest thing I had ever done.

The report about the ITAs was interrupted for some breaking news about a local gangster shot dead at the Copacabana Palace. I looked away before they could show the picture of the guy. It was time to board.

CHAPTER 44
Sunday
ALINA

ONE WEEK LATER

The next week was a big blur. From Miami, I flew to LAX. At the time, I didn't know why I had done it. I told myself it was because there were tons of famous people in L.A. so it would be easier to blend in. Or maybe I just belonged there since it was where all the porn stars lived.

I spent my first few days in Los Angeles hermitting in a crappy motel, only having human contact to order the bare minimum amount of food required to not starve. I screened all my calls, and I didn't even go on my phone again after I received an email from the US ITA Committee informing me that my prize money for my gold and silver medal were being withheld pending a formal review of my disgraceful actions during the tiebreaker. In other words, I was probably never going to see that money, and even if I did, it would be well after my dad had already sold the bakery.

After three days, I finally got the courage to go get tested for every STD in existence. When the tests all came back clean, I was finally able to admit to myself the real reason I had flown to Los Angeles: I had to see Bryce.

I knew it wasn't fair to ask him to ever speak to me again, much less forgive me, but I had to try. I loved him.

What the hell am I going to say to him?

That question consumed my thoughts for the rest of the week. I kept trying to plan out the perfect apology, but the truth was, no apology could ever make up for what I had done. Maybe I just wanted to see him to get some closure. If I didn't try to get his forgiveness, it would eat away at me forever.

I was going to summon an Uber, but my phone had died days ago and my charger was in Brazil, so instead I pulled on my Brazil hoodie and aviators and got the front desk to call me a taxi.

When we arrived at the address I had found by doing some old-fashioned phonebook stalking on Bryce, I handed the cab driver my credit card to pay the fare.

"Alina Smith?" he asked, reading the name on my card. "You're the ITA tiebreaker girl, right? I didn't recognize you with that hoodie on."

"No, that's not me."

He ignored me. "Can I have your autograph? My friends are never gonna believe I met you!"

"You're mixed up. I'm pretty sure the tiebreaker girl was Aliba Stitch, not Alina Smith." *Aliba? That's not even a real name.*

"Are you sure? You definitely look like her." He glanced down at my chest.

"Yup. I'm sure." *Is this what every day is going to be like now?* I was going to need to buy an entirely new wardrobe consisting only of parkas and sunglasses.

I took my credit card back from him and got out of the cab.

Bryce lived in an apartment complex, so the door was locked and there was a call box with a list of tenants. I pushed the button next to the name Bryce Walker.

"Bryce?" I said. "It's Alina. I'm so sorry about what happened. I never meant..." I stopped to choke back tears. "I...I just want to apologize. And then you never have to see me again."

No answer.

"Please, Bryce. I'm so, so sorry."

Still no answer.

It was clear Bryce didn't want to talk to me. I had kind of expected it, but I had been holding onto a small, ridiculous shred of hope that he would forgive me. The reality hit me like a ton of bricks. I couldn't hold back the tears anymore. I collapsed onto the stairs and cried my eyes out, and then I cried some more.

***

A sickly homeless man offered me part of a sandwich - a sandwich he had clearly plucked from a trashcan - while I cried on the stairs of Bryce's apartment was the final straw. Being pitied by a homeless man was horrifying, but that alone wasn't what did it for me. What really did it was seeing how he kept going despite literally having nothing. Yes, I had done something awful, and yes, I had lost Bryce, but I hadn't lost everything. I still had money, I still had my health, and no matter how much I dreaded seeing my parents and my grandma, I knew that deep down they would still love me. I was going to have to face them eventually, so I might as well get it over with. If I took it one day at a time, I could slowly pick up the pieces of my shattered life.

After catching a plane to Philly, I got an Uber to Kristen's apartment.

Kristen had moved into a nice apartment after graduating a few months ago. I had moved home to live with my parents. But if I had to choose between facing my parents or facing Kristen, it was an easy choice.

I pressed on the buzzer outside the building. "Kristen, it's me."

She didn't say anything, but the doors immediately buzzed open. I took the stairs instead of the elevator, and then I stopped in front of her door. *Am I really ready to see her?* She had a front row seat to my handing out blowjobs like lollipops. I didn't know how she could ever look at me the same again.

I considered turning and running away, but before I could, the door opened.

Kristen immediately threw her arms around. "Alina, I'm so, so sorry." She immediately burst into tears. "I didn't think you were ever going to talk to me again. I'm just so happy to see you."

Her crying made me start crying. "What?" I choked through my sobs. "You're the one that shouldn't be talking to me. You saw what I did."

Kristen pulled back and wiped the tears away from her eyes. "I just thought after my message..." she let her voice die away.

"I haven't listened to any of my messages. My phone died. I...I can't."

She grabbed my hand and pulled me into her apartment, closing the door behind me. "Alina, what happened was all my fault."

"No it wasn't. I was like a sex craved maniac." Saying it out loud made me wince.

"No." Kristen shook her head. "Tim planned that whole thing for me. He knew the idea of multiple partners excited me. He choreographed everything that happened. He just didn't tell anyone except the backup dancers about it."

"Tim being crazy doesn't make it your fault. You just said you didn't know about it."

"I didn't know. I swear I didn't. But you don't understand. I lied." She looked down at her ankle.

For the first time, I realized she wasn't using her crutches. She didn't even have a wrap around her ankle.

"I didn't hurt my ankle. I just wanted you to have the chance to beat Gabriela."

"What?" I felt my tears biting at my eyes again. "I saw you fall..."

"I faked it. And I'm so, so sorry. I didn't know what Tim was planning at the end of the dance. I didn't know what was going to happen. But it was supposed to be me up there. When he found out it was you, Tim told the guys exactly what to say to trick you. He used your relationship with Bryce to manipulate you. For some reason he was taking the tiebreaker way too fucking seriously. He completely lost his mind."

I took a step away from her. "Kristen. My life is over. I can't go anywhere. I lost...everything." I felt like I couldn't breathe.

Tears started coming to Kristen's eyes again. "I'm sorry. Alina, please, I'm so, so sorry."

I sat down at a stool at her kitchen counter and put my face in my hands. "I'm not mad at you. I'm not mad at Tim. I'm just mad at myself. How could I let it go that far?" I lifted my face out of my hands. I could feel the tears streaming down my cheeks.

"Because they were encouraging you. And because Coach Hammond didn't let you have sex for a month. And because Bryce teased you all week long."

I laughed and then immediately shook my head. "None of this is Bryce's fault." *Bryce.* Just thinking about him made my chest hurt. "He's lucky he never slept with me. At first I didn't understand why he didn't try to stop me. But then I realized that he couldn't hear what those guys said to me. He didn't know I thought they were him. He just thought I was blowing them to win gold. He must think...God I don't know what he thinks."

Kristen slid into the stool next to mine. "He was too busy trying to stop the whole thing from behind the scenes. Tim didn't tell him what was going to happen either."

I pictured the hurt look on Bryce's face. God, that image was going to haunt me forever.

"Have you talked to him?" asked Kristen.

I shook my head. I knew he had called me. Before my phone died I had several missed calls from him. But I didn't know what to say. Nothing could take back what I had done. I thought seeing him in person would be better. He'd be able to see how sorry I was.

"He tried to go after you when you fled the stage. You have to call him, Alina. You were falling in love with him."

"Which is why I can't. I just can't."

Kristen let my words settle around us. She was quiet for a few minutes while she stared at me.

"Where have you been? Your parents are worried about you. No one knew where you were."

"I went to Pasadena. I thought I could talk to him. I wanted to apologize." I shook my head. During the worst moment of my life, Bryce was the one that I wanted. I needed him. But it wasn't fair to him that I needed him right now. Not after what I had done. What I really needed was a miracle. That's what it would take for him to forgive me.

"Did you try to go see him?"

"Yes." My voice came out as more of a croak. "But he didn't let me into his apartment. He didn't even speak to me." I took a deep breath and looked down. "Kristen. I love him. If I could take it back, oh God, I wish I could just take it all back."

She got off her stool and put her arms around me. "It's going to be okay."

"No," I sobbed into her shoulder. Nothing was ever going to be okay ever again. Not if Bryce wasn't here beside me.

"Did you ever think that maybe he wasn't there?"

I shook my head.

Kristen laughed. "He was probably just out then. He likes you. If there's anything I'm sure about, it's that he likes you. And he's probably just as worried about you as I've been."

I sighed. "You think?"

"Yes. Why else would he have chased you to your dressing room and even found a security guard to help let him in when you wouldn't answer."

"Wait, you mean security wasn't there to arrest me?"

"What? Is that why you escaped out a window and disappeared?"

"Yes. I thought I was going to get arrested for public nudity or something and spend the rest of my life in some Brazilian prison."

Kristen starting laughing even harder. "Why would they let you get the gold medal and then wait until you ran off stage to arrest you? Why wouldn't they just stop the performance?"

"I don't know! Clearly I wasn't thinking straight or I wouldn't have..."

She stared at me for a second. "I'm sorry, I just have to ask...what was it like?" It looked like she was trying hard not to smile.

"You mean, shoving cocks into my mouth on live television?" I cringed as I said it. "Can we please not talk about it? How are you even looking at me after seeing me do that?"

"What, you mean because I'm so jealous of you?"

"Jealous?"

"Yes. And proud. The way you went out there and handled those two beautiful cocks. I don't know if I would have had the confidence to do that. And the way you made Gabriela look like she was about to cry. That was priceless."

I couldn't help but smile. I should have known Kristen would have my back. She was the best. Knowing there was someone in the world who didn't think I was a disgusting whore significantly improved my mood.

"So it was awesome, wasn't it?" she asked.

"No." I laughed.

"Oh my God, you loved it!"

"I didn't love it." I could feel my face turning red. "I don't know, it was weird. I thought it was Bryce, you know? I felt comfortable despite being in front of all those people because I thought it was him. It was...intoxicating."

"See, I knew I should be jealous."

"Ugh," I said with a laugh. "I wish it had been you."

"Me too."

I shook my head. "You're so ridiculous."

"I'm ridiculous? You're the one that doesn't realize how big of an opportunity this is. You could have your own reality TV show now. Everyone gets their start these days by leaking a sex tape. A blowjob tape will do just fine."

I started laughing. And once I had started, I couldn't seem to stop.

"Can I please be on your TV show?" Kristen said as she gasped for air through her own laughter.

"Absolutely." It felt so good to laugh after my week of shame hibernation.

Kristen got up and grabbed a bottle of wine. "Okay, so you know I need all the juicy details, right?"

I put my hand over my eyes. "What details?"

"Like how it felt to have your lips around a stranger's cock in front of millions of people."

We both burst into laughter again.

CHAPTER 45
Sunday
ALINA

"So what are the odds that my family saw the full video?" I asked. Kristen and I had just pulled into my neighborhood. We were on the way to my house for my welcome home dinner, and I was getting more nervous with every second that passed.

"I don't know," said Kristen. "They had to have been watching the tiebreaker, right?"

"Not necessarily. Everyone thought it was going to be you dancing until a few minutes before. But let's assume they were watching. What would they have seen?"

"Okay, so they definitely saw that your backup dancers got naked and that you took your bra off, but that was all censored. I think the broadcast cut out before you started giving head. And then it didn't come back on until Owen Harris gave you the towel."

"Hmm...so they heard what the judges said to me." I tried to recall exactly what the judges had said to me, but I couldn't remember for sure. "I think that French lady said the most. Do you remember if she specifically mentioned that I gave blowjobs?"

Kristen shrugged as she turned into my parents' driveway. "I don't know, Alina. It'll probably be pretty obvious if they know or not. And if it isn't, I'll help you figure it out."

I took a deep breath and we walked to the front door.

"Don't be nervous," said Kristen. "Your parents will still love you no matter how much of it they saw."

Oh God.

My mom answered the door. "Alina." She pulled me into a hug. "Sweetie, we've been so worried about you. Where on earth have you been?" She released me from her hug but kept both hands on my shoulders.

"I just needed some time to myself," I said.

She nodded. "Right. I know how upset you were about the final. But silver is nothing to be ashamed of. That's a huge accomplishment."

Does she really not know about what happened? Or is she just pretending like she doesn't? I glanced at Kristen and she gave me a subtle thumbs up.

"So what's for dinner?" asked Kristen.

"I cooked up a big turkey dinner. I hope that's okay. In fact, I need to go take it out of the oven. Why don't you go put your things upstairs and then join us in the dining room."

My mom disappeared down the hall and left Kristen and me at the door.

"I think she's oblivious," said Kristen.

"I don't know. She was acting kinda weird. And why didn't my dad or grandma come to greet us?"

"They're probably just already at the table. Come on, go put your stuff upstairs and come eat. I'm hungry."

I walked upstairs and dropped my duffel bag on the floor of my room. There was a picture of Chris and me on my nightstand. I walked over and picked it up. Chris had his arm around me, his hand resting on my ass. I always thought his physical affection was a good thing. I had been too blind to realize that it was the only thing that was important to him. I opened up the drawer in my nightstand and tossed the picture inside. *Screw Chris.* Bryce was who I really cared about. But just like Chris had fucked things up with me, I had fucked things up with Bryce. Even though Kristen had cheered me up a little, the thought of Bryce still brought tears to my eyes. I tried to cheer myself up by looking at the other picture on my nightstand, a picture of Grandma and me in front of Nona's Bakery when I was young. But that picture didn't cheer me up either. It just made me think about how I still had to convince my dad to give me more time to come up with the money to fix up the bakery. And convincing him that the money was coming involved admitting that I had participated in the tiebreaker and won gold and that the US ITA Committee was withholding my winnings until a review of my behavior was completed.

Shit.

I turned away from the picture and went downstairs.

Kirsten, Mom, Dad, and Grandma were all seated at the table already.

"Alina!" my grandmother said. "My beautiful, Alina." She was smiling brightly. It was questionable if my mom knew or not, but it definitely seemed like my grandma was in the dark. *Thank God.*

"Hi, Grandma," I said and gave her a hug before sitting down.

"Welcome home, honey," said my dad. He glanced up at me and then turned his attention to carving the turkey.

I looked over at Kristen to see if she had figured out if they knew, but she just shrugged.

We all served ourselves and began eating. With each second that passed in silence, I began to think that my family had seen the video. Usually we had such free-flowing conversation during our family dinners, especially after not seeing each other for three weeks.

"So, girls," said my mom finally. "We want to hear all about the games."

"They were a lot of fun," I said. I wanted to avoid giving any details at all costs.

"What was Brazil like?"

"Hot. Really hot," I said. "You know, in a temperature way." I ate a big spoonful of mashed potatoes and hoped no one picked up on the innuendo.

"Yeah, I saw on the news how hot it was there," replied my mom.

Please be talking about the temperature. "Yup. High 90s and very humid."

"What I want to know is what it was like to be surrounded by all those athletes," said my grandma.

"Intimidating," said Kristen. "And a little overwhelming. But I thought Alina handled it really well."

I kicked Kristen under the table. *What the hell is she doing!?*

"What about that boy you were telling me about?" asked my mom. "Are you two still together despite the tie..." She coughed into her napkin. "...Time difference? You said he lives in Pasadena, right?"

Shit, was she about to say tiebreaker? I looked down at my plate and tried to hold back the mix of tears about Bryce and embarrassment that my mom almost mentioned the tiebreaker. I was pretty sure she knew all about it and was just pretending like she didn't.

"I'm not sure they've talked since the games," said Kristen.

"Can we talk about something else?" I asked.

Kristen nodded. "Can someone pass the white meat? I wanted to get my hands on it before Alina shoves it all in her mouth."

My dad choked on whatever he was eating and my grandma giggled. My mom pretended to ignore it completely.

Oh fuck. They definitely know.

"So uh...what'd I miss in Delaware?" I said, changing the topic as quickly as possible.

"We sold the bakery," said my dad matter-of-factly.

"What?" I asked. "No. You said you wouldn't until I got back..."

"It's done," said my dad. "End of discussion."

I looked to my grandma for help. "Grandma? Are you going to let him do this?"

She looked down at her plate.

I turned back to my dad. "But I'm going to get the money. Just give me a few days."

He slammed his fist on the table, making everyone at the table jump. "What are you going to do? Host a charity strip show to get the money you need to fix the place up? Or maybe you could go do some more porn."

I swallowed hard. I had never been more ashamed in my life. Or more embarrassed. But it wasn't just that. I was mad. I was so mad. "Dad, I made one mistake."

He scoffed. "That's not what I heard."

I winced. It wasn't just one mistake. There had been two guys I had blown. I looked over at my grandmother. She was looking everywhere except for at me. Before she had started getting sick, she loved putting my father in his place, making him feel like the son she still viewed him as. But not even Grandma was on my side this time. Had she really heard about it too? Why were they talking about that in an old folks home? Her lack of support hurt the most. It was her dream to pass the bakery on to me.

"Bill, please..." said my mom.

"God damn it. I can't just sit here and pretend like nothing happening." My dad turned to me. The disappointment in his eyes was heartbreaking. "We heard all about what you did, Alina. You didn't deserve that bakery, not after that. I sold it to the highest bidder."

"She won gold," said Kristen. "You should be proud of her, not slut shaming her."

My dad shook his head. "We didn't raise you that way, Alina."

"What do you mean you didn't raise me that way? You're who I got my competitiveness from. You always told me to do whatever it takes to win. You always said..."

My dad stood up. The chair squeaked across the floor. "To be a prostitute? I can't even look at you!"

I bit my lip. I didn't want to start crying again. "It was a mistake."

He shook his head. "It doesn't matter."

"Then give me more time. Dad, please, I'm begging you."

He finally made eye contact with me. "It's too late. The sale is final. I need some air."

I closed my eyes and squeezed them harder when I heard the front door slam. "I'm gonna go to bed."

"You barely touched your food," my mother said. She put her hand on top of mine.

I opened my eyes. "Did you know?"

"Yes. I saw the video on Twitter..."

Oh my God. The thought of my mom watching that video made me want to vomit.

"I think she meant about the bakery," said Kristen.

My mom cleared her throat. "Oh, right. No, I didn't know. I would have told him not to do it, but I don't think that would have helped. Someone came in with a last minute bid that was way higher than the price he had been negotiating with the developer. Either way, my opinion didn't matter. It wasn't mine to sell."

"It wasn't his either. It was Grandma's."

Grandma continued to stare at something that no one else saw. Clearly she didn't want me to have the bakery either.

"I'm already beating myself up over what happened enough," I said. "I don't need anyone else against me." I stood up.

"Sweetie..." but my mom's voice died away as I ran up the stairs. It felt like I was a kid again, being reprimanded. Only what I had done was nothing like what a child would do.

I collapsed on my bed. I remembered being upset after getting my silver medal. Bryce had held me. He made me feel safe and secure. Like nothing bad would ever happen to me. Like he'd be there making sure it didn't. I needed him. I closed my eyes and tried to imagine what it felt like with his arms around me again. But all I could see was the hurt expression on his face.

Kristen entered my room a second later. She sat down on the bed and put her hand on my shoulder. She didn't have to say anything. I knew she didn't mean to set my dad off like that. She was just trying to help me figure out if my parents knew.

"I can't believe he sold it," I said.

"Maybe it's not final. He was probably just lashing out because he was mad at you. He'll probably come to his senses in a few days and cancel the sale."

"I don't think so. He's never looked at me that way before. He hates me."

"He doesn't hate you," said Kristen. "He's just adjusting to the fact that you're all grown up."

"That's a nice way to put it. But I really think he hates..."

A knock on the door interrupted me. I was about to tell them to go away when my grandma poked her head in. "Can I come in?"

"Of course." I sat up and Kristen scooted over to make room for her on the bed.

She was looking down at her hands. "I'm sorry I didn't say anything in front of your father."

"You don't have to apologize. I know how upsetting what I did was for all of you. I'm so sorry."

To my surprise, Grandma laughed. "That's not why I didn't say anything. I just didn't want to embarrass your father."

I looked over at her.

She laughed again. "I understand what happened completely."

"What do you mean?"

"Do you girls promise that what I say will never leave this room?"

Kristen and I looked at each other. "We promise."

"Well," she said and lowered her voice slightly. "Before I dated your grandfather, I was dating this handsome farm boy." She smiled, remembering him. "Two of his friends worked on the farm too. And they all shared a small house right next to the farm. They were all gorgeous. Tan from the sun, ripped muscles from heavy lifting. Short days, long nights. Very long, very cold nights." She sighed. "Some of the best nights of my life."

I just stared at her and then looked over at Kristen. Her jaw had dropped. "Wait, are you saying..."

"That I know what it's like to give into my hormones? To be shared? That feeling that you're already in so deep?

And that all you want to do is satisfy everyone the same way they're satisfying you?"

"Um, yeah."

"Let's just say those were some of the best nights of my life. Up there with when you were born, my beautiful, Alina." She put her hand under my chin.

I didn't know what to say. "But only you and them knew. Not the whole world."

She waved her hand in the air. "And the next scandal will come soon enough. Everyone will forget. It's a burden that you'll carry alone, making it a monster in your own mind. I carried mine and lived through it. It'll be the same for you. But really, once you settle down and have children, you'll remember it more fondly. You'll think back and know what it was like to be so free with your body. To know what it was like to truly live." She sighed.

Oh my God.

"And your regret will turn into a memory. There's only moving forward. Stop looking back, Alina."

I was still having trouble processing the fact that my grandmother was into foursomes. I shook away the thought. "How can I look forward when Dad just took my future away from me?"

My grandmother shook her head. "Your father is incorrigible. I signed over the lease to him years ago. He didn't even ask me. Don't worry, I'll be giving him a piece of my mind. That bakery was for you. All I've ever wanted was for you to take it over."

None of us said anything for a long time.

"So you think he'll get over it and change his mind, right?" asked Kristen.

"I think the deal closed this afternoon," replied Grandma. "He was serious when he said it was done."

It was what I had been fearing. "I can't believe it's really done. I always thought it would be mine." My voice sounded small.

"There's other ways. You'll start your own bakery somewhere else. You'll make your own legacy."

"But my dream is your bakery."

My grandmother nodded. I knew she understood. The bakery had probably been even more important to her than it was to me.

"One day at a time, dear granddaughter." She patted my knee. "Now, who is Bryce?"

I sighed and leaned my head on my grandma's shoulder. "The most amazing guy I've ever met."

"You know, I got together with your grandfather right after dating my farm boy."

"Did he know about your time on the farm?"

"I told him everything."

"And he was okay with it?"

My grandmother laughed. "I think he liked that I was a little wild."

What I had done was probably classified as more than a little wild.

CHAPTER 46
Sunday
ALINA

I listened to Bryce's message again: "Alina." There was a sigh. "I need to talk to you. Please, please call me back. I..." his voice trailed off. "I need to see you." The recording beeped, signaling that it was over.

He had left that message the day after I had fled Brazil, but I hadn't heard it until today. My phone was finally charged again and I was quickly losing battery from replaying the message over and over.

I was trying not to read too much into it, but it was hard not to. He had wanted to talk to me the day after the tiebreaker. But after a week, he hadn't been as interested. If he had been, he would have let me into his apartment. I knew I should just call him. But right now, I was clinging to that small thread of hope that he might still want me. As soon as I made that call...that would be it. Right now, I just wanted to believe that we could still have a future. Even if I was lying to myself.

"Alina?" my dad said.

I jumped. I had woken up with the sunrise. I couldn't sleep. All night I had dreamed of some developer coming in and demolishing the bakery.

"Hi, Dad," I said as he grabbed a bowl and some cereal out of the cupboard.

He didn't say anything else as he sat down at the table across from me. He ate his cereal in silence as I pretended to look through the mail. His silence was killing me. He dropped his spoon in his empty bowl. But instead of getting up, he looked at me. "I regret selling the bakery," he said.

My eyes started to water. "I regret what I did too."

He nodded.

I wasn't sure there was anything else to say. We were both sorry, but neither one of us was ready to forgive.

"We're handing the keys over tonight. If you want, you can go today and make sure everything is in order." He scratched the back of his neck. "To say goodbye."

"Yeah, I think I'll do that."

He stood up and put his bowl in the sink. Usually he would kiss me on the cheek before he left for work. I so badly wanted things to just go back to normal. He stopped by the chair I was sitting on.

"Sorry, kiddo," he said and awkwardly patted me on the head.

"I'm sorry too."

He cleared his throat and immediately left the kitchen. It wasn't normalcy, but it was a good start. As soon as the front door closed, I replayed Bryce's message. It was the only thing that seemed to make me happy. Maybe I'd call him tomorrow. Today I had to say goodbye to the bakery. I couldn't take another goodbye right now. I needed to hold on just a little longer. Hell, he probably wouldn't even answer my call.

***

I slid the pan into the oven and set the timer. One last dessert. I wiped down the counter that I had just gotten messy. All I could think about was the fact that I had done it a million times and this would be my last.

I turned around and looked back at the ovens. It seemed like only yesterday when I was putting cookies in the oven with my grandma. I closed my eyes and took a deep breath. The bakery always smelled like vanilla and fresh bread. If I saved up and opened up another one, would it smell like this? Or was this the last time I'd be able to breathe in my favorite scent?

I quickly wiped my tears away and pulled out my phone. It wasn't fair, but I needed him. I just needed to hear his voice. I didn't care how selfish it seemed. I loved him. Didn't that mean that we could work through this? Didn't that mean I shouldn't give up?

Before I could chicken out, I pressed on Bryce's name in my phone. It rang several times and then went to voicemail. *I should hang up.* But before I could decide what to do, his voicemail beeped. *Shit.*

"Bryce? It's me. Alina." I cleared my throat. "Alina Smith." *What the hell am I doing?* "I don't even know where to start. I know you don't want to see me anymore. I went to Pasadena to see you after the ITAs. And you made it pretty clear..." my voice trailed off. I was silent for a long time. I just didn't know what to say to make it better. "But I just needed you to know how sorry I am. If I could take it back I would. I just really need to hear your voice. I'm saying goodbye..." the phone beeped.

"Shit," I mumbled. I had been rambling too long. The message had cut me off. He was going to think I was saying goodbye to him. I didn't want to say goodbye to him!

I immediately called back. After a few rings it went to voicemail again. "Hi, Bryce. It's me, Alina Smith. Again. I wasn't saying goodbye to you. I don't want to ever say goodbye to you." I laughed awkwardly. "I know that's what you want. And obviously I'll respect your boundaries. I'm not going to stalk you. I mean, I did kind of already, but I won't come back to Pasadena is what I mean." I sighed. "I was saying goodbye to the bakery today is what I was trying to say in my last message. And I know that's not your problem. But, Bryce, you're the only thing that I can think about that makes me happy right now." I could feel myself choking up. "I just want you to know how sorry I am. And how much I love you." *Oh God.* "How much I'm falling in love with you." I put my face in my hands. "Sorry, that's not true." The voicemail beeped, ending my call again.

"Fuck!" I called him back again. "Bryce, it's Alina again," I said as soon as the voicemail kicked in. "What I meant was that it's not true that I'm falling in love with you. Because I am in love with you. I'm sure you already think I'm a lunatic, so I might as well put it all out there. I can't stop thinking about you. I don't want to stop thinking about you. Please, please just call me back. I need you right now." I let my last sentence sit there for a few seconds. "I love you, Bryce." The phone beeped.

I put the phone down and wiped my tears away with the back of my hand. It took every ounce of my resolve to not immediately call him back. I could apologize a million times and confess my feelings a million more. It wasn't going to fix anything.

I sighed and leaned against the counter. Even if he didn't call me back, I was glad I did it. He had to know. Not that he'd believe me. Who falls in love with someone and then immediately gives head to two other guys?

The oven timer went off. I grabbed a potholder and opened up the oven. They looked perfect. I pulled out the pan and set it on top of the stove. Homemade brigadeiros. I had looked up a recipe on my phone.

I wanted to travel back in time to when I was eating my first one. Back when I was first falling for Bryce. I had hoped that making his favorite dessert would help me feel like I was close to him again. I lifted one off the pan and popped it into my mouth.

It was good. But it wasn't as good as it had been in Brazil. It had nothing to do with the taste, though. I closed my eyes and pictured myself back on our first date. I thought about his fingers grabbing my hips in the car. I thought about the way his hand lingered on my back. I thought about him telling me he liked me. It almost felt like he was beside me again. I could almost feel his arms around me.

The bell on the door jingled, signaling that a customer had just walked in.

"We're closed." I turned around to see who had walked in. I swallowed hard. *Bryce?*

CHAPTER 47
Sunday
ALINA

My hands gripped the edge of the counter. I wanted to run over to him and jump into his arms. I wanted to kiss every inch of his perfect face. I wanted him to know how much I loved him. "What are you doing here?" I said lamely instead. I could hear how breathless my voice sounded. He was going to think I was psychotic.

"You said you needed me." He walked toward me.

With each step, it seemed like my heart was beating faster and faster. He walked around the counter, stopping a few inches away from me.

He was wearing a pair of jeans and a light blue v-neck T-shirt that matched his eyes perfectly. God, was he handsome. His familiar scent engulfed me. I searched his face, but I couldn't read what he was thinking. *He's probably here to serve me with a restraining order.*

"I only just left that message."

"Messages," he corrected me with a smile and leaned against the counter.

All I wanted to do was grab the front of his shirt and pull his lips to mine. I realized I was staring at his mouth. I forced myself to look back up at his eyes.

"You went to Pasadena?" he asked.

"You know I did. I went to your apartment. And you didn't buzz me up. I know you don't want..."

"I wasn't there."

"I didn't even tell you when I was there."

He shrugged. "It doesn't matter when you were there, because I flew straight here from Brazil."

"Why?"

"Because I can't stop thinking about you either."

I shook my head. "You don't have to say that. I know you don't want to be with me anymore. I just needed to apologize. I need you to know how sorry I am. Bryce, I don't even know...I don't have any excuses. I thought that they were you. I just...I lost my mind. I'm so, so sorry. I can't even express..."

"It wasn't your fault, Alina."

"Yes it was." I could feel my eyes getting teary. "Kristen already told me about what Tim did. But it doesn't matter. It was my fault. And you tried to stop it." I reached up and lightly touched the side of his face. I slowly ran my thumb along his cheek bone. He didn't shrink away from my touch.

Instead he smiled.

"Bryce." My voice wavered.

He grabbed my hand off his face and pulled me against his chest. He immediately wrapped his arms around me and put his chin on the top of my head. And I couldn't describe the feeling. It was almost like I was home. He held me tightly for a long minute. Maybe he was breathing me in, like I was breathing him in. Maybe he felt like he was finally home too.

"It wasn't your fault, because it was mine," he said softly.

"No," I mumbled into his chest. I wasn't even sure if he had heard me. But then I felt his fingers brush through my hair.

"Remember when you thought that Uber driver kidnapped me?" His body seemed tenser than it had a second ago.

I nodded against the chest.

"He did."

"What do you mean?" I tried to tilt my head back, but his palm was cupping the side of my face, keeping me nestled against his chest.

Right now he needed me just as much as I needed him. At least, he needed me to listen to what he had to say. And I didn't want to move. I wanted his hands on me forever.

"This thug, Rodrigo, was rigging the games. I think he had a lot of operatives. I'm pretty sure Liam was one of them."

Liam. I closed my eyes. *Oh God. Poor Liam.*

"He threatened to kill Em if I didn't help him. I didn't have a choice, Alina."

His words seemed to settle around me. This time when I moved, he let me take a step back from him and my back hit the counter. My heart was beating so fast it felt like it was echoing around the small bakery. "Didn't have a choice for what, Bryce?" But it felt like I already knew what his answer was going to be. I thought about how the line judges so clearly favored Brazil in the game for gold. He rigged the volleyball game which had resulted in the tiebreaker occurring in the first place.

CHAPTER 48
Sunday

BRYCE

"It's not what you're thinking, Alina." I reached for her hand, but she pulled away from me. I hated seeing her so upset.

"The refs in the volleyball game. Was that you or not?"

I couldn't tell if she was on the verge of tears or about to punch me in the face. She thought I sabotaged her game. That I made her miss out on her dream. It hadn't been me. But if Rodrigo had asked me to do it, I would have. I didn't have a choice. And I felt guilty for what had happened during her game regardless. Because I knew what was happening and all I could do was sit there and watch it unfold.

"No. That wasn't me. I'm sure it was one of the other operatives though. That game was clearly rigged. I'm almost certain of it."

"Then what did you do?"

"Rodrigo wanted me to win my race. And I did. Without cheating. He wanted me to make some ping pong player lose his game. So I had one of the women that worked for Rodrigo have really rough sex with him so he couldn't even walk right." I was hoping that would make her laugh.

Instead she said, "Okay." She was staring at me with her big brown eyes, waiting for whatever horrible thing I was going to say next.

But I didn't want to tell her. I didn't know how she was going to react. The thought of losing her made my chest hurt. The past week had been horrible. I couldn't eat, I couldn't sleep. I felt so guilty for what had happened. And I couldn't find her. She hadn't taken any of my calls or responded to my texts. And it killed me. I had this terrifying feeling that I couldn't live without her. Now that she was in front of me again, I knew just how true that was. I couldn't let her go. I just needed her to understand.

"What did you do?" A single tear had fallen from her eye.

I took a step toward her. Her back was pressed against the counter behind her, so she couldn't dodge me. But she didn't flinch. And she let me reach up and wipe the tear off her cheek. I kept my palm pressed against the side of her face and put my other hand on the counter beside her.

"He threatened Em."

"I'm sorry." Her voice came out as a whisper. That wasn't what I expected her to say at all. She should have been throwing a fit and trying to hit me. Instead, she was staring up at me like she could feel my pain. Did she really love me? She was looking at me like she loved me. And I didn't feel like I deserved it. But I wanted to. I so badly wanted to. I shook my head, trying to clear my thoughts. I had to tell her.

"Alina." I ran my hand down her cheek and the side of her neck. She seemed to shiver under my touch. All I wanted to do was rip her clothes off and finally have her. After everything that happened, all I wanted to do was officially make her mine. I wanted her to know what I was feeling. *Tell her.*

I cleared my throat and moved my hand off of her. I put it on the counter on the other side of her, sandwiching her so she couldn't leave immediately. *Please understand. Please forgive me.*

"The thug, Rodrigo, told me that I had to make sure the US won the tiebreaker," I said. "Tim had already agreed to do the choreography, so I told him to do whatever it took to win. I didn't know what he was planning and I didn't ask until it was too late. Apparently he hacked into the judges computers and found out that they liked multiple partners porn or something. And he thought it was going to be him and Kristen on stage, not us. And I couldn't stop it. I tried and I..." I shook my head. "But it's not Tim's fault and it's definitely not your fault. You did exactly what Tim wanted you to do. The whole thing was my fault. I never meant to put you in that position. I never meant to hurt you. And I'm so sorry."

"Why didn't you tell me you were being blackmailed?"

"Because I didn't want to put you in any danger."

Alina looked up at me in silence for a minute. Finally, she said, "Is Em okay?"

That wasn't what I thought she'd say. After everything I had just said, she was wondering how Em was? God, this girl was amazing. "Yeah. Thanks to you. You won because of your sensuality score. And all the judges made it pretty clear about why they scored you so high in that area."

She laughed. "Ugh."

I loved hearing her laugh. "I'm sorry, Alina. I'm sorry I didn't tell you about being kidnapped. If I had just told you..."

"It's okay. Bryce, I don't care about what happened. All I care about right now is that you're here. And that you're forgiving me?"

I could see the silent plea in her eyes. "Alina, there's nothing to forgive."

She shook her head. "I'd understand."

"What?"

"If you wanted to walk out that door and never talk to me again. I'd understand, Bryce."

That was the last thing I ever wanted to do. Now that I finally had her in front of me again, I wasn't going to let her out of my sight.

"I know what you must think of me," she said. "And despite what you said, it wasn't your fault. I was the one that agreed to all of it. I was the one that completely lost my mind. I wish I could take it all back, but I can't." Her eyes were getting teary. "You must think I'm disgusting."

That was so far from the truth. I thought she was perfect in every way. She was beautiful and sweet. And I hated that she was beating herself up over something that was my fault. I didn't want to see her cry ever again. And I wanted to be the one that was always making her smile and laugh. *God, that laugh*. It was my favorite sound in the world.

"Alina, I think you're perfect. I wouldn't change a thing about you."

"Even what I did?"

"Even what you did. To be honest, I was a little worried about being your rebound."

Alina laughed. "That's kind of you to say, but I don't believe it."

"I'm serious. I wouldn't change a thing about you. When I was a kid, stuck in those foster homes, I used to wish every night that my parent's hadn't died. I would have given anything to have them back. Maybe it was just my way of coping with it, but over time, I formed a theory that everything that has ever happened to me, whether it's bad or good, has played an integral part in forming who I am and what my life is like. Sure, if I could hold all things equal and go back in time and bring my parents back I would, but that's not how it works. Bringing my parents back would change everything. Maybe I wouldn't have been as close to Em. Maybe I never would have started running. Maybe I never would have met you. Same goes for the tiebreaker. I don't know where I'd be at this moment if that tiebreaker had never occurred, but I know for sure I wouldn't want to be anywhere but here."

"Are you sure? Or are you just saying that you wouldn't want to change the fact that I'm clearly a slut?"

I leaned forward slightly, pressing myself against her. "Did you mean what you said in your messages?"

She swallowed hard. "Every word, Bryce."

CHAPTER 49

Sunday

ALINA

Bryce let go of the counter and took a step back from me. For a second I thought he was going to kiss me. He had been looking at me the same way he had in Brazil. Like all he ever wanted to do was stare into my eyes.

"Bryce." My voice came out as almost a croak.

He walked around the counter toward the door. *What the hell? A second ago he was telling me how he wouldn't change a thing about me, and now he was running away.* He did think I was disgusting. I freaked him out for confessing my feelings too soon.

"Please don't go. I'm so sorry. You said you forgave me. You can't leave. I don't want you to go. What are you doing?"

Instead of opening the door and walking out of my life, he turned the lock.

The click of the bolt made me gulp.

He walked back over to me. There was a fire in his eyes that hadn't been there before.

"I'm doing what I should have done in Brazil." He grabbed my ass and lifted me up. I instinctively wrapped my legs around him as his lips met mine.

And there it was again. That spark that made my knees feel weak and my heart beat fast. I grabbed the back of his head, deepening the kiss. He missed me just as much as I missed him.

But we had made out in Brazil a lot. That couldn't be what he was talking about.

As if answering my thoughts, he pushed the bottom of my tank top up. His palms felt hot against my skin.

I pulled my face away from his and watched his Adam's apple rise and fall.

"Are you sure this is what you want?" I asked.

"Alina, I've never wanted something so badly in my life." There wasn't a single doubt in his voice or in the way he was looking at me.

I wasn't sure how I deserved him. But I was never going to question his feelings again. He wanted me despite everything. And I had never stopped wanting him. I grabbed the hem of my tank top and pulled it over my head. His eyes fell to my breasts. I wasn't wearing a nice push up bra like I had during my performance, but he was looking at me like I was his favorite thing in the world.

He immediately grabbed his shirt by the collar and pulled it off, revealing his perfectly sculpted torso. I vowed to memorize each contour of his muscles. I vowed to memorize every inch of him.

He grabbed my waist and pulled me to the edge of the counter, kissing me again. And this time there wasn't just want there, there was need. He needed me just as much as I needed him.

He unhooked my bra in one fluid movement and looked down as he slowly pulled it off my arms.

"You're so beautiful, Alina."

After days of thinking I was the most disgusting person on the planet, his words were music to my ears.

He leaned down and kissed the side of my neck as his hand slid up my thigh. Each inch his fingers moved up, the wetter I became. I had been wanting him ever since I first saw him in the men's locker room. He lightly kissed my collarbone.

A moan immediately escaped my lips.

I felt him smile against my skin as he kissed down the front of my chest. He took my nipple in his mouth, gently biting down on it.

Fuck.

His fingers traced the bottom of my cutoff jean shorts, teasing me. Another moan escaped my lips as his fingers slid slightly under the fabric. He pressed the center of my chest, making me lean back on to my elbows.

He released my nipple and left a trail of kisses down my stomach as he massaged my left breast with his hand.

"Bryce," I moaned. My whole body felt alive. Every time his lips touched my skin, I got even more aroused.

"You have no idea how long I've wanted to hear you say my name like that." He easily unbuttoned my jean shorts and hooked his fingers in the belt loops.

I immediately lifted my hips. He pulled off my shorts and thong, letting them slowly fall down my legs. He kissed the inside of my knee and made a torturous ascent of kisses up my thigh. His fingers trailed up the inside of my other thigh.

I spread my thighs wide. I needed him right that second.

He stopped right where I needed him most. I could feel his hot breath between my thighs.

"I'm trying to savor this moment," he said. His voice was low and husky. "But if I don't taste you right now, I'm going to lose my fucking mind."

Holy shit.

His warm tongue thrust deep inside of me.

"Bryce," I moaned. My hips rose to meet him. He pushed down on my thighs to hold me in place and spread my legs even wider.

His tongue swirled around inside of me. It was like I was his favorite dessert in the world and he couldn't get enough.

My head dipped back as he devoured me. That's what it felt like. Like he was completely devouring me.

His nose brushed against my clit as he thrust his tongue even deeper.

And I shattered. Completely. I wasn't sure I had ever orgasmed so fast in my life.

I grabbed the back of his head to keep him in place. But clearly he had no intention of stopping. His tongue continued to lap up my juices, somehow transforming me from just orgasming to feeling like I could again at any moment.

His lips moved to my clit and he sucked hard.

I moaned again. It was like it was his mission to make me come more times than I ever had before.

His hand traced up my thigh, making my whole body tingle. He sucked on my clit again as his finger filled the void that his tongue had left.

"Fuck, you're so tight."

Oh God. His lips found my clit again as another one of his fingers quickly joined in. He pumped his hand in a rhythm that matched his tongue encircling my clit.

All I could think about was the building pressure in my stomach.

He curved his fingers, hitting a spot that I didn't even know existed.

"Bryce!" *God!* I closed my eyes as another orgasm washed over me.

He gently kissed my clit and pulled his fingers out of me. "I love when you say my name like that." He kissed the inside of my thigh and looked up at me. "And I love the way you taste." He slid his fingers that had been inside of me into his mouth.

Holy shit. I wanted him to know how I was feeling. I sat up and slid off the counter. He looked down at me as I slid my hands down the contours of his abs. Watching his Adam's apple rise and fall was the sexiest thing in the world. I unbuttoned his jeans and pulled his boxers down with them. I tore my eyes away from his and looked down at his cock.

CHAPTER 50
Sunday
BRYCE

A smile formed on Alina's face. "I should have known you were the biggest one out there."

"I'm pretty sure Python had me beat by an inch or two."

"That doesn't count. That was more like a baseball bat than a penis. I wouldn't want that thing anywhere near me." Alina dropped to her knees and locked eyes with me as she licked the length of my cock. Then she wrapped her soft lips around it and started bobbing up and down.

"Alina, you should..." I was going to tell her that she should let me fuck her before I cum, but she interrupted me by pushing my cock against the back of her throat. "Fuck," I moaned.

I grabbed a fistful of her hair. For a second it was tempting to fuck her face, but there was something I wanted to do much more than that. I pulled her head back.

"You better stop before you make me cum in your mouth," I said.

She smiled. "I don't mind." She took me into her mouth again.

"But I'm going to lose my mind if I don't fuck you right now."

"Even better," she said.

I reached into my pants on the ground and pulled out a condom, but Alina grabbed it and threw it across the bakery.

"No condom," she said. "I'm on birth control. And I got tested for STDs after..."

"I know. Tim had screened them to make sure they were STD free."

"I want you to cum inside of me. It'll be my first time. For that."

"Mine too." *Wow.* I had never had sex without a condom, much less cum inside a girl. "I guess I better make it memorable then." I grabbed Alina's hand and helped her to her feet. I took a second to admire the full beauty of her body. Her long blonde hair, her big brown eyes, her tiny little waist, her big soft tits, and best of all, her perfect volleyball ass. If I could create the perfect woman, it would be her. "God, you're beautiful," I said.

CHAPTER 51
Sunday
ALINA

I started to blush. Bryce was looking at my body so intently. And he thought I was perfect.

I stood on my tiptoes and kissed him while my hand gravitated to his cock. He grabbed my ass and lifted me up, wrapping my thighs around his waist.

I laced my fingers behind his neck as he turned around and pressed my back against the cold steel of the refrigerator.

It felt like I had been waiting all my life for this moment.

"Alina, I was made for loving you."

I moaned as he slowly slid his length inside of me. He silenced my moan with a kiss. Soft and gentle like his strokes.

He wasn't fucking me. He was making love to me. No one had ever done this to me either. No one had ever loved me before. The realization made my whole body feel warm. Or maybe it was just the feeling of another impending orgasm.

I wrapped my legs tighter around his waist as he slowly thrust in and out of me. And I respected the fact that he was a disciplined athlete. Because this wasn't a sprint. This was a fucking marathon.

He pushed my thighs farther apart, thrusting deep inside of me.

"Bryce," I moaned. I ran my hands down the muscles on his back, savoring every second of this moment, as the intensity started to build. All I could focus on was the friction inside of me and how complete I felt in that moment.

He pulled my hands off of him and intertwined his fingers in mine, pressing the backs of my hands against the cold steel of the refrigerator.

I wasn't sure how much more I could take. His lips moved to the side of my neck as his hips began to move faster. I could feel my ass banging against the fridge as I grew closer and closer to the tipping point.

"Come for me, Alina," he whispered in my ear and lightly bit my earlobe.

And just like that, I lost control. "Bryce!" It was the most mind-blowing one yet. I felt my toes curl. "Oh God, Bryce!" It was everything I had ever imagined. He was absolutely right. He was made for loving me. And I was made for loving him.

He pressed my hands more firmly against the refrigerator. "Alina," he groaned.

I felt his hot cum shoot up inside of me, filling me completely. I had never felt so full in my life. It was like every happy emotion crashed down on me. Love, joy, bliss. I never wanted to let go of this feeling.

He must have felt the same because he groaned and my back slowly slid down the refrigerator as he kneeled down, still buried deep inside of me.

"Bryce, that was..." my voice trailed off.

"Incredible." He pressed his forehead against mine. We were both quiet, listening to each other catch our breath, savoring the feeling.

"I was just hoping that I could make you forget all about the other options out there."

"Oh God." I put my arm in front of my eyes.

"Too soon?" He laughed and pulled my arm away from my face.

"Bryce, the only person I love is you." I immediately blushed. It was the first time that I had said it to him face to face.

He smiled and grabbed both sides of my face in his hands. "I know it's fast and crazy, but I'm never, ever going to delay anything with you ever again. I love you too, Alina."

He slowly pulled out of me, but I didn't feel empty. *Bryce loves me. Bryce Walker is in love with me!*

"I love you so much." I could feel the tears coming to my eyes.

"Why are you crying?" He pulled my face against his chest.

"I thought I had lost you. I never felt so alone in my life." I breathed in his cologne. I was wrong before. The bakery wasn't my favorite scent in the world, Bryce was.

"Alina, you'll never be alone again." His fingers combed through my hair. "I'll never let you go."

I pulled back and shook my head. "I can't ask you to deal with all of this. I don't know when everything is going to settle down. I'm such an embarrassment."

He laughed. "Do you know how much every guy in the world wishes you were his?"

"I don't think that's true."

"It is true. And I'm the lucky one." He grabbed my waist and pulled me in close. "Because you're all mine."

All his? I smiled. "I love the sound of that."

"I hope so, because I'm never sharing you again. Whatever backlash you're going through, we can go through it together. You're not alone, Alina."

"Except for when you go back to Pasadena."

He stood up and pulled me to my feet. "I want to show you something." He grabbed his pants off the ground and pulled them on.

"What are you showing me?"

"The apartment I'm renting down the street from here."

"You got a place here?" *He's moving here for me?* I started to get dressed.

"I told you I wasn't going to move slow anymore. I meant it. I don't want to live across the country from you. And I'm not planning on going anywhere without you ever again." He smiled as he grabbed a brigadeiro off the pan and popped it into his mouth.

"What do you think?"

He finished chewing. "I knew there was a reason I fell for you so quickly. These are amazing."

I laughed. I grabbed a container from under the counter and put the rest of the brigadeiros in it. I placed the last one in and closed the lid. These were officially the last thing I'd ever make here. I could feel the tears biting my eyes.

"It's going to be alright." Bryce said and slipped his hand into mine.

I looked up at him. There wasn't a doubt in my mind that it wouldn't be. Now that I had him? We could figure it out together. My hand in his made me feel safe and whole. He was all I needed. I could live without the bakery. "I know."

His fingers tightened around mine and he led me toward the door.

I turned around to get one last look at the bakery I had grown up in. Before whatever horrible owner swooped in tomorrow and changed everything.

"I know what you need," Bryce said.

I looked up at him.

"Cheer up sex."

I laughed. "I don't think that's a thing. I've heard of makeup sex, but not cheer up sex."

"Trust me, it's a thing."

"But we just..."

"Oh, that's not a problem. I hope you're ready for a fun night." He grabbed my waist and lifted me over his shoulder.

"Bryce!" I laughed as the door to the bakery closed behind us with a thud.

CHAPTER 52

Monday

ALINA

I slowly opened my eyes. For a moment I thought it had all been a dream. But my head was definitely pressed against Bryce's chest. It wasn't a dream. I breathed in his heavenly scent and listened to his steady heartbeat. If it had been a dream, it really would have been more of a fantasy than anything else.

It was tempting to close my eyes again and fall back asleep, but I was too giddy. *He's really here.* I wanted to kiss every inch of his perfect body. But I didn't want to wake him up. I tried to focus on how secure I felt with his arms wrapped around me. I had no idea what the future held, but I knew I wanted to wake up every morning intertwined with him. Maybe I was being naive. Bryce seemed just as eager to be with me as I was to be with him, though.

I looked up at his face. He looked like he was sleeping so peacefully. I couldn't believe everything he had been through in the past few weeks. And he had kept me out of the loop to protect me. He was trying to keep me safe. *Because he loves me. Bryce Walker loves me.*

I couldn't resist touching him anymore. I reached up and ran my palm across the scruff on his chiseled jaw line. *God, he's so sexy.*

Bryce groaned in his sleep.

I didn't bother moving my hand.

He slowly opened his eyes and smiled. "Are you watching me sleep?"

I shrugged. "Maybe."

He laughed and rolled over on top of me, pinning me to the mattress.

"I really like waking up next to you."

He smiled and ran his hand down my back until he was grabbing my ass. "I love waking up next to you, Alina." He kissed the side of my neck.

"Is this place really yours?" For some reason I had this fear that he was going to say, "Just kidding," and hop on a plane and leave forever. This apartment was really nice. I knew how expensive real-estate was on this street. That was part of the reason why I couldn't afford to keep the bakery without the money for winning gold.

He kissed the side of my neck again and rolled onto his back, pulling me on top of him.

I loved the feeling of his muscles beneath me.

"Actually, I was hoping to talk to you about that," he said.

I swallowed hard. I shouldn't have said anything. I should have just savored this moment. "You're not staying?" *Of course he's not staying.* I tried to sit up, but he grabbed my waist.

"Alina." He smiled as he reached up and tucked a loose strand of hair behind my ear. "Of course I'm staying. What I was hoping was that you'd want to stay here with me."

I looked into his blue eyes. The way he was looking at me made me feel warm and fuzzy. "Are you asking me to move in with you?"

"Too fast and crazy?"

I pressed my lips together and shook my head. If I let him see the huge grin I was holding back, he'd think I was a lunatic.

"So, is that a yes?"

"But I don't have a job. I don't even know what I want to do."

"And I don't know what I want to do either. Maybe we can figure that out together."

The smile that I was trying to hold back was escaping. Before he had walked into the bakery, it felt like my life was over. And now it felt like it was just beginning.

"I love your smile."

His words just made me smile even more. "I think I like fast and crazy."

"So that's a yes?"

I nodded my head.

"And just so we're 100 percent on the same page here, I want to be exclusive. So, no more giving random guys blowjobs."

I winced and laughed at the same time. "I swear that was just a onetime thing."

"I just wanted to make sure."

I lightly shoved his shoulder. "Let me make you the best breakfast of your life to help make up for it." I climbed off his lap and grabbed the clothes that I had been wearing yesterday.

He sat up in bed and watched me get dressed. "Yeah, I could get used to this."

I smiled at him and walked out of his bedroom. It looked like the apartment had been recently remodeled, especially the kitchen. Dark wooden cabinets and marble countertops, topped off with brand new stainless steel appliances. I hoped he didn't use too much of his gold medal winnings on this place. He said it was for Em's college tuition.

I opened up the fridge. It was completely empty except for a case of water bottles.

"I literally don't have anything to eat in there," Bryce said.

I looked over my shoulder and watched him walk into the kitchen. He was pulling a T-shirt over his head. I could definitely get used to this too. I smiled to myself. "I can't exactly make anything out of water. Except boiling water."

Bryce laughed. "I've heard about this place that has great pastries down the street. Do you want to check it out?"

"My grandma's bakery had the best pastries."

He wrapped his arms around me. "It's going to be okay."

"I know. And I'm sure this other place is good too. I just..." I let my voice trail off.

He placed a kiss on my forehead.

"Let's go check it out. Maybe I can get a job there in the meantime."

He looked down at me and smiled. "Maybe I will too. It would be cool to be able to walk to work."

I grabbed his hand. "I didn't realize that you were so passionate about bakeries."

"Well, I'm passionate about you. And eating baked goods."

I laughed.

He kept his hand in mine as we walked along the sidewalk. It was a beautiful summer day. It was like we had walked along this path a million times together. I just felt so comfortable with him.

"Close your eyes."

"What?"

"I have a surprise for you."

"But I'm going to trip."

He laughed and picked me up in his arms. "Close your eyes now."

I followed his instructions. "You showing up was the only surprise I needed. Asking me to be your girlfriend and to move in with you was pretty great too though."

"I think you're going to like this one too."

"Well, you're whisking me off my feet."

"Keep your eyes closed." A few seconds later he placed me back down on my feet. "Okay, open them."

I opened my eyes and looked up at him. "You're very handsome, Bryce." I clasped my hands around his neck.

He smiled. "Turn around, Alina."

I looked over my shoulder. We were standing in front of my grandmother's bakery. Only, it had a fresh coat of paint. It looked amazing. Maybe the new owners were going to take good care of it. And then I realized that Kristen, Tim, Alex, and some slutty looking girl that I didn't recognize were inside, painting the walls.

"Bryce, what did you..."

"I bought it for you." He grabbed my chin and turned my face back to his.

I thought about his fancy new apartment. And how much money it was going to take to put into the bakery. "Bryce, you can't buy the bakery for me. I can't pay you back."

"I don't want you to pay me back. And the sale was final." He reached into his pocket and handed me the key. It was the same one I had been using ever since I was a little girl.

"Bryce." My eyes started to water. He really was my knight in shining armor.

"I was hoping to make you smile, not cry." He ran his thumb under my eye, wiping away my tears.

"I don't...I don't understand. I thought you were using your money from winning gold to help pay for your sister's college tuition?"

"I did. But I recently came into a lot of money."

"How?"

"Remember how I mentioned Rodrigo last night? Well, I got Isadora to steal his betting ticket." He nodded toward the window. I looked over my shoulder. He must have been talking about the girl that was currently making out with Alex.

"The one with Alex?"

"Yeah, Alex has a thing for Brazilian prostitutes." Bryce cleared his throat. "Shit, I wasn't supposed to tell anyone that."

I laughed. "So...she stole his ticket and...?"

"And split the winnings with me."

"What were the winnings?"

"Millions."

I laughed. "Right."

"No, really. It was a parlay. Rodrigo needed all these super unlikely things to occur in order to win. And the payout was huge."

"So, you're a millionaire?"

He shrugged. "Yeah, I guess I am. But without you winning the tiebreaker, we wouldn't have won anything." His arms tightened around me as he smiled.

"That doesn't mean you had to buy my bakery back. Bryce, that's your money. I can't accept this."

"Well, I was kind of thinking we could run it together. My degree is in marketing, and I think I could help make it grow."

I shook my head. "You're the fastest man alive. You're a millionaire. Any minute, people are going to be calling you for endorsements and all sorts of stuff. Why on earth are you in Wilmington, Delaware hanging out with me?"

He laughed. "There isn't any other place in the world that I'd rather be."

"I don't understand it, but I am so glad that you're here." I stood up on my tiptoes and kissed him. "Why didn't you tell me last night?" I laughed. "I was so upset about losing the bakery."

"I wanted to make sure you wanted to be with me for me. Not just because of this. Despite what you seem to think, you're the one that's out of my league."

I laughed and moved my hands to the sides of his face. "Bryce Walker, I am head over heels for you."

He pressed his forehead against mine. "I love you, Alina."

"Yo!" Alex said, poking his head out the door. "While you two were shagging all night, we've been doing all the work. Get in here."

Bryce laughed. "That's actually pretty accurate."

I lightly pushed his arm and laughed. "Is Isadora really a prostitute?" I whispered to Bryce before we walked into the bakery.

"Not anymore. I'm pretty sure Alex and her are together. She's a millionaire too. If there's one thing Alex wanted besides a prostitute, it was a sugar momma."

I laughed. "I don't know why that doesn't surprise me at all."

Everyone turned toward us with huge smiles on their faces when we walked into the bakery. Except for Tim, who was kind of hovering behind Kristen.

"Guys, thank you so much."

"Just hit me and get it over with," Tim said and stepped out from behind Kristen.

I glanced at Bryce. "Um...what? I was saying thank you."

He looked nervously at Kristen. "I was in Kristen's bedroom the other night when you two were talking."

Kristen nodded and put her hands about a foot apart. "He's huge," she mouthed.

Oh my God. "Wait, Kristen, did you know that Bryce was in Wilmington?"

"Yeah, but I couldn't ruin the surprise."

I laughed and walked over to Tim. "I don't want to hit you." Instead I gave him a huge hug.

"I knew it," he said, once I released him from my hug. "You did appreciate the perfect men I found. I was telling Bryce that you'd like their above average length and girth. You're welcome, Alina." He beamed at me.

"Yeah...don't push it."

"I told you it would work out, my love," Tim said and slapped Bryce on the back, completely ignoring what I had just said.

Bryce laughed. "Now when I tell you to stop saying that you should actually listen, or Kristen will get jealous."

"Nonsense. Kristen is fine with our relationship."

Alex cleared his throat. "You should listen to Bryce, man. Oh, and Alina, this is Isadora."

"It's really nice to meet you," I said and shook her hand.

"Nice to meet you as well," she said in English with a Brazilian accent. "And you never have to worry about Rodrigo again. I killed him. I love your bakery! It is so cute."

"Aw, thanks. Wait, what?" *Did she just say she killed Rodrigo?*

Alex laughed awkwardly. "English is her second language. I'm sure you didn't mean that, right, Isadora?"

"No, that's what I mean," she said. "I shot him in the face."

We were all silent for a second.

"You're so funny," Alex said. He turned to Isadora and whispered something in her ear. "Anyway, back to painting."

She shrugged. "Sure...I'm just kidding," she said and grabbed a paintbrush. "That's what you all say when you make a lie?"

"Mhm. See, she was just joking." Alex picked up a paintbrush too.

When they were out of earshot, I turned to Bryce. "You don't really think..."

"I'm pretty sure she was serious. Look it up. Rodrigo was shot at Copacabana Palace the day of the tiebreaker."

I put my hand over my mouth. "Oh my God, I saw a news report about that."

"Anyway, let me show you the new ovens." He grabbed my hand and pulled me behind the counter. "Aren't these great?" he asked.

My phone started buzzing. I pulled it out of my pocket. It was my agent. He probably wanted to terminate our contract. There was no point in delaying it. I lifted up my phone.

"Hey, Scott."

"Alina! The phones have been ringing nonstop. Why haven't you been answering my calls?"

"I've been out of town."

"Yeah, well, we need to talk. I know you wanted to retire after the ITAs, but you have a ton of offers for pro teams."

I looked over at Bryce. He was examining the new oven. He turned to me and put his thumb up. There was no way I was going to drop everything and move to some other city to play pro. I had never wanted to do that. And with Bryce right in front of me, the thought was even less appealing.

"Scott, I haven't changed my mind. I'm officially retired."

"Okay, well, there's other offers on the table too. Reality TV, endorsements for sex toys, adult films..."

Adult films? God no. "Actually, Scott," I said, cutting him off. "I think I'm good. Remember the bakery I told you about? It's all worked out."

"Wait, what? Alina, this is a huge opportunity. Any one of these would get you a signing bonus in seven figures."

I looked over at Bryce again. He was pulling ingredients out of the fridge. He hadn't stocked his own, but apparently this one had everything we needed. I never thought whisking eggs could look so sexy. But everything Bryce did was sexy. "I'm exactly where I want to be," I said into the phone.

"Alina, you're making a mistake. You have to ride this wave. People are going to forget all about what happened soon."

"That's actually what I'm hoping for. I really appreciate everything you've done for me, Scott."

He sighed into the phone. "Just think about it. I'll call you again in a few days."

"Sure," I said and hung up the phone. But I had already made up my mind. I was standing in my dream, right beside the man of my dreams.

"Everything okay?" Bryce asked as he turned on the stove.

"Everything's perfect."

"I almost forgot!" Tim said as he joined us behind the counter. "I have the perfect picture of you and Bryce to hang up on the wall in here." He lifted up a framed photo of me crawling on all fours in front of the eight backup dancers with their erections all over the place. "Where should we put it?"

"What is wrong with you?" I grabbed the frame out of his hands. "This is a family friendly establishment."

Kristen laughed and leaned against the counter. "I tried to stop him. But he insisted that you'd want the memento."

Bryce took the picture out of my hand and placed it face down on the counter. "I have a better idea," he said and wrapped his arms around me. "How about we get a picture of all of us together?"

"See, Tim? Now that's a good idea," Kristen said.

Tim shrugged and pulled out his phone. "Fine, but I don't see how it will be as good as the one from the tie-breaker. Everyone get together in front of the counter." He put the camera on his phone on a timer and set it against a ladder. "Ten seconds, people!" He ran over and started moving everyone around so that we'd be in perfect formation.

But all I cared about was the fact that Bryce's arms were around me. I smiled up at him. Yeah, I was exactly where I wanted to be.

ABOUT THE AUTHOR

Ivy Smoak is the international bestselling author of *The Hunted Series*. Her books have sold over 1 million copies worldwide, and her latest release, *Empire High Untouchables*, hit #10 in the entire Kindle store.

When she's not writing, you can find Ivy binge watching too many TV shows, taking long walks, playing outside, and generally refusing to act like an adult. She lives with her husband in Delaware.

Facebook: IvySmoakAuthor
Instagram: @IvySmoakAuthor
Goodreads: IvySmoak

Made in the USA
Monee, IL
30 July 2022